SHADES OF LIFE

AMARENDRA PATTNAIK

WORDIT ART FUND

This book has been fully funded by the Wordit Art Fund. Wordit Art Fund helps deserving authors publish their work by providing monetary support. To apply for funding, please visit us at www.BecomeShakespeare.com

First published in 2017 by

Becomeshakespeare.com
Wordit Content Design & Editing Services Pvt Ltd
Unit - 26, Building A-1, Nr Wadala RTO, Wadala (East),
Mumbai 400037, India
T:+91 8080226699

©
ISBN 978-93-86487-60-5

2

DEDICATION

This collection of short stories and monologues is dedicated to my parents and to my wife Ruby.

ACKNOWLEDGMENTS

Learning is a never ending process and everyone we meet in our life teaches us something. I have learned from everyone, including strangers. Each one of them has touched my life in their own way. I thank all of them.

CONTENTS

1. Dream Job   08
2. Sweet Memories   11
3. Save My Soul   15
4. Grass is greener on the other side   22
5. No Dowry   26
6. Men and Animals   31
7. Nostalgia   34
8. Sales Tricks   37
9. Guide   39
10. Sibani   45
11. Setting Sun   49
12. A Simple Act   53
13. Cost of Samosa   56
14. Basement Parking   59
15. Supermom   62
16. Morning Walk   65
17. Strange Encounter   70
18. Miss Call   75
19. The Naïve Cameraman   79
20. Sadhu-The Driver   83
21. Mineral Water   87
22. Innocent Wishes   94
23. Naughty Boy   98
24. Heartless   102
25. Looking Back   107

26. Sarada   113
27. Insomnia   118
28. Marriage Invitation   123
29. Food for Thought   128
30. Innocent Aspiration   133
31. Whisper at the Mortuary   137
32. No Time for Rest   142
33. Gratitude   147
34. Gourmohon   152
35. Florist Shop   157
36. Destiny   162
37. Puppy   168
38. Crazy Ambitions   174
39. Circus Girls   180
40. Bitter Pill   186
41. Young and Uninterested   190
42. Old Fashioned   196
43. Just for few Bucks   200
44. Bank Locker   205
45. Strange Interest   210
46. Silver Jubilee Celebration   215
47. Dangerous Neighbor   219
48. A Simple Question   226
49. We meet to part   236
50. All well that ends well   244
51. Life is like that   254
52. Wise Retreat   264
53. Prince of my heart   273
54. Virtual Flirting   281
55. Love in the air   294
56. Honour of my father   303
57. How Blue is my Sapphire   312

DREAM JOB

Ramu reached home with a packet of sweets and few gifts for his family. He has a loving wife and two daughters – one aged five, studies in the nearby government primary school in class-I and the other one is just a year old. The little one just started taking baby steps. He has brought a cotton printed sari for his wife, a bobby printed frock for his elder daughter and a teddy bear for the baby. He is very happy today; five years back on this day, he got his most desired job and since then every year he celebrates this event.

His wife was very caring. Though he stayed at a small rented asbestos roofed house, she had maintained it quite nicely. The house had two rooms – one room at the entrance and then an adjoining room inside. They used the adjoining room as a bed room which the daughter also uses as a study room. The front room is used as a lounge for the visitors. In this room, at one corner there is an elevated slab and a sink with a tap. This space is used for cooking. They used to have a coke stove but last year Ramu got a gas connection, which his wife has been pleading for quite some time.

Ramu was the only son to his parents, and so has grown up with lot of care and affection. His father worked in the local government hospital for long thirty years but he is no more. His mother had also died in the meantime. Ramu had passed matriculation from the same government school where his daughter is studying now. He had very limited friends in his youth. He remembers, on Sundays, he would accompany his father to the hospital to see how his father attends to his duty. His father's job was mentally stressful but nevertheless a government job.

His father, while he was alive and was working in the hospital, had got Ramu a sweeper's job. Ramu could get this job because of his qualification and also because of the good rapport that his father used to have with hospital administration. Chief District Medical Officer (CDMO Sahib) used to like his father for his sincerity to the work.

As a sweeper, Ramu's job was very easy. He used to sweep the cabins, wards and the corridors of the hospital. At times, when the latrine sweeper is absent, he takes care of that job also. He wears a brown half pant and a shirt of same color when on duty. He was happy with his job, but the salary was not good. He was getting just three thousand rupees a month consolidated amount as he was a contractual employee. With the rising price and with a baby child at home, it was a tight rope walking for him all the time. At times, he had to take hand loans from colleagues to meet some emergency expenses, though he really did not like taking loans.

After the demise of his father, Ramu approached CDMO sahib to take up his father's job, but sahib was non-committal to put him in the permanent roll. He met the local MLA, got his recommendation for the job, but it was of no avail. Then an intelligent advocate suggested him to file a case in the local labor court, claiming his father's job on compassionate ground. He filed the case and with many visits to the court and with God's grace, he won the case. Court's order reached CDMO's office shortly and they issued the appointment letter soon after. Ramu could not keep himself waiting for the letter to reach his house. He instead personally visited the hospital administration and collected it on the day of its issue. He opened the letter with delight, the post given was as per his wish: Sweeper-in-Charge, Port-Mortem Dept. The legacy of his father rightfully inherited by him.

Ramu has been working as a sweeper at the postmortem department since then. He takes a peg or two before he gets into the action. With his chisel and hammer, he cuts and tears, the heart and head of the dead bodies, and then leaves the body to the presiding doctor for the report. Later, he stitches and packs the body so that relatives can carry that for last rites. He executes his job like a robot without any emotional feeling, though he feels sad when he sees a child lying on the table for his service.

Ramu now earns ten thousand rupees a month and leads a happy family life.

SWEET MEMORIES

Mohonbabu aged fifty-five spends most of the time on the bed. He is suffering from memory loss for the last five years. He does not recognize any one; rather he recognizes all with mistaken identity. He calls his friend as his own brother and his own brother as his friend. He will address a small child as his uncle and will bow down to touch his feet. He and his wife stay in a 2BHK apartment in a city. They actually belong to a suburban town 200km far, but have shifted to this city as medical facility is better here. He displays emotions like a child. He will run away from food; will not wash his mouth after eating food; if he wants something, it has to be provided instantly; else he will start crying uncontrollably. These are some of the childlike traits that one sees in him. His wife Manaswani takes care of him. She does everything, like a mother would do to his child. But Mohonbabu recognizes her as his sister.

Mohonbabu was a normal person few years back. He had a happy family. He, his wife and his two children made up his small family. Both Mohonbabu and his wife used to work in a bank in clerical positions. They had two sons. Both of them are IIT pass outs and are now settled in USA with their families - one works in corporate sector and the other in academics. Sons visit India during Durga Puja and spend time with their parents for a week or so. Everything was going fine till one day when Manaswani noticed minor abnormal behavior with Mohonbabu. She ignored those for few weeks; but later it became apparent to her that

11

something is wrong with him. She took him to a local psychiatrist for check-up. What she heard from the doctor stunned her. The doctor told this memory loss is not because of age, but because of non-functioning of a particular nerve in the brain. And, this disease is not curable and will aggravate with time. He should not be allowed to go near fire and water bodies. Sharp items like razors and knives should be out of his bounds. He should also not be allowed to go to the rooftop or to a busy road alone. Essentially he should be escorted by someone to prevent any untoward incident. This led both Mohonbabu and Manaswani take voluntary retirement. They started living a retired life at home. While Mohonbabu would spend time with newspaper and TV, Manaswani would keep herself busy with cooking and other household work.

Two sons are very concerned about the health condition of father and the difficulty of mother; yet they are unable to make regular trips to India because of professional commitments in USA. Last year, when the elder son visited them, he has arranged installation of a computer and provision of high speed internet at the flat. This will help them talk with their mother over Skype. He has also explained his mother how to log-in and use Skype. When she talks to her son over Skype, Mohonbabu looks at the computer screen indifferently. There is no hint on his face that he is seeing his son, thousand miles far, talking to his mother.

Manaswani has brought only the essentials to the city – two single bed cots, two plastic chairs, gas stove and some utensils. She has left behind all furniture and many non-essentials that they have accumulated in the prime of their life at their sub-urban home. But what she has not forgotten to bring are two small trunks, each one containing the childhood memories of their two sons. Once in a while, she would open these trunks and would look at the many items inside it to revive her old memories.

Today she has opened the trunk of his elder son and looking at many items stuffed inside it .The cutest of these items is a Jaipur print tiny frock. Manaswani always wished for a girl child and little before her delivery she had purchased this frock from an exhibition. But she delivered a baby boy. Notwithstanding the gender, Manaswani made the kid wear this little frock and he looked pretty in that outfit. Inside the trunk, there are also parts of a Barbie doll. She purchased this first Barbie for his son to play. But as he grew-up, he distanced himself from all these girlie items. Cricket is what attracted him first. Mohonbabu had purchased a plastic cricket bat and a ball for him, when he was just three years old. The drawing room used to be the cricket field then. Mohonbabu would make the bowling and the son batted. That red color small cricket bat is there inside this trunk. Now, she finds a goggles, the frame is red in color. Just one glass is there, the other glass is missing. This one she had purchased him during in a local mela and he looked stylish wearing that goggles on his small face. There are many other items there – a plastic wrist watch, comic books, a cap, a plastic gun and many prizes that he won in school . She now comes across, his first mark sheet, the LKG exam mark sheet. He had got A in all the subjects except Math, where he got just a C. She had rebuked him for this poor show and he cried. That day Mohonbabu was upset not because the child got a C but because Manaswani made him cry. Mohonbabu stopped talking to her for many days for this fault of hers.

All old memories were crossing Manaswani's mind and she was trying to hold her tears. The fact that Mohonbabu was standing behind him and looking at the items had escaped her notice.

She recovered from her thoughts and quickly asked him "Anything you want?' to which Mohonbabu responded "Getting a C grade once in a while is OK"

SAVE MY SOUL

Flying has always been scary for me and after a gap of nearly three years on 22nd April 2015, I had to fly from Bhubaneswar to Hyderabad for official work. I reached the airport an hour before the scheduled time for departure and completed the formalities of collecting the boarding pass and luggage check-in. Waited at the lounge. Passengers were trickling in. One could segment the passengers into two types by looking at their faces – frequent flyers who projected a matter-of-fact kind of look and the occasional fliers who displayed a gloomed face veneered with forced smiles. I can quite compare their faces with cloudy sky interrupted by occasional lightening.

Flying is no more a privilege for the rich; one would find more hoi polloi than the rich and famous at the airports now a days. While I was watching the passengers, two sadhus (saints) neared the Indigo counter for the boarding pass. The elder sadhu, perhaps in his late 50's was wearing an orange colored vesti and had covered the upper part of his body with a shawl of same color. He had well groomed white beard. The other sadhu in his late 30's was wearing similar attire but the color was yellow. His vesti had a black printed border. He was clean shaved and was wearing a turban of yellow color. Each of the two sadhus was holding a small hand bag, no luggage.

There was a long queue at the counter. Sadhus joined the line. At this point, I saw a uniformed girl from Indigo reached the Sadhus and spoke briefly. Later, the Sadhus came out of the queue and followed the girl to a less crowded place of the lounge. The girl was holding a small machine of the size of a camera; she collected the tickets from the sadhus, punched something on the device she was holding and then handed over printed slips to the sadhus. Later, I understood from the girl that the tiny machine is called crowd busters and is used to provide boarding passes to those who have just a handbag with them and no luggage. The learning is, when one reduces his worldly belongings, the humanity conspires to make his life hassle free. Someone has rightly told, "Life is a journey, travel light"

Before I forget , when I submitted my ticket to at the Indigo counter for the boarding pass, the girl at the counter asked " Do you have any seat preference...window or aisles; I replied intuitively 'any place you like' . In any case, I am not going to look down through the window. Floating in the air is scary in itself.

Completed the security check and waited at the boarding lounge. I noticed two pilots standing at one place of the hall and talking to each other. I thought these are the two fellows who will take charge of my life for the next one and half hours. Why not meet them and have a chat? I went up to them and started the conversation "Hi, Captains. Are you piloting the Hyderabad bound Indigo today", "No, we are the pilots for a helicopter that Odisha Government has hired and we would be flying to Raipur" they replied. Then I started quizzing them with all kinds of questions - what is the cost of the helicopter , who is the owner , what is the operational cost , what is the market hiring rates, how may flying hours they have accumulated , at what height and speed they fly and finally "Is not it scary to fly at such a height?"...They answered all my questions and with obvious pride told 'we have been flying for last twenty years now, we love the sky and trust us it is much safer to be in the sky than to be on the road'. I briefed them about what I do, KIIT University and the purpose for which I am travelling to Hyderabad. We exchanged contacts.

I could not postpone the fear of being inside the aircraft anymore. There was an announcement for the passengers to board the aircraft and I notice people forming a queue to hop unto the bus which will drop them at the doors of the aircraft. I entered the aircraft from the tail end and occupied my seat at a window. By God's grace it was a seat near the wings; so even though I will be at the zenith, the nadir will be out of my visions. After the initial confusion, hustling and bustling, passengers settled down in their respective seats. Some started adjusting the air-conditioner knob. The middle seat adjacent to me was vacant. At the aisles was sitting a young girl in her late twenties, wearing dissatisfaction in her face for some issues. From her body language, I could make out she is a frequent flyer; and she must have made out the opposite about me.

In the opposite side the aisles, were sitting the two sadhus and a gentle man; the gentleman was sitting at the window. I noticed, the sadhus read two newspapers one after another – one Hindi daily and then The Economic Times. After reading the newspapers, they fell asleep.

17

The pilot made the announcement about the names of the two pilots and the four airhostesses. Post this, two airhostesses stood at different places of the aisles and started describing the safety tips – first in words and then in action. The fear which had retired from my mind briefly resurfaced listening to the safety tips. The tips sounded like 'what you need to do if you are standing opposite to a tiger in deep jungle'.

The wait got over. The flying machine roared like a hungry lion and started rolling on the run-way. As the wheel rolled, my heart throbbed with the most intense fear. After a playful turning at a place , the aircraft took position on the straight path , picked up speed...more speed...and then with a jerk took off and scaled thousand feet in few seconds , like a rocket on fire. Settled down briefly at an altitude but again rose vertically upwards. All this sudden happenings made me say "Never again will I travel by air. Save my Soul this time"

There were four air hostesses, all pretty, young, well groomed and well mannered. But one of them was the centre of attraction, for many obvious reasons. I leave those to the imagination of the reader.

Knee length blue scot with a matching tie is what they wore. The tie resembled a bow-tie but the knot looked like a big blossomed flower and instead of being at the neck button, it was fixed near the collar bone. There was a cut at the lower part of the scot at the back, to allow the legs free movement. It was not really a cut, but a pleat from inside deceptively looking like a raw cut and this must have disappointed many hawkish eyes. Transparent knee length stockings and black half shoe adorned their feet. Each of them had applied liberal amount of lovely pink face gloss and ravaging red lipstick. Hairs combed tightly and the long silky hairs made short in the shape of a ball at the back, protected with a soft black net. At the ears, they were wearing small tops, embedded with a glittering white gem stone.

One of the girls was perhaps wearing a wig. May be she is a South Indian and had recently visited Tirupati and gifted her hairs to the God. The prettiest, who was the show stopper, had a very small defect, a temporary defect though. She had steel wires knitted at her teeth, perhaps to bring in better alignment. The dentist must have had a good time while knitting the wire and he must have taken unusually long time to finish his service.

Most of the young travelers in the aircraft would confess that they had a crush on these hostesses. Rest would be definite liars.

I heard an announcement: 'Any passenger who wants more leg space may please contact our hostesses. Such seats are available for extra charges'. I smiled. Luxury and comfort has no limits.

Yet another announcement 'The pilots have observed bad weather condition and have given advisory to all passengers to fasten their seat belts'. Every time, I attempt to forget the fear, these people remind me the worst.

Air hostesses ferried their trolleys – first with eatables, then gift items for sale and finally to collect used paper glasses and trays. Eatables on sale included beverages, sandwiches and noodles. Each item conveniently priced in multiples of Rs50. I saw one lady sitting in front of me buying a glass of noodles. She handed over a Rs500 note to the hostess and she in turn refunded Rs250 and a big thank you. Gift items included Barbie dolls, key rings, imitation jewellery etc. I wondered why people don't buy these stuffs from their neighbourhood shops and think of buying them at 25000 ft altitude.

I found it a little awkward to watch the pretty girls collecting used paper cups and trays in a big polyethylene bag. Why God create such mermaids and compel them to work as maids.

I was looking at my watch again and again and eagerly waiting for the pilot to make landing announcement. After a long wait, the aircraft approached Hyderabad. Pilot announced "In spite of our best efforts we could not be on time. The plane is ready for landing. All passengers are advised to fasten their seat belts, switch of their gadgets and keep the window shutter open".

The plane landed safely. Passengers started taking out their handbags from the overhead rack and moved towards the exit. Some young corporate executives, with laptop at their shoulder, were deeply annoyed that the plane landed fifteen minutes late. I was happy, as I landed alive. At the exit, were standing one pilot and a smiling hostess. Both of them were conveying "Thank you "to each passenger.

I thought , actually the passengers should be thanking the pilots and the crew for taking care of their life during the time they were air borne.

GRASS IS GREENER ON THE OTHER SIDE

Namrata, Sweta, Manisha, Priya and Bhanupriya are all colleagues in a private bank. All of them are young and are of similar age group. In terms of education and experience, they are all contemporaries. Namrata, Sweta and Manisha studied at the same university. Namrata is one year junior to the other two.

They got married one after another, but all continued to work at the bank excepting Bhanupriya who opted to become a housewife. Bhanupriya's husband works in Army and now posted at Jammu bordering Pakistan. It was a childhood love affair that culminated into the marriage of Bhanupriya. There was resistance from the families of both the sides; but the saying goes "Mia bibi raji to kya karega kaji". After some years of stalemate, both the families realized that they can't stop this fire of love with their parochial thoughts. They willingly solemnized the marriage and after marriage Bhanupriya moved to the border area and now stays at a Defence colony.

It was a case of arranged marriage for Manisha and Priya. Manisha's hubby is a software engineer posted at Bangalore. He frequently travels to different foreign countries to work on overseas projects. Priya is married to a marine engineer. He voyages in ships six months a year and gets next six months as rest. He spends this time with Priya.

Sweta had an affair with one of his batch mates who were studying law in the same university. Sweta fell for his childlike look. He was also a very bright student. After he cleared judicial services exam, they got married. He is now posted as Judicial Magistrate at an interior town, but in the same state where she works.

Namrata's hubby is a corporate executive and is a wizard in finance. He is an engineer-mba and loves finance as a profession but automobiles are his passion. He spends lot of time reading and writing about bikes and cars. He is now posted at Mumbai.

Namrata, Sweta and Priya stay alone at rented 2BHK houses; Manisha stays with her in-laws.

Once Bhanupriya visited the city and wanted to meet all her old friends. A plan was chucked out. A kitty was organized at Sweta's house. Each of them brought some eatable and the host Sweta was made responsible for non-stop provision of cold drinks and coffee. All reached the venue on time and occupied the sofa at the drawing room.

The gossip started.

Bhanupriya: I envy you all. You are all lucky to be in the city you like. I am in the border town with no relatives nearby. I wish I could stay in this city.

Namrata: But you know our life is very much a routine here. Everyday go to bank, count currency, make data entry, comeback home, cook, eat and sleep. TV and Mobile are our only companion. On the contrary, you have picked-up many good things. You now play snooker, badminton and golf. You are also into gardening. We don't have space here even to keep few flower pots. You also go to Army club and meet many interesting ladies there. All these are bliss dear.

Manisha: But I think, Namrata you are the happiest. As a corporate honcho, your hobby is minting money and you can buy everything that money can buy. When you shop, you don't have to look at the purse.

Namrata: Oh come-on, what about things that money can't buy. He is all the time stressed with work. I think, Manisha you are the happiest. You stay with your in-laws and have a good support system. They have dedicated a car and a driver for you. You wear sari and ornaments and look like a queen in the house.

Manisha: Oh God!!! , Namrata you are so naïve. You have to stay with your mom-in-law to know the difficulty. I am always under scanner. I don't have freedom. You can wear a shorts in your room, I can't.

Priya: The happiest person is Sweta as she is the home minister of Judge Sahib. Government bungalow is where she stays when she visits him and no one gets more social respect than her hubby in the town. Office car with red light is always ready to ferry Sahib and Memsahib. Servants and attendants are always there to take orders from Madam. What more one wants in life?

Sweta: I agree, there is social respect; but there is no social life. As a judge he can't socialize and remain insulated from public. He has to read a lot as there are new judgments everyday and he has to be up to date. As such books are his first love, not me.

Bhanupriya: I bet the happiest is Priya. Her husband stays with her full six months uninterrupted and attends to all her wishes. And imagine having free cruise to any country you wish with your hubby. After all he is a marine engineer and ship is his second home. Moreover, he must be bringing her all kinds of gifts from across the globe. World at her feet...ha-ha.

Priya: Oh no!! , nothing like that. You can meet your hubby anytime you want. At best you have to take a flight and in an hour or two you are in the arms of your hubby. I can't have that. I have to wait for six months.

The coffee that Sweta had served to everyone has only been half consumed. Sweta reminded "Finish the coffee before that gets cold"

Bhanupriya philosophically said "We all are in the same boat. The grass looks greener on the other side"

NO DOWRY

Mayadharbabu is a clerk in a bank and lives in an urban city. He earns reasonably good amount to take care of his family. He has twin daughters – Dimple and Twinkle. Both are bright students. Dimple studied Engineering in a government engineering college and Twinkle Humanities in one of the very reputed university. Since their childhood, they were very good in everything they do. They were good at studies. Both of them were also good classical dancers and used to perform in the annual day functions of their school regularly. They were also black belt holders in karate. Mayadharbabu purposefully trained them in this martial art so that they can protect themselves physically at the time of need. Mayadharbabu's wife Minati taught her daughters elementary cooking….how to cook rice, dal, some curries, tea and coffee. This skill would come handy when they get married.

Dimple and Twinkle were both very pretty. Though they were twins, their physical features were all different. Dimple was short and fair. She had curly hair on her head and used to sport a pony tail at the back. She was shy and reticent. Twinkle was tall and dusky. She had long hair and most of the time allows them a free fall at the back. She had straightened the hair through laser treatment recently. Unlike her sister, Twinkle is very extrovert and garrulous. She can talk and talk on any topic.

On graduation, Dimple got a job at a multinational software company. She stayed alone at another city where her office is located. For convenience, she stays as a paying guest with an elderly couple. This couple had two sons, who were software engineers and are settled in USA. They have a maid servant who takes care of house-keeping and also cooking. The couple treats the PGs as their own children. Twinkle, is back at home after post-graduation. She spends time reading novels, chatting with friends on phone and watching movies at the multiplex. She wanted to become a teacher and is looking for options at the many private schools in her city.

While Mayadharbabu wanted his daughters to get married, he was not in a hurry. He thought, his daughters should enjoy their life and as and when they think it right, they should get married. But Minati thought just the opposite. As per her, daughters should get married as soon as they complete their studies. This difference of opinion between the husband and wife many times escalates into hot arguments and most of the time the argument closes with the statement from Mayadharbabu , " I don't want to argue with you. Do whatever you want"

The profiles of both the daughters were posted in the matrimonial sites and friends and relatives were also discretely informed that they are looking for prospective grooms for their daughters. Many proposals came. And after the never ending paraphernalia of visits of boys, their parents and sometimes other siblings and friends, the grooms were finalized. As fate would have it, the grooms were also twins and belonged to a very respectable family. They are separated in age by just an hour. They look almost the same. Both of them are IIT grads, software engineers and settled in USA. Father of the boys is an orthopedic doctor and the mother a housewife.

There was no demand of dowry or anything else from the parents of the boys, excepting a very small one. The marriage has to be organized in a five-star hotel. In the barat, there will be one hundred and fifty members. Mayadharbabu agreed without immediately knowing the cost implications.

The marriage date was finalized and Mayadharbabu had just fifteen days time to organize everything. Lot of things to be done- invitee list to be prepared, cards to be printed and distributed , venue to be finalized, costumes and other essentials that the daughters will carry to be purchased, Priests to be contacted and accommodation for close relatives coming from distant places to be arranged etc.

Mayadharbabu and his wife prepared the list of guests to be invited; it added up to 350; these included relatives from Mayadharbabu's side and his wife's side, office staffs, neighbors, friends of their daughters and some people on whom they are dependent on their day-to-day life.

Mayadharbabu, calculated the total number of guests as 500 – 150 in barat and 350 own guests. Then he thought it is better to be conservative while arriving at the number, as a shortage of food will cause huge embarrassment to him. So he finalized the headcount at 600.

Mayadharbabu called his best friend in the town and both of them started the search for a venue – A five star hotel.

Mayadharbabu was driving his 25 year old Bajaj Chetak scooter which he got as a marriage gift when he got married....and his friend was on the pillion. He has never stayed in luxurious hotels and never had an occasion to visit their restaurants . The closest he has done is passing through the roads in front of some of the star hotels in the city.

In one such star hotel, they parked their scooter and started walking towards the reception. The huge Italian marble floored lobby, the exquisite sofas, the indoor fountain spring and the breathtaking chandeliers hanging from the ceiling left Mayadharbabu dumbfounded. This is his first intimate encounter with luxury.

The man at the reception directed Mayadharbabu and his friend to the event manager's cabin. In the wooden floored nicely decorated cabin was sitting a young man with his eye on the laptop. He was perhaps engrossed in come intricate calculations and was tapping his fingers on the calculator lying on the table.

The Youngman welcomed Mayadharbabu and his friend with "Good Morning Sirs", offered them chairs and asked "How can I help you Sirs".

Mayadharbabu narrated the requirement –A hall to host the event, private sitting places for the bride and the groom before they come to the altar for the marriage and dinner for 600 guests. The Youngman listed down the menu. It has to be elaborate as per the wish of the parents of the groom : 4-5 types of welcome drinks, a spread of starters...and in the main menu Prawn, Mutton and Chicken ...and at the end 4-5 varieties of desserts. ..And everything has to be served liberally.

The Youngman made some calculation in his laptop and said…

"1200/- per plate and you get the hall and other facilities free. So total, 7.2Laks plus service tax...You can think of an upper limit of 8Lakh."

Mayadharbabu felt like sweating inside that cold air conditioned cabin…8Lakh is what he has saved in his provident fund in his entire service career….

MEN AND ANIMALS

Sunday afternoon…2PM.

Amzad Ali, the butcher had brisk business in the morning at his roadside shop. He did not go home for lunch as he wished to do some more business in the afternoon. His wife had packed lunch for him in a three tier steel Tiffin box. After the street got deserted and there were no more customers to attend to, he had his lunch. After lunch, at about 2PM he spread an old rexin sheet on the floor and took rest. The shop is an open asbestos roofed 10ftx10ft space and there were some essentials like a short rounded log pegged onto the ground like a center table, a stool for the butcher to sit and 2-3 sharp knives. At the back side of the shop, a cubicle veil has been created with stitched cement bags. Amzad uses this place to slaughter animals and then transform their bodies to eatable meat.

The butcher had brought twenty goats of assorted sizes today morning , have killed them one after another and the customers have snatched away their flesh , like vultures would do to a corpse.

Today's survivors are just two goats – a matured well built black goat and a small tender goat. The small one is almost half the size of the bigger one. Its skin is light brown with white patches all over the body. Just these two innocent animals have survived the forenoon slaughter.

31

Big Goat and the Small Goat have been tied to a bamboo pole. The Big one asked the Small one, "Where are your parents and siblings? I didn't see them at the shop in the morning when we came here loaded in the mini truck".The Small one replied, "Yesterday night, one big fat rich man came to Amzad's house in a big car; he spoke to Amzad regarding his daughter's marriage party at a mandap and while leaving asked him to send the "Mall" directly to the site. Early morning today, Amzad sent my parents and siblings in a small auto; I guess they have been sent to the mandap. The rich man was telling he has invited 200 guests"

Small goat asked the Big goat, "what happened to your five children; I saw them at the shop when we all were brought down from the mini truck and then tied to the poles." The Big goat replied," All of them gone. Amzad has killed them one after another ...I could only hear their helpless groans .Later, I saw their cut-off heads kept at one corner of the shop for quite some time. The skins were also drying on the boundary wall adjacent to this shop; but during noon time, a customer came , purchased the heads and the skin. The man was telling another customer "the juice extracted from goat heads is very good for the development of brains of young children."

The Small goat told the big one "You know, while large number of customers was waiting at this shop to buy meat today, they were discussing something regarding animal sacrifice at the temples. They were all against such sacrifice. Some of them were even thinking of organizing a protest march against such sacrifice of innocent animals. One person who seems to be a lawyer was telling that he will file a PIL."

Big goat responded..." These human beings are very clever. They know where to shout and where to remain silent."

It was 4PM...And the butcher woke-up. He washed his face...Caught hold of one big knife and started rubbing it on the edge of the log to sharpen it....

NOSTALGIA

Harinarayan was a barber and owned a shop 10ftx10ft in a suburban town. To make it look different he had painted the outside wall of his shop red, but there was no sign board. Everyone in a radius of 5km knew him. He had served three generations of customers. Some of the old man who bring their grand children to the saloon today, had been coming to his saloon when they were young. His was a mens' saloon, but people also bring their girl children for a haircut. Inside the saloon, there were three chairs for the customers. He had added cushion to the chairs for the comfort of the customers. He and his youngest son took care of hair cutting and shaving of customers. At any point of time, two customers could be served and one more could wait at the third chair. He also had two long wooden benches, each of which can accommodate 4-5 customers. Customers in queue occupy these two benches.

Harinarayan's saloon is famous for hair cutting and intellectual discussions. Two leading native language newspapers and one English daily will always be there on the bench to keep the customers-in-waiting engaged in reading. One also finds 2-3 months' old Stardust and Filmfare magazines lying on the rack. Young people don't read much and keep looking at the pretty faces in those magazines, while giving an impression that they are reading something.

Harinarayan was quite an aware man. He knew who are the potential winning candidates at the local municipal elections and also what is happening at the White House in USA. All the local, national and international political news were at his finger tips. While he craftily moved his scissor on the heads and the razor on the chins, he would be initiating and discussing all these news with the waiting customers. One will always find few elderly men engrossed with such discussions, with points and counter points. Many of these elderly people are either senior government servants or respectable people of the society because of their professional achievements. One would often find customers more interested in the discussion, than the actual purpose of their visit to the saloon...and many of them spend hours at the salon, just like that.

Harinarayan had three sons and one daughter. He had been able to get his daughter married off to a peskar who works in the nearby tahasil court. Youngest son had joined him in the profession. The eldest and the next one, were reasonably good students and have passed intermediate with second division marks. They were sitting at home without any work. Who will give them a job without a recommendation? One day Harinarayan expressed his plight to a customer-in-waiting, who was incidentally an engineer occupying a high position. Next day, the eldest son was posted at the engineer's office as an NMR. With God's grace, next year the younger one also got a government job, as constables in the police department.

Times have passed and all his three sons are married now and have their own families. Harinarayan has grown old and can't work anymore. His eye-sight poor and hands shaking. But he comes to the saloon daily, early in the morning .Sweeps and cleans the saloon properly; keeps two bucket full of water at one corner of the room and covers it with a cardboard. All these he does to ensure that his son starts his work at the saloon without any hassles.

Harinarayan notices, these days' customers don't read newspapers and also don't talk to each other. Each one of them carry a smart phone in their hand and fiddle with it during the waiting time.

He thinks aloud ..."Times have changed, People also have changed."

SALES TRICKS

It was a Saturday afternoon...I was very happy, no more classes. I had opened Facebook and was reading postings from different friends. At this time, phone rang and without bothering to look at the number, I put the set at my left ear. "Good afternoon , I am calling from Tanishq ;Are you displeased with us Sir" , prompted a lady with a sweet voice.

With naughty tone I quickly responded, "Why should I".....and she replied back, "Sir you have not visited us for last two years". I did not know how to respond to such a sweet statement. I told, "Don't have money, and will visit when able". I thought she will be distressed at my financial status and will stop. But No, she was after me..."Sir, we have an installment scheme, you deposit a small sum of money every month for 11 months. 12th installment we will deposit and you can buy any item with the full amount". I got bitter, "Don't have money even for installments, and please don't disturb me"

This was in the month of Dec. Two months passed. On 3rd March, a lady called me "Happy Anniversary Sir, I am calling from Tanishq. Please visit us with Madam today evening; we would like to celebrate your anniversary at our show room". I felt awkward, why should a jeweler show room is so enamored with my anniversary? . But later I could visualize their agenda and promptly asked, "Do you have my wife's mobile number?' "No" is what she told...I breathed a sigh of relief and I disconnected the phone without further deliberation.

If jeweler shops are smart, sari shops are not far behind.

Purchase of sari is a very elaborate and cumbersome activity. My wife's interests lies in variety, design, texture, color etc, but my mind always gets riveted at the price. While the sales man spreads the saris on the desk one after another and my wife gets busy scrutinizing them, I secretly look at the price tag stapled at some corner of the sari. 2-3 saris get shortlisted only after a heap is created on the desk and these 2-3 are later put on the shoulder to check how that looks on the body....and in each such exercise , the salesman remarks "This is a sober color, suits you madam "...Smile flashes on wife's face signaling final choice.

My wife was taking more time. The selection of the saris was not getting over and I was impatiently looking at other couples busy in similar exercise. My goodness! I heard the same prompt is being used by all the salesmen for all the ladies...""This is a sober color, suits you madam". After a gruesome search operation, finally selection of saris got over and I turned towards the cash counter...But from behind, a salesman called, " Sir, we have a good collection of sober shirts for you. Have a look". I quickly replied, "I only wear tailor made shirts. Thank you".

Long back I had read a book titled "What they don't teach you at Harvard". If I ever meet the author, I will ask him to add our sales techniques as a chapter in his book.

GUIDE

Raju is a twenty-five year old boy from a village. His father is a farmer and mother a housewife. He is the only son to his parents. The income that his father makes from the small farm land was just good enough for them to meet the necessities of life. They have two cows. The milk that the cows give is sold to the well-off families in the village to earn little extra money to take care of the vagaries of life. There is no sign of any luxury in his thatched house, excepting a second hand motor cycle that Raju has recently purchased on loan. By God's grace, neither of his parents have any big disease though both of them have crossed fifty now. Occasional cough and fever doesn't bother them.

Raju studied at the village school and passed matriculation in 3rd division. His parents don't understand the meaning of divisions. They only know pass and fail. The fact that Raju passed matriculation was a matter of joy and pride for his parents. Raju joined the nearby Government College and studied Arts and cleared his +2Arts in 3rd division again. Raju's parents did not want him to toil in the field and wanted him to pick up a job. But Raju was not too good a student to get a government job in competitive exams. He also did not choose to do a private job as they make one work like dog and pay very small amount. More over there is no job security and also no respect. The owner will misbehave with you if you don't dance as per his whims.

5km far from Raju's house, there is a tourist place. A place of worship for Buddhists but a tourist place for all. This is located at the top of a hill. Throughout the year, tourists pour in this place. Many of his village friends make a living by doing business at this place like tea stalls, juice point, handicraft shops etc. There are also some who work as photographers and tourist guides. One of his friends is into a parking space business there. While Raju didn't quite know what to do to earn some income and support his aging parents, one day he met a friend who works as a tourist guide. After listening to Raju's plight, he suggested him to work as a guide. He told Raju, "You can easily make 2-3 hundred rupee everyday if you can get just one foreign tourist as a client."...Raju responded "But neither I can speak English nor I have any knowledge about the tourist place". His friend smiled "You don't need any knowledge, whatever you tell, they will believe...And with regard to English I will teach you some key words, phrases and sentences..Come with me tomorrow for on the job training."

Raju accompanied his friend the next few days and learned the tricks of the trade. Many of the foreign tourists are from Tibet and China.

It was the day of Buddha purnima; there would be lot of crowd at the tourist place and Raju decided to make his maiden attempt as a guide on that day. He got up early in the morning, took bath in the nearby village pond and had his breakfast. He wore a black full pant and a white half shirt. For the 1st time in his life, he also wore a black shoe and a red printed tie. He has to work throughout the day and would sweat. So he kept an over-sized hanky in his pant pocket. He touched the feet of his father and mother; kick-started his motor cycle and drove towards the tourist place.

There is a huge crowd and there are many foreign tourists also. They are recognizable by their skin color and the kind of informal dress they wear- a half pant and a T-shirt. At their shoulder, a back-pack. Some of them wear a cap with a flat border around it.

Raju waited at the main gate where tourists enter the premises. Like him many guides were also waiting at the gate to get a client, but they were all experienced. Raju is a novice, a guide with zero experience, waiting for his first client.

He started wishing to all the tourists, with particular emphasis on foreigners "Good Morning Sir , Would you like to have a guide?". Many were ignoring his wishes; Some were shaking their heads in negation. He is there at the gate for last one hour or so without any success. Rest of the guides have got their catch and have moved into the premises.

Raju was wondering, "Perhaps my first day will be a disappointment."

But, good news can come anytime. A foreigner, perhaps a Chinese asked him "Are you a Guide, Can you help me tour this place". Raju got perplexed at this unexpected turn of events and intuitively told "Yes Sir, My pleasure". Raju did not tell his charges as anything will be better than earning nothing.

41

Raju escorted the tourist around the spot and made him see everything. The tourist bowed at the statue of Buddha . Both the tourist and Raju were tired of walking in the scorching sun and sat down under a tree just outside the tourist spot. At the instance of the tourist, Raju brought two glasses of fruit juice from the nearby stall . They both drank the juice.

As they were resting, the tourist asked Raju," In all religion, there is just one God. I read somewhere that in your religion, there are many Gods, more than thousands if I am not wrong...Is that correct?

Raju responded" You are partially correct.....We have many Gods , not thousands but in crores...33 crores to be precise...A Crore means seven zeroes after one"

Tourist," But do you have space and time to worship so many Gods"

Raju," We worship only 8-10 important Gods. Rest is worshiped in a lump sum basis. When our priest makes offerings, he makes individual offerings to these important ones and to the rest he gives single offering by saying "Sarva Devadebyai Namah"...meaning, take our offering of prayer as a team.

Tourist," Oh...I understood.., but who are these important ones"

Raju, "Before I tell you their names, let me tell you, unlike in other religions, we have different Gods for different work. This reduces their work load. For example , for Knowledge

42

Devi Saraswati is responsible and for Wisdom, Lord Ganesh...Understood?"

Tourist, "Yes, that sounds very scientific and rationale"

Raju, "Among the top order Gods we have Shivji; He gets angry very quickly and once angry he will dance and that dance number is called Tandab. He wears the skin of a tiger at his waist which stretched up to his knees. He wears snakes as his necklace. He also smears ash on his body as a talcum powder. He has long hairs like ladies and makes top knot. He sits at the top of the icy mountain and holy Ganga river emanates from his hair knot...He is also fond of opium. He has a bull as his pet. Everyone worships him because he is the God of Destruction"

Tourist," Who are the other Gods?"

Raju," We have Laxmi for Wealth and Biswakarma for Engineering. Also we have a God for Love, Krishna. In the heaven, all the beautiful ladies cherish to become the beloved of Lord Krishna."

Raju continued, "Ganeshji, Lord for Wisdom, has a head like an elephant"

Tourist," Head like an elephant? Tell me more about that"

Raju," Our lord of destruction Shivji was married to a beautiful goddess named Parbati. They had a cute little child named Ganesh, but he was too small to recognize his father. One day what happened, Parbatiji went to take bath in the bathroom and kept Ganesh as the gatekeeper of the house. She asked him not to allow anyone into the house till she finished the bath. But as bad luck, Shivji who normally sit at the mountain top came to the house for a visit and the little boy did not allow him. He got angry and cut his head. When Parbatiji finished bathing and came out she saw her son without head. The cut-off head could not be rejoined. She got angry and asked Shivji to get a head as soon as possible. Like all husbands, Shivji was very scared of Parbatiji. He directed his servants to search for a head and gave them some specification. The servants after thorough search got an elephant's head. This elephant's head was implanted to Ganesh's neck. Ganesh grew up and became Ganeshji, God of wisdom"

Tourist, "These stories are very interesting...Raju, tell me which God you worship"

Raju," My Father and my Mother. They are the reasons of my existence. My father toils in the field to see smile on my face...and my mother would not touch food till I am back at home at night"

Raju continued "At workplace, customers like you are my God...I survive on your payments"

The tourist took out a five hundred rupee note from his purse and handed over to Raju....

SIBANI

Sibani was a beautiful girl studying at a village school in class-VII. In those days, there used to be Board exams for class-VII and students were given grades like O, A, B, C and D. While O is considered the best grade, D graders are the students who have managed to cross the fence. Sibani appeared class-VII Board exam and scored O-grade. Not more than one percent students get this grade and considering her superlative academic performance, her father decided to admit her in the best government school in the neighboring town in class-VIII.

She got admitted at the Town High School and stayed at one of her close relative's house.

1st day in the school:

In class-VIII, there were four sections-A, B, C and D. Brightest students are clubbed into section-A and as such Sibani got into that section. In those days the ratio of boys to girls in the class was generally 70:30. This is the first day in the class and all the students are strangers to each other. At 10AM, the class teacher entered the class room. He was wearing a dhoti and a light sky colored panjabi. The class teacher is known to be very tough yet a great math teacher. He took the attendance and every time he called a roll number, he looked up to see the face of the student.

Teachers have a penchant to know the best students in the class. With this objective in mind, he instructed "Students who have got O-grade, please stand-up". There were just five of them in the class of fifty students – four boys and one girl, the girl being Sibani. Everyone's attention turned towards her.

She was beautiful. A rustic innocent charm was on display to the whole class. She was wearing a deep sky colored scot, which went few inches beyond her knee. Scot had a stitched captive long cotton belt made of the same cloth. She had tightened the scot at the waist with that belt and made a knot. The excess of the belt on both sides of the knot was dangling at the belly button. She was also wearing a buttoned white shirt, the lower part of which was tucked inside the scot at the waist. The shirt had small rounded collars to give a feminine impression. Sibani had waist length hairs. Those had been beaded to make it look like a tapered rope at the back. At the end, a white ribbon has been craftily tied to look like a flower. White stockings and black half shoes at her legs.

That day the sight of Sibani completely eclipsed the four boys who also got "O" grade – Kailash, Pratihari, Dillip and Ranjan.

Sibani maintained her academic excellence and passed 10th class board exam with higher first division marks. She got admitted into the best college in the town and pursued science, with biology as an optional. Perhaps she aspired to become a doctor.

This big college attracted many bright students from far and wide. But Sibani remained the centre of attraction – now less for academics and more for her beauty. With youth, the curves became more prominent and she looked more attractive than ever. All and sundry harbored ambition to woo her. An affair those days meant a girl maintaining an eye-contact for few more seconds and if there is a smile on her face, it is a bonanza. Boys adopted different strategies to win her, but nothing really worked. Some would discretely follow her to the college every day, as if it is a coincidence. But this coincidence meant long wait at some corner of the street or at the bench of a tea stall. Some, in the afternoon, would make rounds in their bi-cycle in front of her house to get a glimpse of her in the balcony. Some others would lend her books and notes, even though many times the notes are of sub-standard quality. One would salute the audacity of hope of these young boys, but Sibani would not yield. She maintained a respectable indifference for all their advances. Perhaps she was too innocent to understand what a crush is or she was too matured to handle such hazards of being pretty.

But one day miracle happened.

Breaking news spread among all boys. "Sibani has given a B&W passport size photograph to Basanta". Not getting your affection reciprocated is tolerable, but knowing that your friend has won the jackpot was painful. It was more painful because Basanta was not good looking, had a skin color as dark as a mustard seed and wears a specs to make it more clumsy. He was very average in studies.

Time passed and this breaking news became daily news. Friends started seeing Basanta and Sibani together in different places in the campus. Sibani started spending less and less time in studies, but Basanta maintained a balance between the book-affair and love-affair. Both appeared +2Sc Board exam together. Basanta came out in first division, Sibani in third division, unbelievable news to all. This academic fault line brought cracks in their love affair and later they choose to become strangers to each other.

Time passed. Sibani pursued Arts and completed her PG. She could never get back to her great academic roots; she just sailed through the exams and passed. Sibani had developed weak feet. She again fell in love; this time with a matured individual working as a station master in Railways. He was staying alone in a rented accommodation near her house and she lost her heart to him. This man was no match to Sibani in terms of looks or credentials. But marriages are made in heaven. After initial family reservations, she got married to him. All her old suitors, thought Sibani deserved a much better marital partner and this marriage was a kind of anti-climax of her life.

Twenty years passed in the meantime. All her brilliant suitors are now married and have their own families. When they meet, Sibani is the common topic for discussion. Nobody quite know where she is these days. She is an enigma.

SETTING SUN

This is the state office of a big insurance company. Mr. Nayyar is sitting at the customers' lounge at 10AM. He has taken medical insurance from this company. Recently due to a mild heart attack, he got admitted to a hospital and has spent nearly 1.70 Lakh and he has submitted the bills to the insurance company for reimbursement. But the insurance company did not honor his claim with the reason "pre-existing diseases not disclosed". Perhaps the insurance company meant "blood pressure" as the pre-existing disease. Mr. Nayyar thought a person not having blood pressure can also get a heart attack. He wanted to meet the concerned official of the insurance company and pursue his matter.

As per the advice of the security at the gate, he had made necessary entry in the visitors' register and is waiting at the lounge. He wanted to meet the Head of the office, but the security said, "Sahib doesn't meet anyone from 9AM-11AM". The security has informed someone else over phone "A customer is waiting at the lounge". More than thirty minutes have passed. Neither any officer has come to meet him at the lounge nor has he been asked to get into the office to meet anyone. In the meantime, he has already reminded the security guard twice. Each time the guard rebutted "Sir is busy, please wait"

Mr. Nayyar drank a glass of water that was available for the visitors on the centre table. Later he picked-up The Economic

Times lying on the table and started looking at the headlines. Though his eyes were on the paper, his mind was traversing in the past.

Mr. Nayyar used to head this office a year back. He used to come to this office by a company provided chauffeur driven car. It was a completely different response from the ex-security guard then. The security guard would salute him as soon as he comes out from the lift and nears the office entrance at the fourth floor. As he would walk towards his cabin and pass through many work stations, staffs would stand up and wish him "Good Morning Sir" with smiling faces. He would smile back and reciprocate "Good Morning".

He had a nice wooden floored spacious cabin. Walls of the cabin were made of opaque glass, but the door was left transparent. At the centre of the cabin, an expensive table; a more expensive revolving chair for him to sit. For the visitors, there were four cushioned chairs. Before he reaches the office, the house keeping staffs make the cabin clean and tidy and ensure that the vessel on the table is adorned with the flowers he loves – yellow roses. They would also keep the newspaper The Economic Times on the table. Adjacent to his cabin, there is a small cabin where his Secretary used to sit. She was pretty, disciplined, and sharp, in that order. As he takes his chair, Secretary would come, wish him and then brief him the appointments of the day. No one is allowed to meet him for the first one hour as he makes his plans for the day.

He was actually working in another insurance company and the above cited company hired him with thirty percent hike in remuneration. In the insurance industry, he had earned a name as a high performer and so the premium. And the new company had made the right judgment in poaching him. He took the topline and bottomline of the company to new heights in a spread of just three years. From just "yet another player" in the market, his company became the market leader in the state with forty percent market share. He used to get regular compliments from the CEO. Among the peers he was the envy of all...Jealousy is the byproduct of success. For his superlative performance, he got salary hikes, which many of his peers thought unbelievable and also unreasonable. He was also given the membership in the best club in the city. Celebration of his birthday at office used to be mega event. For Mr. Nayyar, life was smooth sailing.

But life has turns.

One day while Mr. Nayyar was traveling to office by car, he met with a severe accident. A lorry hit the car from behind, throwing him almost to the jaws of death . He survived with multiple bone fractures . The driver escaped unhurt. Mr. Nayyar got admitted to a big hospital and remained there for long six months. During this stay he also suffered a mild heart attack . This insurance company where he worked could not keep his chair unoccupied that long. A new person was hired to head the office.

Though Mr. Nayyar recovered after six months, his mobility got restricted. The doctor advised, he shouldn't sit and work for long hours. He should also cut down on his long travels.

Considering all these, he wrote to the CEO for a suitable posting. But in the meantime, a new CEO had taken over. He did not give much importance to his past credentials. After many follow-ups, Mr. Nayyar got a posting at a far off branch office in a junior position; he could not accept the assignment because of health concerns.

Since then, he has been looking for an academic assignment in the city where he has a house. Teaching jobs are less demanding and would suit him, though in terms of salary it would be peanuts. He neither has any PhD nor any teaching experience. But hopefully someone will value his work experience and will take him as a faculty.

It is almost an hour since he is waiting at the lounge. Mr. Nayyar was thinking aloud "No one salutes a setting sun"

A SIMPLE ACT

Asutosh is a professor in a university and is a diabetic. Doctor has advised him to take up morning walk every day. He has avoided the advice for quite some time now. But he can't any more. The recent blood sugar report shows that his sugar level has increased to an alarming level. Last time when he met the doctor, he had hinted, if the sugar level doesn't remain in control, Asutosh has to shift from tablets to insulin. He is very scared of injections. They are very painful and then these have to be taken twice daily before food. Though ultra thin needles are available now days, pain is always a pain. He has seen this pain when his father used to take insulin. In those days, needles used to be thick and he remembers the worry in his father's face when he has to take lunch or dinner.

Asutosh has set the alarm at 5AM in his mobile and keeps it near his pillow before he sleeps at night. Mobile is ruthlessly disciplined in its work. It rings exactly at 5AM and Asutosh wakes up. He washes his face, changes the night dress to a track, puts on the sports shoe and goes out for the walk to the nearby park. The park is located quarter of a kilometer far from his house. He does not disturb his wife and kids with a request to lock the house when goes out. He instead locks the house from outside, as he will be back in a while and by that time all his family members will still be asleep.

53

On a nice cool morning, while he was walking towards the park, Asutosh noticed a five hundred rupee note lying on the road. He bent down and picked that up. Kept that inside his pant pocket and resumed walking towards the park. His mother has taught him in his childhood "if you ever get such unclaimed money on the road, never make personal use of it. Give that to a beggar sitting in front of any temple". She has told him many times, if you possess something that doesn't belong to you, it is stealing.

Asutosh wondered who could probably drop this money on the road. He started thinking of many possibilities:

Perhaps he is a poor labor who was walking down the road, in the evening, after a day's hard work, towards the nearby slum where he stays; the loin cloth that he wears must not be having a pocket, and may be the money has slipped from the knot at his waist. If that is the case, he must have wept at this loss after reaching home and not finding the money at the knot. His wife must have consoled him saying "whatever happens is as per God's wish"

May be the person is a servant of a rich person, who had come to the neighborhood shop to buy a packet of cigarette for his master and has dropped the note. If that is the case, the master must have rebuked him a lot and must have warned him against such negligence. The master might also deduct the loss from his salary.

Or....It could be one of the many five hundred rupee notes that the members of the Barat party threw at the hired professional dancers while they danced to the raunchy numbers on the street. Or it can be a drunkard who has dropped the note, while returning home in his slumber.

As Asutosh reached the gate of the park, he saw a beggar sitting there with his bowl. He took out the note from his pocket and left that on the begging bowl.

The beggar smiled and blessed Asutosh with the words "May you live for hundred years"

COST OF SAMOSA

1983..Bijay passed +2 science with first division and secured 5th position in the state. Friends were after him for a party. A party those days meant a visit to a nearby asbestos roofed Jamuna canteen and eating of samosa and sweets with friends. But parents did not finance such luxuries and Bijay has to meet the expenses from the small savings that he had accumulated from the pocket money that he got sporadically from his mother. Asking for money from father for such parties is like chanting the name of Ram in Lanka.

Bijay mentally calculated the cost ...it should be one samosa, one alu-chop and a rasogolla...total Rs5 per head...So for five friends and himself, the total money required is Rs30.

He invited all for an evening party at the canteen. All sat round a squared table. Being the host, Bijay signaled the waiter to come and take the order. Both the owner and the waiter were in their bare necessities...means owner was wearing a dhoti and the canteen boy a half pant. Waist upward all bares...Nothing surprising in this dresses up though, in those times. Anticipating that the friends may consume more than the budget, he advised the boy to serve each of his friend whatever they want with an upper limit of Rs5. After the boy receded to the kitchen to fetch the ordered items, Bijay clarified friends that they can eat more than the budget but have to pay themselves. All nodded as none was carrying even a paisa in his pocket.

Ordered items were served and each one started taking small bites. By the way, Jamuna canteen was famous for the sweet handmade sauce that they serve as an addendum to snacks. You might come across an ant or a two swimming on those viscous orange colored sauce, but sauce used to be very tasty.

Though there were just six tables in the canteen, all were lying unoccupied that evening excepting one opposite Bijay and his friends. An aged man may be forty-five years old and a young men of thirty something were sitting and were having snacks. Looked like the aged man is a lower level clerk in a government office and the young one, a well placed officer, may be in a Bank or an Insurance company. At first they ate a plate of samosa each. Later, Bijay noticed the young man ordered kachori and alu-chop , though the aged man was saying "I can't have more"..After some time ,the young man again ordered chenapoda in spite of the aged man having serious reservation about his taking anything more. And that was not the end..The young men again ordered the canteen boy to give two rosogolla each and the boy obliged. The aged man appeared to be worried but finished the items quickly.

The young man was eating slowly , very slowly. The aged man waited at the table for some time and then excused himself to wash his hands. After washing hands , the aged man reached the counter of the canteen hoping that the young man will finish eating and will pay the bill. But he was eating as slow as a tortoise will walk. After a protracted wait , the aged man understood the mystery behind slow eating of the young man and without waiting any further took out the money purse from his pocket and handed over few notes to the canteen owner.

After the financial transaction was over , the youngman reached the counter . He took a handful of snuff from the tray kept on the counter and threw those into his mouth in style. Old man signaled him , let's go .

Standing at the counter , the youngman signaled back "let me pay the money" to which the aged man said "I have already paid"...The young man displayed a mock anger with a statement "Why Did You Pay?"

BASEMENT PARKING

11 PM in the night.

It is a five storey newly constructed apartment and there are ten flats in it. Out of the above , only five flats have been occupied till date. Kasi is the caretaker-cum- security of the apartment.

At the portico inhabitants have parked their vehicles. There are four cars : one Matiz , an Alto , a Honda City and an Innova ; three Bajaj scooters , four Hero Passion bikes and five little bi-cycles of the kids. While all are asleep and it is quiet all around , there was a chat among all these vehicles. Alto initiates the chat, "Hey, we have been here for 2-3 months now , but we don't know each other. Let's introduce ourselves and try to know each other. Let us start with Matiz.

Matiz: My owner is an advocate. He purchased me ten years back because madam liked my cute look. He used to drive that blue Bajaj scooter which is parked at the corner. My body parts are not available now days. The other day , I heard my owner telling to his junior that he will sell me off. The junior who his learning advocacy from him , evinced interest to buy me and they discussed the price. The advocate agreed to sell me at throw-away price. Looks like I will relocate to Junior's house shortly. The junior was telling , he will use me for 1-2 years and then will sell me off to a Kabadiwala.

Honda City : My owner is a CEO of a company. He doesn't drive me. He has a driver who drives me. The driver takes good care of me. Every day morning he washes me clean and removes all dust from inside by using a vacuum cleaner. The owner gets very upset if there is any sign of dust inside. Therefore the driver is very careful. I have a dedicated parking place at the office. Since I am CEO's car , rest of the four wheelers respect me a lot. At my sight at the office gate , the gate keeper comes running to open the gate. My owner loves to listen to gazals and so the driver puts the CDs accordingly. Honda looked towards the bikes and said "Hello group of four bikes' how is life?"

Bikes: We are all same. All our owners are software engineers working with Infosys. They have purchased us a year back and all of them stay in one flat and each one pay a rent of five thousand rupees a month. We ferry them to office and different food joints like Domino's. McDonalds, Subway etc. Friday evening , we either go to a pub or a bar. Many times , we also bear the extra load of their girl friends.

Innova: My life is pathetic . My owner works in a bank and uses the bottle green colored chetak scooter that is parked near me. He has purchased me for business purpose and has employed a driver also. Every day morning , I go to different travel agent's offices and get parked there. I ferry different customers to different places. Most of the time I carry people in groups. Some are good but many are very bad. They make me dirty. Some even vomit on me. Due to over work , I break-down frequently and have to visit garage .Life is difficult.

Now it is the turn of the Alto.

Alto: My owner is a professor in a university. I came to his home twelve years back. He loves me very much and every Sunday he cleans me personally. Once I overheard Madam telling my owner to sell me off as I have grown old. But my owner did not agree and said "Never ever this car has stranded us on road , then why should I sell it off". I have seen his kids grow-up from infants to now high school going children. Many times the little daughter of the owner also joins him to clean me on Sundays. I love them all. He also has a Bajaj scooter which is 17-18 years old now. He had got that as a marriage gift. Every Sunday , my owner also cleans the scooter , though he uses it very rarely.

Last but not the least, the bi-cycles introduced themselves:

Bi-cycles : We don't know who our owners are. But our users are the small little kids who stay in this apartment. We have no work except in the afternoon. During that time , they make us run like crazy. They bang us against the walls . Drop us on the floor ,and dash against each other . Kids are like that. We get injured , but we love their energy and innocence.

Honda city made the closing statement:

Good to hear you all. It is quite late now. Let's take some rest. Good night to all.

SUPERMOM

This is Chiraranjanbabu's house . This is an old model bungalow with a big central courtyard , of the size of a badminton court . Around this courtyard, there are living rooms, study rooms and kitchen, all single storied. If one will stand at the entrance of the house, all the rooms in the left are made of brick with concrete roof . Rooms on the right are made of mud with thatched roof.

At the entrance, parallel to the frontage of the house , there is a wide verandah. Two wooden benches are placed at the verandah for visitors to sit . These benches have backrest as well as armrest. At the front court, there is a small garden where one can notice variety of flower trees and a number of decorative plants . On the backyard, there is a half a acre pond and adjacent to it half an acre of land where seasonal vegetables are grown.

On this land, but with a respectable distance from the main house, there are two latrines and one bathroom. There is municipal water connection to this bathroom. Inside the bathroom there is a brick partitioned tank, where water is preserved for emergency use. This bath room is meant for females; males take bath in the pond. For the purpose of the latrine, one has to carry a bucket full of water from this tank. Adjacent to the field where vegetables are grown , there is a cow shed. In this cowshed there are three cows and two calves. Towards the extreme part of the backyard, there are three small thatched houses where three tribal families stay.

Chiraranjanbabu has an aristocratic lineage, but he works as a clerk in a bank. He has a bi-cycle to go to office and other places. At a later part of his career in the bank , he purchased a moped, which is a sign of his wealth in those times. In the evening, he either goes to a club or to a friend's house to play cards. He enjoys smoking, but later left it due to heath issues. On Sunday afternoons, he would go fishing with a fishing stick in his own pond. Few feet inside the pond, there is a small platform on which he will sit and in the evening he comes back with the catch in a small rounded cage made of bamboo sticks. He loves growing plants – both vegetables and flowers. He had a pet dog , which spends its time lazily at the verandah. Little before the dusk , it takes the stairs and gets seated at the conical peak of the thatched roof , so that he will be the first to see his master returning home from office. As he gets a glimpse of his master from the distant street , it will jump from the height and will be at the main gate to welcome him and licks his leg as a token of his love.

Nirmaladevi is the wife of Chiraranjanbabu, and mother to four children – one daughter and three sons , daughter being the eldest. She is the superwomen of the house. In terms of education, she can just read her language and count, nothing more than that. But tell her any work to do or any problem to solve, she can do that in a blink. Children are pampered with all kinds of homemade food, as per their choice. She milks the cows in the morning; even the unruly cow stands calm in her sight. When a snake or a reptile sneaks into the house or the central courtyard, it is she who dares to finish them with a stick. When Chiraranjanbabu was required to take insulin injections , she learnt how to do that and would give the jab effortlessly. At the dead of the night, if a child need to go to the outdoor latrine, she will stand guard.

At the end of the tiring day, before she goes to sleep she brings out her diary. In the diary, she takes down all the expenses made in that day, including the coins of smallest denomination. She knows , everything matters, so also money.

Each home has a Nirmaladevi and we call them Supermom now a days.

MORNING WALK

It is early morning. Darkness is still there. Yet there is a gathering of people , young and old , at the gate of the Lumbini Park. The park opens at 4AM and closes at 9AM. This is a beautiful park with greenery all around. There are big lawns at different segments of the park ; concrete chairs are also available almost everywhere , each of which can accommodate 4-5 persons. At the center of the park, there is a small artificial lake and across this lake there is a foot over bridge. There are two entry gates – one in the west and the other in the east. The eastern part of the park is the foot hill of a hillock and one can see quite a deep forest there. Near the entrance, there is a playing area for children . There are sea-saw, swings and other games. There is a sign board that only children up to twelve years age can play there. Concentric to the boundary of the park , there is a jogging track which will be approximately 500mtrs.

On the jogging track, quite a good number of people are having a morning walk. Walkers are predominantly men but there are also some women and young girls on the track. Most of them are in small groups of 3-4 friends but there are few who are also alone. Gossiping while walking is fun and therefore many love to walk in groups – both men and women.

I reached the park little late at about 5AM and took to the jogging track. Lot of people are there on the track. I am a fast walker and hence overtaking different groups of people one after another. At the same time I am also able to hear the content of their gossip . I first overtook two young people – one boy and a girl, both are in their late teen . They have earphone plugged into their ear drums and wires running over their chest up to the mobile inside their pant pocket. They are enjoying music and walking. Both of them are of sound health and perhaps they are into this morning work-out to maintain the good physique that they possess. I am now seeing a women secretly plucking flower from a tree at a distant corner of the park. In spite of her skillful quick hand movement to snatch away flowers from the tree, the guard has seen her misdeed and is whistling and running towards her. She surely needed these flowers to offer to the gods and goddesses at her house , but this security will not allow her to do that.

I notice, in one portion of a lawn , a number of people , men and women , have congregated. All of them are wearing white dress. Each of them has spread a bed sheet on the lawn and is sitting crossed legged. One aged man seems like an instructor is giving some tips to all these people. Later he sat down on a mat and started doing some physical postures, by stretching and bending his legs and hands. All the other members of the group were following his actions. Later, I noticed they all stood up and burst into loud laughter and they were laughing in a rhythm. They did this activity for 10-15 minutes. I read somewhere, this is a new therapy called "Laugh Therapy". Basically means , when one laughs many nerves get excited and the blood flow improves, thus contributes to better health. I wondered if one needs to come to a park to laugh. Can't these people laugh at home or at office.

I returned my notice from these laughing crowd and sped up to overtake one group of three old men walking in front of me. As I neared them, I heard them talking about their latest medical reports and different medicines that they are taking. They also spoke how difficult it is to spend time at home. The only things they do at home are read newspaper and listen to some informative programs on the TV. Some of them also disclosed how their sons and daughters-in-law are finding them as a burden at home. Also they spoke about some of their friends who died last week. One of them was telling , life was better till his wife was alive; at least she was showing some concern for him though physically she was too weak to do anything for him.

I overtook this group of old people and am walking behind a group of four ladies. They are aged and must be in their late forties. As I neared them, I heard them talking about the irregularity of their maid-servants , how they provide poor quality of service and that they will not attend to even a single extra work. They also spoke about their mother-in-laws. While one was talking how even though she is old she supports her in all her work , the other lady was bad mouthing her mother-in-law as lazy and how she has spoiled her grand children with too much of pampering. One lady was telling what all she has done to find a suitable match for her daughter and how nothing has worked.

Ladies were walking slowly and so I overtook them and now behind a group of men in their late forties. I heard them talking about the problems at their office, how there is too much of favoritism in promotion and posting at office. And then they also spoke about how their children are doing academically in their professional colleges and what kind of jobs they are expected to get. One of them perhaps has taken a study loan for his child and was telling his headache of repayment will get reduced only after his son gets a job and takes care of repayment.

I overtook this group and now following a fat man accompanying a very smart looking person. I know both of them. The fat man is a businessman and owns 2-3 manufacturing units and the smart looking man is an IAS officer. This fat man was discussing some permission related matter with the smart man. I thought, the business man is quite intelligent. It is better to meet a babu at the park than at the office. Babu will be receptive in the morning hours as the mind is free and the businessman can also discuss everything with him without any inhibition.

I overtook this business man and started approaching an equally fat man walking alone. He has disproportionately large butts and was releasing sounds in installments from his back. Perhaps he has eaten too much previous night and has not attended to call of nature before visiting the park. I quickly overtook him to escape the human bombardments.

I have already made eight rounds and am tired but will make two more rounds to complete my daily quota. Now I am few meters behind a young lady. She is wearing a light colored salwar and kameez. She is slim and shapely from behind. She has lifted all her hair and has made a beautiful top knot ; her smooth neck looks quite attractive. Due to excessive sweating, impressions have become apparent. I wondered, many must be coming to the park just to see this damsel early in the morning.

I am now through with my walk and am taking a brief rest at one of the cement benches near the playing area for the children. Two young couple have brought their kids to play here.

Two girls on the swing are enjoying their ride and giggling. No worries on their face...they looked as charming as morning dews.

STRANGE ENCOUNTER

Deepak is a Chartered Accountant in a private company and is newly married. He stays in a rented house 200mtr far from the office. This saves him travel time . Since the house is nearby, he doesn't bring lunch box to the office. He instead goes to his house during the lunch break. Besides having food at home , it helps him spend some time with his dear wife. His in-law's house is in the same town where he works. Once in a week his wife goes to her parent's house and spends a night there. During her absence, Deepak takes lunch in office canteen and dinner at a restaurant in the neighborhood of his house. Deepak enjoys this occasional solitude. He spends time watching TV and at times also cooks the dinner to keep himself engaged.

Soumya works in the same office as an office accountant . This is her first job and she is on probation. She is very young and beautiful. She is very diligent in her work and everyone likes her because of her sweet behavior and disciplined work. There are few other female workers in the office, but all of them are elder to Soumya by at least 8-10 years. Everyday Soumya commutes by bus from a nearby town , 30km far to reach the office.

Soumya's parents are very educated but at the same time are very conservative also. They were planning her marriage as soon as possible. Since she was good looking and was also having a job, her parents could quickly get a groom without much of difficulty. He was an agricultural engineer and was working in a government department in another state. After the initial reluctance, Soumya agreed for the marriage. The groom wanted her to leave the job and become a housewife. Soumya had no other option. Engagement function was held and the marriage date was finalized. The news that Soumya is getting married and may consider leaving the job spread to everyone in the office.

It was a Saturday and Soumya reached office at 9am as usual and attended to her regular work. She was wearing a pink colored printed salwar kameez .

Little before the lunch break, she went to her Boss's cabin and submitted the resignation, with a request to relieve her from the job same day. She cited marriage as the reason for her quitting the job. Boss understood her predicament and assured to do the needful. She being on probation, the clearance was ready by 2PM. At 3PM all staffs assembled and bid farewell to Soumya. Though she has worked just for six months in this company, she felt very emotional. She was very close to her immediate boss Deepak and has learnt a lot about accounts from him. During the farewell, eyes of Deepak also got wet.

Soumya intended to leave office at 5PM . But little before this time, the sky got clouded with the darkest cloud. Wind started blowing and picked up intensity . It started lightening also. In an hour , all this moved towards a heavy cyclonic storm. Wind was blowing at 180-200 km/hour and was giving a feeling that it will break the glass paneled windows of the office. The power went off and there is no fuel in the generator . So it is all dark inside the office. It is no better outside. Coconut and other tall trees were on the verge of getting uprooted. Big and small trees could not sustain the pressure anymore. They got uprooted one after another. Electric poles got bent like hairpins and the electric wires netted all over the road. Huge banyan and papal trees adjacent to the office also accepted defeat and are lying like a dead monsters on the road. Heavy rain added to the devastation. It poured cats and dogs. With the choked drains, all the roads virtually became drains and water flew over them with heavy current .

Staffs in the office were sitting at different places in groups and were waiting in the darkness for the storm to subside. At one corner of the office are standing Deepak and Soumya , little isolated from other staffs. Soumya's dad called her and she responded " I am at office , don't worry. I am fine here".

It is already 8PM and there is no sign of the storm to subside, though the intensity of rain has reduced. Soumya has realized that it will be impossible now to reach her home 30km far , perhaps she has to spend the night at office. She is worried and insecure now. She can't expect her parents to come to this office and rescue her also.

At this weak moment, Deepak told Soumya " My house is 200mtr far and I have a guest room . May be you can consider staying at my house tonight . Tomorrow early morning I will drop you at your home in my bike" , and then he added , "My wife has gone to her parent's house and I am not sure if she is back at home or not ". Soumya knew Deepak very well . He is a thorough gentleman and always helps others. She thought for a moment and agreed. They came out of the main entrance of the office building. It is all dark outside. Trees, electric poles and wires are lying everywhere and there is knee deep water running on the road. Deepak held Soumya's left hand tightly and they started their walk. They navigated the gruesome obstructions with the help of each other and at last reached the doorstep of Deepak's house. It is all darkness and the house locked, meaning his wife has not come back. Deepak opened the door with the duplicate key and they entered the room. Both of them are completely soaked in rain and drain water. Rain water has also entered the floor of all the rooms of the house.

Deepak traced a candle in the kitchen, lighted it and make it stand on the dining table. Later , Soumya called her father and informed that she is staying back at one of her colleague's house.

Deepak changed to a dry dhoti that was lying on the rack. He could not get any night dress of his wife to give that to Soumya. After lot of search , he could locate a chiffon sari and gave that to her. Soumya has never worn a sari before. She went to bath room and came out somehow covering her body with that thin transparent sari. When Depak's eye met hers, she looked down shyly unto the floor.

Deepak brought out bread and butter from the fridge. They sat adjacent to each other at the dining table, and ate those eatables. After food , it is time to sleep. Deepak escorted Soumya to the guest room ...but alas , the bed is completely wet . The water has splashed unto the bed through the window which Deepak has not closed properly before leaving for office. Deepak quickly inspected the other bed room ; found the bed to be dry and fine. He asked Soumya to use that bed room and told her that he will somehow manage in the guest room.

Soumya felt awkward . How can she trouble Deepak whole night and sleep comfortably alone. He has already taken lot of trouble for her.

She intuitively asked, "Is there not adequate space for two persons to sleep on that bed?"

MISS CALL

Aditya and Divya are lovers. Both of them study in the same engineering college and in the same branch. While Aditya is from Uttar Pradesh , Divya is from Andhra Pradesh. Both of them are in the same year. It was a case of love at first sight. The affair started on the first few months of their joining the college. Now they are in the final year.

Yesterday , they had an argument at a secluded place of the college lawn . The issue was informing their respective parents about their affair. Divya has already told her parents about her interest in Aditya. She has been asking Aditya to also tell about their affair to his parents for quite some time now . But Aditya was evading this suggestion. Yesterday Divya again raised that matter and gave an ultimatum to Aditya. He has to inform his parents then and there, else she will walk out from his life. Aditya knew his parents, both are very conservative. His father is a burning coke when he gets angry. He again tried to buy some time from Divya , but she was unmoved.

They sat at the lawn for an hour or so. But Aditya could not muster the courage to call his parents. Divya got up and started walking towards the girls' hostel. Aditya followed her, pleading for few more days' time. But she has become deaf by that time. She did not listen to him. Aditya followed her till she reached the hostel with the hope that she will cool down , but in vain. She entered the hostel gate without even looking back once.

Aditya came back to his hostel and lied down on his bad. He thought about the nice time he has spent with Divya and promise of marriage that he has made to her many times. That he will marry her is a foregone conclusion, but he is scared to tell his parents at this point in time. May be after he gets a job and starts earning money, he will tell his parents. Perhaps, his parents will be more receptive then.

It is evening time now . Aditya knew Divya's anger is short lived . He thought he will call Divya at about 8PM or so. By that time , hopefully her temper must have come down. He went to the Boys' common room and tried to keep himself engaged in reading some magazines and playing carom. But his eye was on the big rounded wall clock hanging at the common room at a height.

Little before 8PM , he came back to his room and dialed Divya . There was no response. He called again , but same result. He waited for few minutes and tried again, but Divya was not picking the calls. He continued with this effort for half an hour or so. Towards his few last attempts, the rings were getting cut at the other end. Divya did not yield that day. She is serious this time.

Aditya thought of an idea. Calls she may reject. But if he writes a mail , she will surely read. Aditya went to hostel mess , had his dinner and came back to his room. He took rest for some time and then sat before his lappy to write the love letter. The letter goes like this:

Hello Beautiful Divya - I never knew, you look so beautiful when you get angry. Today, you looked like a fairy from the heaven with those puffy cheeks glowing red with anger.

Divya , I understand your displeasure dear but hopefully you also understand my difficulty. You know , I love you like mad and can go to any length to marry you. But everything has a time. Please bear with me for few more days. By the way , you have to bear with me whole of your life , once you marry me. Do you remember our first day ?....and how we fell in love.

On your first day in the college, you were not wearing the college uniform of black salwar and white kameez. Rather you were in a pink salwar with a matching bobby printed kameez. Pink is my favorite color and this pink in you floored me that day. You looked simple, calm and poised. When you were sitting on the opposite side of the class , I was looking at you again and again....and you caught one of my such innocent adventure with your eyes. I turned my eyes towards the white board with an attempt to give an impression that I was not really looking at you. But I must confess, I was not in my control that day. I thought God has created you just for me only.

The next day , you came to college wearing college uniform , black salwar and white kameez. Even this mundane colors could not take away the charm from you, the beauty just got moderated...little bit.... and you remained the star of my eyes.

You remember the dress you wore on that first Saturday?... this being the day for informal dress..Forgot?..I remember , you were wearing a body hugging jeans with a pink tank top , again my favorite color. And you were wearing a low heel shoe that day . Dear , you looked stunning that day.

I saw you in sari for the first time on Saraswati puja. I was wearing a brown punjabi and a black pant and was standing at the pandal. I was looking at the goddess but frankly waiting for the other devi 'you' to appear before me. And after a long wait , you reached the pendal with other girls. You were wearing a copper sulphate color printed chiffon sari with a matching long sleeved blouse. You had left those long hairs free at your back and it appeared like a river on the flow . You looked divine that day dear.

And on the annual day DJ night , it was an anti-thesis of you . You were wearing a black scot little above the knee with a contrasting red top. A beautiful red hair band with white dots , at your head . I could not believe my eyes when I saw you on the dance floor. You were a show stopper that day.

Dear Divya , I remember how you looked in all such occasions. I love you dear and I love you like mad.

Mail sent at 10PM after which Aditya went to sleep.

When Aditya woke up in the morning , he saw a miss call from Divya at 1AM in the night.

THE NAÏVE CAMERAMAN

Sovon is a Christian young man married to a Hindu girl. It was a love marriage. The marriage was solemnized in a church as per Christian tradition. There was lot of resistance from both the families , but later parents of Sovon accepted the marriage. But the parents of Sima , wife of Sovon , were dead against this marriage and cut-off all relationship with Sima after she went off to Sovon's house.

Sovon was into variety of businesses. He had a cable TV business and provided cable TV service to nearly hundred customers. He also had a small hotel in the town , where a middle class person can have a bellyful of food at a very reasonable price. His hotel business had good reputation because of the quality of his food and the hygiene he maintained in the kitchen. Based on this reputation and also because of his Christian connection, he also had a catering contract from a nearby Christian hospital, to provide food to all its indoor patients. This contract was not very lucrative but Sovon had a social service mindset and he liked this business very much. Patients in this hospital are treated free of cost as it is a charitable institution. To get associated with such an institution was a matter of pride for Sovon.

Sovon also had a video recording business. People take his service for recording of important events like marriage , birthday party , school functions , seminars and corporate events. He had two costly cameras and accessories for the purpose. Sovon was very popular in the town for the quality of video he makes and also the promptness of his service . He will be always on time for recording and does his best to keep the customer happy. Sovon has employed two boys for cable TV business and another four boys for the hotel and catering business. He undertakes the recording business himself. As per need, at times he pulls in one boy from the cable TV business for video recording work.

Once an executive of a not-so-reputed company from Kolkata called Sovon and inquired if he can provide recording service for their product launch in a hotel. He agreed and rate was finalized. The product launch was scheduled at evening 8PM. On the appointed day , Sovon reached the hotel with one camera at 7.00PM . Based on the advice from the reception, he reached the conference hall . In the conference hall , he found the elementary arrangements for a function. Nearly two hundred chairs have been laid on the floor. On the dais, there are four chairs for the guests arranged alongside a long table. The table is covered with a white cloth. On the backdrop there is a banner mentioning the name of the company, the product to be launched and the chief guest of the evening. Two well dressed young men , with black shinning shoe at the feet and red printed tie at their neck , were present in the hall. They appear to be busy checking the arrangements for the function.

Sovon met these two persons and introduced himself. As per their advice, he started arranging the camera on a tripod stand and connected the power cord to the nearest plug point. At this point in time , one of the tie-wearing fellow reached Sovon and inquired if he has brought just one camera for the recording to which Sovon conveyed yes. Listening to Sovon's reply , he showed some signs of dissatisfaction and told him that they actually needed two cameras in the hall for recording – one for the activities at the dais and other for the audience. He suggested Sovon that since there is still half an hour left for the event to start , he can go and fetch another camera and also a operator for the same. Sovon innocently agreed to their suggestion as his house was just 2kms from the hotel.

Sovon drove his bike towards his home. He is half a way to his house , when he got a call from the customer- "Can you please bring ten strings of marigold flower while you come back with another camera. We want to decorate the venue little bit , but don't find any florist nearby". Sovon always believed in customer service; so he once again agreed to their request.

Sovon collected the camera from his house and then went to his assistant's house to pick him up. On the way to the hotel, they halted at one of the florists and purchased ten strings of marigold flower. All these took some time but there is still ten minutes left for the event to start. So there should not be any problem for installing the 2nd camera and start recording on time.

They reached the hotel , got down from the bike and rushed to the conference hall in a hurry. But there is no one in sight. Sovon got confused. He also did not find the camera in the hall that he had fixed at one place of the floor half an hour before. Sovon went to the reception to find out where are the two gentlemen who were coordinating the event. As per the advice of the reception, he went to the room where these two persons were staying since two days. There was no one in the room. No sign of any luggage in the room also.

Sovon got the shock of his life. He had purchased the camera last month at a price of one Lakh.

He remained standing like a statue on the corridor of the hotel and was telling himself "I paid a price for my innocence"

SADHU – THE DRIVER

Misrababu is a senior officer in a Government undertaking . This is a commercial establishment and Misrababu heads the Projects division. This division participates in various tenders for civil and mechanical works and executes those projects by engaging subcontractors. Being the head of the division , Misrababu takes all major decisions of the division and extensively tours the project sites to ensure timely execution and adherence to quality. Whenever he goes to any site, the contractors take care of his hospitality and are very careful not to annoy him any way.

At office , Misrababu is a very respected and feared officer. He does not tolerate any kind of lapse on any one's work and doesn't hesitate to take stern action on them. The action can be as small as calling for explanation to as big as deduction of salary. He has even gone to the extent of suspending some staffs for dereliction of duty. Misrababu talks less and his action speaks. He has a lady private secretary. She is very careful in deciding when and who can meet Misrababu at his cabin. He returns files and rejects bill payments if he notices a single mistake anywhere. He is very honest and upright. So no one ever tries to bribe him as that will adversely affect the work.

Misrababu had a dedicated office car and a driver. Name of the driver is Sadhu. He is an aged person and a good driver.

He will sit at the drivers' waiting room and never goes anywhere without the permission of Misrababu. For him Misrababu is almost like his god . His happiness depends on the wish of Misrababu. In the morning he reaches the residence of Misrababu to pick him up and makes sure he reaches office on time. Same way, in the evening he ferries his boss from office to residence.

Tours of Misrababu was very frequent and he prefers to travel by office car if the distance is within 3-4 hundred kilometers. Many times he travels over night as the traffic is less during that time. He used to stay at government guest houses located near the project sites.

Once Misrababu had to go to a far off project site , nearly 400km far . He asked Sadhu to reach at his house early in the morning so that they start early and reach the project by noon. The driver was on time and Misrababu started the journey as planned. They took 2-3 breaks en route and reached the project site in the afternoon. During the break, they took tea and also coconut water at one place. As soon as Misrababu reached the spot, the contractor came running and bowed before him. He accompanied Misrababu to different parts of the project site and showed him the progress. After the visit , Misrababu went to the project camp office , sat there and noted down all progress made in execution of the project. He was happy for the good work done by the contractor. Inspection work got completed by 5PM. The contractor served some snacks and cold drinks to Misrababu at the camp office.

Originally Misrababu had planned to stay back at the nearest government guest house and start return journey next day morning. But since the work got completed early , he thought of returning in the evening itself so that he will be back at home by midnight. So he instructed Sadhu to get ready for the return journey. Sadhu cleaned the vehicle with water spray and Misrababu started the return journey at 6PM.

400 km will take them nearly six hours as there is a patch of bad road on the way and also they have to scale some hilly ghat road. But the fact that he will be back at home by midnight rendered all these issues on the road insignificant . The first 150km was easy and smooth. Before the car has to take on to the rough patch of 50km or so , Misra babu instructed Sadhu to halt near a road side tea shop so that they can have tea. Sadhu accordingly stopped. They took tea. Sadhu also got few pouches of gutkha so that while he drives , his mouth remains engaged. The rough patch was harsh on Misrababu , it strained his entire body. Now there is a good patch of 50km , after which there is ghat road of 10km and then there is smooth national highway. It is 8.30PM now , and Misrababu has dozed off. Sadhu knows that his boss , who seats at the comfortable back seat of the car , generally falls asleep while he drives in the night.

Sadhu covered the good patch , while Misrababu is asleep at the back. Then he took to the ghat road. Half a way through the ghat road, he halted the car and went for a leak 6-7 meters ahead of the car. It was dark all around. Misrababu woke up at this very instant and decided to go for a leak. He got down from the rear seat of the car and went few meters behind the car for the purpose.

Sadhu returned to the car , occupied the driver's seat and drove off. By the time Misrababu realized this action of Sadhu , he is gone.....gone far.... and Misrababu's frantic calls were of no use.

After the ghat road , it is the NH , Sadhu picked up speed and drove 100km/hr so that they reach home by 11PM or so. It was a smooth drive and he reached the house of Misrababu at the expected time. He honked the horn 2-3 times .Madam came out, opened the main door of the house and stood at the verandah to welcome Misrababu back home.

Sadhu got down from the car and opened the rear door for Misrababu to come out..

But...there is no one there...Sadhu was wondering when and how his boss vanished from the rear seat......By the way , there was no mobile phone those days.

MINERAL WATER

Narayan graduated from Ravenshaw College last year having economics as the specialization. He hails from a village named Singada located at Bengal-Odisha border. After completing his schooling from the local village school , he went to the nearby town to do his intermediate , after which he went to Ravenshaw for graduation. For him studying at Ravenshaw is almost like doing an MBA in an Ivy League school in USA. Though he was a so-so kind of a student , he had a fascination for economics. How the economy works and how the political system influences economics always intrigued him.

Narayan gets 1000/- every month from his father , who is a farmer. A small land holding is the only asset they have to fall back upon. They stay in a thatched house , where there were just two rooms to accommodate his parents , his two sisters , and himself when he visits his home . His mother runs a small grocery shop from the verandah of their house to generate some extra income. His two unmarried sisters take care of the household chores . Narayan gets the money from his father through money order . His village doesn't have a bank nearby and hence his father sends this money from the nearby post office. This amount is just enough for him to take care of his messing at the hostel and essentials. He didn't have any money to buy books , so he depended entirely on the college library. In the evening, Narayan used to work as a tutor for 2-3 high school children to earn some pocket money.

He had plans to do PG at JNU after graduation , but his financial constraints forced him to try for some jobs. While he was preparing for his graduation exams , he concurrently prepared for different examinations – Banking , Railways and SSC . He appeared in the written tests of all these but as luck would have it got an interview call only from Nabard , a bank which caters to the needs of farmers and other stake holders in the agricultural sector.

The venue of interview was in Mumbai .He had to buy a railway ticket as soon as possible. The railway station is located very near to his hostel , but he had no money to buy the ticket. Travelling such a long distance without reservation will be very difficult and so he planned to buy a 2nd class sleeper ticket which costs 1000/- approximately for onward and return journey . For Lodging and boarding at Mumbai for one day , he will need another 1000/-. He called his father and narrated why he needs money and how much . Father, consented to send money through money order as soon as possible.

Money received on time , ticket booked. Narayan boarded the train on the appointed day. He did carry a small suitcase wherein he had packed a pair of good dress for the interview , a towel , tooth brush , paste and the shavings kit. Also , in a two liter plastic bottle he carried drinking water...for ease of carrying he tucked the water bottle in a white plastic bag .

The long journey was safe and without any hick-ups ; the train reached the mega city on time early in the morning.

Narayan's interview was scheduled at 12PM . He got down from the train and started moving towards the exit , carrying the suitcase in one hand and the water bag on the other. Mid-way he found the water bottle to be too heavy. Halted at one part of the platform and evacuated the bottle on the track. He thought , it is wise to stay in a lodge near the interview place , so that he can locate the venue without hassles . Initially he was confused and tensed as to where to get a bus to travel to the destination , but later with the guidance of some persons on the footpath , he could take a bus . It was all stampede inside the bus and he struggled to hold on to his suitcase and plastic bag , while being sandwiched among the passengers. Requested the conductor to call him when it reaches Vile Parle . The conductor gave him a call accordingly and Narayan got down at Vile Parle at about 7AM .

Narayan started the search for a lodge in the area . He had heard before , that many film stars stay in this area and got awed looking at the beautiful bungalows on either sides of the lanes and by lanes. His budget for the hotel 200/-. After a brisk walk , he noticed a hotel , which he thought might give him a place within his limit. No!!!, when he checked the tariff , he is shocked. Non-A/C 1000/- and A/C 1500/- . Next hotel , no better 800/- for a non-A/C . The lowest he could come across is 600/- , with common bath room. Common bathroom was not an issue with him , rate was. A good idea stuck him. May be he should find out if there is a dormitory in any hotel , that should be available within his budget.

Narayan had already walked 2-3km and spent more than an hour searching for a place. Finally, he came across Santi Bhavan lodge. A very old three storied building , in a precarious condition . At the counter was sitting an old man wearing a white dhoti and a vest. Narayan asked " Can I get a room : and what rate"..The man said yes , but available after an hour. Rate 200/-, just within his budget . After an hour of wait , he got the room , of size of a toilet at his hostel . Inside the room , there was a functional cot placed at the centre . On the cot , there was a cushioned bed covered with a white sheet and a very thin pillow . The sheet had many brown spots on it and also small holes at some places. The pillow cover was pale and oily. Walls of the room were made of plywood and one could sense the activities of the people in the neighboring room . Narayan gathered, that in the vicinity there is a famous cancer hospital and most of the customers of this hotel are attendants of patients who are being treated in the hospital. Considering the condition of these customers, the hotel had been charging rock bottom rent to the customers. How else one can get a room at 200/-. Narayan thought , in these commercial times , there are still some people left with a heart.

Narayan quickly got ready , had biscuit and tea at a roadside stall and rushed to the interview venue. His interview was well and fine. It was a 15-20 minutes interview and got over at 1PM.

He was very hungry by that time. Without wasting much time , he got into a restaurant , a very modest kind of restaurant. No Darwan at the entrance to salute. Narayan felt happy as he knew even salutes are accounted for while fixing the cost of service. It is dimly lit inside the restaurant, 8-10 tables placed in different places of the big hall . Each of these tables was surrounded by four chairs . There were also two small tables . Each of these small tables had just two chairs placed opposite to each other , perhaps meant for couples. At one corner , two tables have been joined and there are ten chairs placed around that ..Perhaps to take care of big families or a group of friends.

With an intention not to block bigger space , Narayan occupied a two seater table. A uniformed waiter arrived with the menu and left it on his table. On the table , there are two glasses and a tissue paper holder . He looked at the beautifully designed menu. There were different segments – Indian , Chinese , Thai and Continental. He could understand the meaning of the first three menu , as they are the food mostly eaten in those countries . But what is this continental . He thought , there are five continents , but this menu says just Continental ; they should have segmented the menu based on different continents ... ; Without wasting time on the menu of foreign countries , he glanced at the items at the Indian segment...he did not find "Thali" options . Therefore , he has to order the menu on pick and choose basis . He glanced at the rates. His budget for the lunch is 150/-and no three items in the menu are getting limited to this cap. A bowl of rice -50/- , Dal-50/- and lowest priced vegetarian curry is 80/-. Narayan was not sure what to order.

In the meantime , the waiter reached the table , left a cold mineral water bottle on the table , and waited for the order with a small pad in his hand. Narayan hinted the waiter to come after some time. He looked at the mineral water bottle ..." Kinley" priced 30/-. He then looked at the menu. The water actually costs 40/- as per the menu. If he retains the water bottle , he can eat rice only...it seemed. The waiter arrived again at the table. Narayan , asked " You don't have plain water? Give me that..And give me rice and mixed vegetable curry". The waiter exclaimed "No dal sir?"..Narayan said.."I don't eat dal"..But sir " It will be too dry to eat without dal"..Narayan got annoyed" Just get me what I told.."

Waiter delivered the items on the table and later brought a glass of water... and then left after giving a suspicious look towards Narayan.

Narayan had a hard time eating the rice and the dry curry without any gravy in it. After somehow gulping the food , Narayan asked the waiter for the bill. After a brief wait , the waiter brought the bill concealed in a bill holder....kept that on the table and waited for payment.

The bill was as per his budget , Rs134/- including the service tax . Narayan took out one 100/- note and a 50/- note from his purse and gave those to the waiter . With the money and the bill , the waiter left for the cash counter and came back to Narayan's table after few minutes. Kept the bill holder on the table and remained standing at the table , perhaps for the tips.

Narayan opened the bill holder , counted the money in the flap.....a ten rupee note , a five rupee coin and one rupee coin... ...no mistakes in refund amount . Took out the purse from his pocket , kept the money and then got up from the chair to leave the restaurant. The waiter gave him a stern look , but Narayan was indifferent..He moved towards the exit.

From behind he overheard..."Kahan Kahan se aisa log aa jate hey"

Narayan boarded the train in the evening for his return journey. He ate some biscuits at night and then lied down on his sleeper and started recollecting the events of the day. He wondered why is that in restaurants they serve mineral waters instead of common water.

At this time he overheard the tagline of an ad promoting a brand of mineral water , "Bund Bund Mein Sacchai".

INNOCENT WISHES

Indrajitbabu has a small family . He is forty-five now and his wife is five years younger to him. They have two children – one son and one daughter, son being the first child. Both the children go to the school. There is a gap of five years between brother and sister. Daughter's name is Mira and she is in class-VI. Indrajitbabu works in a bank as a PO and earns an amount that gives them a descent leaving. He is now posted at a city and stays in a rented apartment. His wife takes care of home.

Both the children of Indrajit babu were born in the same month, but on different dates. Birthdays of his children are celebrated in a very simple and traditional way . It starts with the visit to the nearby temple in the morning and ends with a small dinner for friends of the child in the evening. Small return gifts are given to all the friends when they leave for their home after the dinner. A cake cutting is organized before the dinner. After the cake cutting, cake, potato chips and cold drinks are served to the friends.

Between the two children, daughter is demanding in term of what she wants on her birthdays . As per her wish, last year three of her friends were invited to spend a whole day at the house. The parents of the friends dropped them at Indrajitbabu's house in the morning and then took them back at late evening.

Mira celebrated her 12th birthday yesterday. But no friend is around who could be invited. All of them have gone on vacation. Some gone to their native places and others to some interesting locations for holidaying. So the birth day was celebrated in a different way from the previous years. Every year , Mira dictates what gift she wants on her birthday. This year it was a pencil box that she wanted. Her parents always tell her, a gift should be a secret and the receiver should know it when she opens the wrapper. But Mira thinks otherwise. As a practice, every year, once she falls asleep the previous night, her gifts are kept near her pillow, so that when she wakes up she first sees her gifts. As per her wish, a new pencil box wrapped with golden paper and pink flat thread was kept near her pillow. Another gift unknown to her was also kept....a fiber frame blue colored wrist watch. Mira had a similar looking pink colored wrist watch, but she had lost it at school play ground few months back. Since it was a costly item, she never asked for any more watch from her parents.

5 AM , Mira woke up briefly and found all those items near her. She opened the wrappers and saw each item and smiled. She kept those items near her head and slept again. She woke up at 7AM finally. In the mean time, his father has kept a big red balloon near her , almost equal to her own height. She embraced the balloon and played ping pong with it on the bed. Mother, father and brother wished her "Happy Birthday" and Mira reciprocated with "Thank you". Phone started ringing. Her grandfather, grandmother and cousins wished her "Happy Birthday".

The first thing Mira has to do in the morning is to visit the temple. She took bath and wore her new dress , a long scot black in color, with two thick golden borders at the bottom and a red top with polka dots . She accompanied her father to the nearest temple. Before she left, her mother instructed her to light a clay lamp before each of the gods and goddesses in the temple and also distribute sweets to all the beggars sitting at the entrance of the temple. It was such a coincidence. She lit nine lamps at the temple and there were exactly nine beggars at the entrance also. She distributed sweets to all of them.

Mira had two more wishes for her Birthday. She wanted to watch a movie and want to have dinner at a restaurant. Her mother took her to a nearby multiplex in the afternoon. The theatre is at the second floor and there is an escalator to reach there. Mira wanted to use the escalator but her mother is not very comfortable. So she took the stairs and Mira has to follow. At the entrance of the film hall , Mira noticed there are few shops in the waiting zone selling popcorns and ice creams.

It was a nice air-conditioned hall and the film was hilarious. During the intermission, Mira wanted to go to the lounge area alone and buy popcorns. But her mother did not allow her as she may get lost in the crowd. Instead, she took her there and purchased the stuffs she wanted. They came back home in the evening.

In the evening , Indrajitbabu and his family went to the nearby restaurant for the dinner. The menu was selected by Mira and they had a nice dinner.

Back at home, Mira switched on the TV and watched a popular dance reality show on the TV. While she was looking at the TV , her mother asked her "Mira , did you enjoy your Birthday today?"

Displaying sadness on her face she responded " Yes , But I couldn't ride that escalator at the multiplex."

Indarjitbabu quickly responded , " Coming Sunday , I will take you to the nearby shopping mall and you will spend as much time as you want on the escalator...I promise"

NAUGHTY BOY

Biswajit stays in the state capital but his native is 200km far. He is a young man and works as a development officer in a public sector insurance company. He is not yet married and his parents are searching for a suitable match for him. He visits his native place twice a year – Durga puja and Saraswati puja. Visit to the native place beyond this mandatory two occasions is need based , particularly when either of his parents is hospitalized. Last Friday night, he got a call from his father that his mother is hospitalized for treatment of her broken ankle. She had slipped in the bathroom and had fractured her ankle. Biswajit had no time to reserve a railway ticket and travel over night. So he decided to travel home by the train early in the morning and reserved a seat through online booking. The train was at 6AM.

On hearing the alarm on his mobile phone at 4.30am , Biswajit jumped out of the bed and got ready. He took an auto and reached the station at 5.30AM.

One has to take a downward stair to reach the entrance of the railway station. While Biswajit was walking down the stair, he noticed the beggar about whom he has heard lot of interesting things. This beggar is popularly known as Bamana. He is dwarf but well built . He always wears a brown half pant and a red half sleeve shirt. At his head , he

98

wears a red colored Gandhi cap. He has been begging at this spot for last 25-30 years now. He was young when he got into begging, but now looks old. There are wrinkles on his neck and his beard is white. Every time he sees a passerby , he forks out his cupped palm and makes a peculiar sound in his mouth for the alms. Most people ignore him but there are a few who slow down and leave a coin in his palm. Thousands take this stair and Bamana accumulates good amount of coin every day. In the last twenty five years, with this income he has built a marble floored two storied building. He stays at the first floor with his family. The ground floor has two independent blocks and those have been rented out for a monthly rental of Rs10000/-each. He has accounts in 2-3 banks and maintains good cash balance all the time. Many of the shops and hawkers who do business at the station area take loan from Bamana . Even if the loan amount is few lakhs , he rarely disappoints a loan seeker.

Biswajit reached the designated platform half an hour ahead of time. He looked at his ticket and saw the seat number to be B2/30 . In the electronic display, he figured out where this bogie-B2 will halt and accordingly walked towards the area. On reaching this area , he noticed there are marbled elevated sitting places for the passengers to sit and wait for the train. These sitting platforms were octagonal in shape and can easily accommodate 7-8 persons . On all these sitting places, only 4-5 persons were sitting and on rest of the space there were luggage. Biswajit noticed many people are standing nearby , women and children included. He wondered why can't these people keep their luggage on the floor and offer the seats to the people standing nearby.

The train entered the platform and started slowing down. It took its own time to come to a halt. But passengers did not wait. Many started running neck-to-neck with the train as if they are in competition with it , with an wish to be the first few to get into the train. There are few others who were even more adventurous. After few meters of chasing, they caught hold of the door railing of bogies and perched themselves on the footrest. It appeared as if they are showing some kind of gymnastics to the onlookers free of cost.

Biswajit entered into the bogie and took his seat. At this time he saw a young person walking down the aisles. He was wearing a T-shirt with a tagline "There is no space at hell, so I came here" . This young man went up to the upper berth carrying the shoe in his hand. He kept his shoe on the cage of the ceiling fan , sat cross legged on the berth and started listening to some songs on his mobile phone. Dust from the shoe was falling on the people sitting at the lower berth. Biswajit thought people like these come back from hell to make Indian Railways a hell.

As Biswajit was trying to turn his attention away from this nuisance , he saw another young person wearing a black T-shirt with a tagline "My favorite place in the world is next to you".. This young man slowed downed near Biswajit with the hope that he will accommodate him by squeezing in , but there was just no space left. All the seats near Biswajit were filled up. Biswajit looked at him in negation and told to himself ' "intelligent guy , dressed for the occasion"

Walking behind this young man was a pretty young lady . She was also wearing a T-shirt. At the chest of the T-shirt was printed a barcode in big font . Above this barcode it is written "No machine can read this barcode" and below the barcode it said "Because I am priceless"...Biswajit smiled at this interesting catch line.

Train picked up speed and moved fast. After half an hour or so it slowed down at a station. A good number of passengers crowded at the door to get down from the train. Biswajit noticed , there was a mild tussle between the people who were getting down from the train and the people who are trying to board the train.

It will take another two and half hours for Biswajit to reach home. He was looking at the new set of people who just entered the bogie and searching for a vacant seats. At this time he spotted a pretty young girl in the crowd. She was wearing a blue denim jeans and a black rounded neck T-shirt. Something is written at the chest in white , but not readable form a distance as the letters were small. She was walking down the aisles ; her youthful charm was turning many heads . But Biswajit's mind was stuck at the message written on the T-shirt. He was trying his best to read that but in vain. The letters were too small...

At last the girl came closer and stood almost in front of Biswajit . Now he can read it......"Naughty Boy"...is what is written there.

Biswajit's face turned pink when his eyes met hers.

HEARTLESS

Ashok is an MBA and works in a telecomm company as a sales executive. He is from another state and has come to this city for the first time. He stays in a paying guest(PG) arrangement. PG provider is an aged couple in their late 60's. Their only son works in USA as a software engineer. They have a fulltime maid servant at home. She is a widow and has a child aged eight years or so. His name is Babu. While the old couple stay in a one storied bungalow, the maid servant stays in the outhouse. This is a single room outhouse with an attached toilet. The name of the maidservant is Maya. Though Maya is a servant, the aged couple treats her as their own family member. Maya takes care of everything in the house – cleaning , cooking , washing clothes and watering the plants in the garden . Maya's son studies in a nearby government school in class-III. The aged couple treats the boy as their grandchild and showers on him all their affection. Ashok has a separate room in the bungalow and he has been staying here for last three years. He likes the aged couple very much particularly because the way they treat their servant.

Ashok is a very disciplined and dedicated employee. He has been achieving the sales target every year and all his superiors think very high about his ability and his contribution to the organization. Every year he gets salary hike at the highest slab. But this year he has more reasons to be happy. He has been promoted to the position of Sales Manager. Now he will be supervising the work of 8-10 sales executives. The day he got promotion, everyone in the office congratulated him. He felt very happy. He brought sweets from a nearby famous sweet stall and personally distributed to all. He also called his parents and informed them about the good news.

In the evening he went back to his PG house and also carried sweets for the aged couple, Maya and her son . Everyone felt very happy about the promotion of Ashok. That day, as per the instruction of the aged couple , Maya cooked an elaborate dinner and everyone had it together. Ashok felt as if he is having the dinner with his own parents and siblings. He got very emotional. After they finished the dinner and sat in front of the TV to listen to the news of the day, Ashok thanked the aged couple for the treat.

Next day was a Saturday and it is a half day at office. Before Ashok left for the office in the morning, he told the aged couple, "Today evening, I would like to take you all for dinner at Dolphin Restaurant" . After showing initial reluctance, the aged couple agreed to the suggestion. Ashok came back home at about 3PM and took rest.

At about 8PM, Ashok called an auto to take the couple, Maya and her son Babu to the restaurant. All were ready by that time. They got seated in the auto and the auto moved towards Dolphin Restaurant which is 2km far from the house. Ashok followed the auto in his bike.

103

Dolphin Restaurant is a haunted place for all food lovers. It is centrally located in the city. There is adequate parking place for customers to park their vehicles and a person is always on duty to guide them where to park. This restaurant has four sections, each serving a specialized menu of food – Chinese, Continental, Indian and South Indian. There is also a coffee house which serves variety of coffee, tea, fruit juice and cold drinks. The ambiance of each section of the restaurants has been created keeping in mind the liking and profile of the customers. For instance, the section which serves south Indian menu, one will notice a portrait of Balaji hung at some place of the wall and carnatic music being played.

They reached the restaurant and entered the section that serves continental food and occupied a six-seater table. Waiter came , served water and left the menu on the table. Ashok sought the choices of all and placed the order with the waiter. While all wanted to have soup at the beginning, the little boy wanted coca cola. Items reached the table shortly.

At this point in time Ashok noticed a group of ten people arrived at the restaurant. There was a table reserved for them in advance, evident in the form of a conical signage on the table. All of them occupied the table, excepting the small girl who stayed back at the waiting lounge near the cash counter. She is a girl in her pre-teens , looks rustic and is wearing a frock. The frock is faded but looks clean, and perhaps the best she has for such visits to restaurants or other functions. She remained seated on a sofa. Ashok made out that the girl must be the maid servant of this group of people.

In the group there were one old couple in their 70's , one aged couple in their 50's , one young couple , two young school going children and one baby. The youngest lady was carrying the baby in her lap. Ashok could see three generations at one place - grandparents, parents and grand children. The waiter arrived and after elaborate discussion with each other, they ordered the items. Each one has a different taste and so the list of items ordered was very large. Before the waiter turned back to proceed to the kitchen, the aged man instructed him to give nine mineral water at the table.

Mineral water bottles kept on the table. Soup was served and each one started having spoonful of hot soup. At this moment, the baby started crying. The young mother could not drink the soup in peace. So she hinted at the little girl seating at the lounge near the cash counter. She came running , took off the baby from the lady and returned to the seat where she was seating. The baby stopped crying and was sitting on the lap of the little girl.

After the soup, the ordered items were served. Everybody got busy in eating. Occasionally they were commenting on the taste of the items and were also comparing that with the taste of similar items in other restaurants. They had perhaps ordered for more quantity than they can consume. So lot of food items remained on the bowls. The aged men called the waiter and asked him to pack the leftover items. The waiter obliged. In few minutes, all left over items duly packed in aluminum foils and polyethylene pouches, returned to the table in a big polyethylene bag.

They washed their hands in warm lemon water. In the meantime the waiter brought the bill and it was instantly paid. After throwing some snuff to their mouth, all of them got off from their chair and moved towards the exit door of the restaurant. The little girl waiting at the cash counter followed the group.

Ashok was wondering if the leftover in the polyethylene bag is meant for the little girl tonight or for this joint family next day.

LOOKING BACK

Amitav is a young boy who has just completed his engineering in electronics from a very reputed government engineering college. Every year , companies make a queue at this college to take the best of students . Large number of students gets multiple offers. But Amitav opted out from campus placement. Amitav never wanted to work as an engineer. Though he was among the toppers in his batch, he had no liking for the course. Engineering appeared very mundane to him and he never wanted to work in a factory. The thought of shift duty and the factory environment was too repulsive for him. He had particular aversion towards dust inside the factory and the sound of machines.

Amitav wanted to work in corporate sector . In many movies, he has seen the nice environment in which people work in corporate. Air-conditioned offices, classy conference rooms , suited-booted executives , pretty receptionist etc appealed to him very much. So while he devoted time for the engineering course, he also prepared for MBA. Amitav was good at mathematics , so he found the quantitative and data interpretation questions quite easy. English language and reasoning were somewhat difficult and so he spent more time for these two subjects. He started this preparation while he was in second year and therefore by the time he was in final year , Amitav was very thorough on all subjects for the entrance.

After the final year examination , he came back home . His father was aware of the career aspiration of Amitav and therefore did not get upset seeing him back at home without a job. But on the other hand his retirement from the banking job was few months away. Amitav had a sister and was studying in class-XII and was preparing to get into a medical college. Everyone was very happy to have Amitav back at home. But his father looked worried as the retirement date was very much in sight and he has no alternate source of income to take care of the family. Money is also required for admission of Amitav in MBA College, assuming that he clears one.

Amitav has since applied for the best management institutes , namely IIM,XLRI and FMS. The entrance tests are staggered over next 2-3months. The earliest one is the entrance test for IIM which is scheduled next Sunday and Amitav is eagerly waiting for the admit card. It is afternoon time and Amitav is taking a nap after lunch. Someone rang the calling bell. Amitav opened the door and was pleased to see the courier boy. He opened the envelope, went through the admit card and doubly verified the date of entrance examination.

The examination centre is at Kolkata , a place 400km far from his native place. There is an early morning train and this train reaches Kolkata in the afternoon. Since the test is scheduled on Sunday , Amitav decided to travel on Saturday . He got up early in the morning , got ready and reached the railway station in an auto . He had a small handbag with him . Previous night his father gave him Rs1000/- to meet the travel and lodging expenses. There was a long queue at the booking counter. Amitav patiently stood in the queue till his turn came. He got the ticket and rushed to the platform where the train will be arriving. On arriving at the platform, he heard the announcement that the train is thirty minutes late. So he looked around and sat on one of the wooden benches at the platform.

Train arrived. Amitav got into the train and occupied a seat. This is an unreserved bogie .Generally such bogies carry passengers double its sitting capacity; half get a seat and rest have to stand and travel. That day was little different. There was not much of crowd. Half of the seats were vacant. Amitav is going to the big city for the first time and is unfamiliar with its addresses . He thought, after getting down at the station , he will go to a area where the test centre is located and in that area he will stay in a lodge. The test centre is Ballygunj Girls High School and the test will start at 10AM.

Amitav looked out of the window and was watching how quickly the trees and houses are moving away from his sight in the opposite direction. He returned his eyes and looked at the co-passengers . Adjacent to him were seated a Muslim family – an elderly couple and their two high school going sons. Opposite to him was sitting a man in his early thirties and three young boys in their early twenties. They were talking among themselves. From there discussion , Amitav could make out that the young boys work as skilled workers in some factory at Kolkata and the elder one has some catering business in the same city. He has partnered with a Bengali fellow and is into this catering business for last 5-6 years and makes a reasonable income. This income is not adequate to sustain a family at the big city. So his wife and two small kids stay at the village.

Amitav introduced himself to this aged man and told him the purpose of his visit to the city. After he got friendly with him , Amitav asked him " Can you do me a favor. I am new to the city. Can you help me get a lodge at Ballygunj?" The person smiled and told , "Don't worry. My business is few miles far from that place. So I will leave you at a proper lodge and then move forward...By the way my name is Gajanana"..Amitav felt relieved at this assurance.

The train reached Kolkata at 4PM. Gajanana accompanied Amitav out of the railway station. They took a town bus and reached Ballygunj . Amitav hinted Gajanana that his budget for the lodge is Rs400/- . They started looking for a hotel. Gajanana knew it is difficult to get a place at that budget , but kept on checking the rates of hotels one after another . Even after two hours of walking down the lanes and by-lanes in the area , a cheap lodge was nowhere in sight. Tired and exhausted Gajanana made a suggestion to Amitav ," We can't get a lodge at this budget. I have a proposal. I stay with the family of my business partner. They have a very small two room house where 7-8 persons stay together including me. If you don't mind, you can come and stay with me for a night". Amitav was too tired and had no energy to haunt for a lodge. So he agreed to the suggestion, though he was worried about his decision of staying with an unknown family at an unknown city.

They reached the house late in the evening. It was a LIG kind of house. Catering business runs from the asbestos roofed portico. There are big utensils stacked at one corner and two men were busy cooking food in gas stoves. Amitav and Gajanana washed their feet at the outdoor tap point and got into the house. The room is a cluttered place. A big cot is lying at the centre ; a steel almirah and a rack placed at the walls. Amitav got seated on the cot , hanging his legs down. Mr. Banerjee , the business partner came to the room. He is a men in his late forties. Amitav said him Namaskar , to which he nodded his head. Later he started some business related conversation with Gajanana. The daughter of the Mr. Banerjee , a pretty young girl brought snacks and a glass of water for Amitav.

Rest of evening , Amitav listened to the TV kept at one corner of the room.

It is dinner time. The pretty girl came again to the room and laid a squared plastic mat on the floor and asked Amitav to sit down. She served rice , variety of curry and rasagolla in a steel plate. Also kept a glass of water near the plate . Amitav was delighted at this hospitality.

Later , Amitav noticed all the family members sat at one portion of the verandah and had their dinner.

After dinner, it is time for the bed. There was just one single cot on that room. Gajanana laid a cushion on the cot and spread a bed sheet and then asked Amitav to sleep on that bed. Amitav laid himself on the bed , but it being a new place he was not getting the sleep. He noticed , Gajanana spread a big mat on the floor and both he and Mr. Banerjee slept there. Amitav felt awkward for putting the host into such trouble. Next day morning , after breakfast , Gajanana accompanied Amitav to the test centre in a taxi. On reaching the test centre , he wished Amitav good luck and then bid adieu . Amitav was overwhelmed with Gajanana's help ; He held his hand and said "I will never forget this help of yours" .

Amitav cleared the entrance test and got admitted at IIM,Bangalore.

After 10 years:

Amitav is now the CEO of a software company . He travels across the globe. Once in a while, he visits Kolkata for official work. Every time the taxi takes him through Ballygunj roads , he is reminded of Gajanana .

SARADA

Misrababu is a senior officer in the central government . He belonged to finance cadre. He gets a transfer every 2-3 years . Though every relocation brings with it problems of adjustment, he actually loves such regular transfers. Transfers give him an opportunity to see new places, meet new people and experience different culture. Misrababu enjoys talking to people and can keep anyone hostage to his interesting anecdotes and life stories. Books are his constant companion and he has a memory of an elephant. Misrababu had a loving wife and a high school going son.

Once he got a transfer to Kolkata. Being a senior officer , he was allotted a big bungalow in a posh locality. His previous posting was at Patna. Misrababu and his family traveled to the city by air. He had engaged a Packer & Mover to shift his household items to the new house and the truck has left two days before . By the time he and his family reached Kolkata , the caretaker had already offloaded the items from the truck and had arranged everything inside the house. Office car received Misrababu and family at the airport and ferried them to the bungalow. As they reached the gate of the residence, the caretaker came running and saluted the new boss. Misrababu and family entered the house and had a look at the rooms and the facility. Madam Misra liked the clean and tidy house. She also appreciated the way the caretaker has arranged the items inside the house; it seemed

113

as if the caretaker knew the taste and preferences of madam. There was a small garden in front of the house. The garden has an oval lawn at the centre encircled with flower-bearing low height plants. This bungalow is built at the centre of a big plot of land , nearly an acre in size . There is a concrete boundary wall around this land. Large number of aging neem and banyan trees dotted the campus. The shed of the big trees was creating a soothing environment. Looking at the trees Misrababu thought...."nice place to casually sit and read books".

The name of the caretaker is Mangal. He is an NMR in the office which Misrababu will be heading and is attached to the residential office . He has been working at this office for last six years and Misrababu will be the third officer he will be attending to at the bungalow. He is a simple and sober young man in his early twenties. Bengali is his mother tongue but he has learnt Hindi to some extent. He is a matriculate and had to stop studies due to the death of his father. His mother had died when he was ten years old. His father was working as a Subedar in Defence and died of cancer while he was still on the job . Mangal would have got a job in the Defence on compassionate ground but due to some procedural issues he could not get one. In the records of the office, his father has not mentioned the names of his nominees and hence the problem. People in the office who could have helped him, wanted bribe from Mangal and he had no money with him that time. Mangal thought it is his bad luck that he could not get his rightful job in Defence and accepted his fate.

Mangal had a sister who is twelve years old then. After the demise of his father , Mangal had to earn the bread for him and his sister . With the help of a gentleman, he got this NMR job . Mangal and his sister were staying at an LIG flat which his father had purchased . His sister cooked food and looked after the house. Mangal's income was inadequate for necessities of life ; but they were able to eat two squares of meal a day and for that he was very grateful to the Almighty. Name of his sister was Sarada.

Misrababu settled down at the new bungalow and took over the responsibility at the new office. Mangal was always a call away. Besides working as a caretaker of the residential office, he acted as an errand boy to fulfill the needs of sir and madam. Whether it is vegetable to be fetched from market or kid to be picked up from the school, Mangal was the answer. Both Misrababu and madam were very happy with the kind of obedience and sincerity Mangal displayed.

Once Misrababu was taking a morning walk in the garden of the residential campus and Mangal was waiting at the lawn with a glass of lemon water. Misrababu loves to drink lemon water . After finishing the walk , Misrababu sat down on the plastic chair at the lawn and took the glass from Mangal. Drank it and felt very happy. At this instance, Mangal seeing the boss in good mood , prompted ," I understand madam is looking for a help for household chores; I have a sister who is skilled at that; if you please , maybe she can work at the bungalow. By this she will earn money and that will help us live a better life".

Misrababu never makes a decision on such household matters without consulting madam or rather taking her due permission . Same day evening ,he told her about Mangal's suggestion. As per madam's wish , Mangal brought Sarada to the bungalow for an interaction . Madam spoke to Sarada and found her acceptable. Sarada is short in height compared to her age, skin is black , body skeletal but features are sharp and sweet. She talks at a low voice.

Sarada worked at the bungalow and she did everything that madam wished for. Misra couple also treated her like a family member. With time , Sarada put up weight, looked healthy and pretty. When she came to the bungalow she was fourteen years old , now she is eighteen . Lot of things happen during this teen-age. Sarada was no exception. She fell in love with a young boy and many times found talking to him at the temple adjacent to the bungalow. This activity became frequent later and at times madam would not find her at house. This affair did not remain secret too long. Misrababu got to know this development and spoke to Mangal. The boy works as a machine operator in a factory nearby. Mangal had already checked his credentials through his friends. The lover boy has no bad habits and is a good soul.

Misrababu and madam decided to get Sarada married to the boy through a formal marriage; else there is a chance she will flee with him. They decided to organize the marriage at the Jagannath temple , as the cost will be less . Mangal was part of the decision. Marriage cards were printed and distributed. Misrababu invited all his colleagues and some of his seniors. In total nearly two hundred guests were invited. Mangal did not have to worry about the expenses as everything was organized by Misrababu and madam. Normal prasad at the temple used to cost @15 and the special one that included a dessert @20. Special Prasad was ordered for the guests.

All guests came to the mandap at the temple . Misrababu was very happy to see that most of his colleagues were accompanied by their wife and kids to the function. For the guests, it was a nice break. Marriage function also gave them an opportunity to have a darshan of the lord at the temple.

Marriage was solemnized at the mandap by the priests of the temple. Parents of the groom were present when the couple took the marriage vow and made seven rounds around the altar. When the priest called for the parents of Sarada for a ritual , Misrababu and his wife acted as her parent. Seeing this, tears rolled down from the eyes of Sarada and Mangal.

Misrababu arranged a honeymoon for Sarada and her hubby at Manali.....after all she is like a daughter.

INSOMANIA

Club Town is the name of a luxury apartment in a happening city. It is a famous address in the city. This apartment is divided into four high rise towers . Each tower is ten storied and in each floor there are four flats. In total, there are one hundred and sixty flats. Opposite facing towers are connected with a foot bridge at the fifth floor and looks like a doctor's cross from a distance. There are two lifts in each tower- one for the residents and the other for service staffs and helpers. This apartment has been constructed over a piece of big land, must be more than five acres. The apartment is located at the centre and there is greenery around it. There is a mini-park and a small pool inside the campus. Around the boundary there is a concentric lawn of the width of a road. Beautifully designed cast iron chairs have been placed at different places of this lawn. Each of these chairs can accommodate 3-4 persons. There is a community hall where meetings and get-togethers are held. There is also a club room where one finds different indoor games like table tennis, carom, chess etc. Some aged people also play cards at this place. At the gate, there are security guards 24x7. At the basement, there are four single rooms and attached bathrooms to house the service staffs like plumber, electrician, sweeper etc.

Club Town is a symbol of diversity. People from almost all the states of the country stay in this apartment . Residents are mostly married people and stay with their kids. But there are a small number of bachelors also. These bachelors stay in groups of 3-4 persons in each flat . There are also a small number of aged couple who stay here along with their maid-servants. The children of these old couples either work at distant places or abroad. They come once or twice in a year and spend a week or two with their parents. Residents maintain functional relationship with their neighbors. More than half of the residents are tenants and one finds new faces almost every day . Since tenants are not permanent residents in the flats , many owners who stay in the flats , do not really cultivate a relationship with the tenants.

Club Town witnesses lot of visitors in the day time but by late evening the apartment becomes less noisy and by 11PM or so it becomes silent. Most of the residents are indoor by this time and prepare to go to bed. Only on Saturdays, youngsters return to the apartment late in the night. Perhaps they spend time at restaurants and pubs to enjoy their life with friends. Once in a while, a few residents return from their official tour and reach the apartment late in the night.

12PM in the night of a regular day....

The lights of almost all the flats have been switched off . Probably people have fallen asleep on their beds and are trying to forget the tiredness of the day. For the next 6-7 hours they will remain oblivion that there is still a world which has remained awake , and one never knows when they will also take rest. The lights at the parking area have remained ON to prevent any thief to enter the premises and steal. The Security has pulled in two chairs and have put them in front of the gate. He is sitting on one chair and has stationed his legs on the other. He is also trying to relax a little, while keeping his eyes open.

While the world has fallen asleep, lights at four flats are still on- Flat: 100, 203, 301 and 409.

Flat 100 : Mr. Kapoor and his wife stay in this flat. He used to work in a bank and now retired. He gets good amount of pension. Swati is their only daughter. She has done her PG in history and then B.Ed. She was working as a teacher at a nearby school. She had crossed marriageable age , must be 32-33. Kapoors , have not been able to get a suitable match for her. But as fate would have it , they got a match through a matrimonial site recently and married off Swati last week. The groom is an architect and is an established person. His first marriage did not work and his wife got separated from him. So Swati is his second wife. The man seems to be of good habits. Swati shifted to the neighboring city where this man has his profession and house. Kapoors are worried about the adjustment issues and welfare of their daughter at the new place. For them Swati is still a little kid. They call Swati 2-3 times a day to check her comfort .Since Swati has left them , Kapoors are not getting sleep at night.

Flat 203 : Misra family stay here. Mr. Misra is a senior IAS officer and works at the secretariat . He is a well known person in the literary circle also. He has written a number of novels, anthologies and travelogues. He has one son and one daughter. In terms of age son is elder to the daughter by 4-5 year. Mr. Misra is very clear in his mind as to what his children should become in their life. He wanted his daughter to become a doctor and son to follow his footsteps. Son has completed is graduation in Economics and preparing for civil services. Daughter got through medical entrance this year and has joined AIIMS at Delhi. Son had cleared prelim in the first attempt. Last year he lost out at the stage of personal interview. So he has two more attempts left. He is working hard and studies very late into the night.

Flat 301 : Mr. Gupta and his wife stay in this flat. Mr. Gupta has got married only last year and the couple has been blessed with a premature girl child last month. Since the date of her birth, the baby has been sleeping whole of the daytime and remaining awake in the night. The baby is intolerant of darkness and starts crying at a loud voice if the lights are switched off. The baby wants to see her mother all the time. So the light in their bed room is ON whole night. Only in the early morning, the baby sleeps after which the couple takes some rest.

Flat 409 : Mr. Jaiswal and his family stay in this flat. He owns a popular restaurant in the city. Mr. Jaiswal has one son and two daughters , son being the eldest. All of them are studying in the college. Old parents of Mr. Jaiswal have been staying with him. They are very old and regularly need medical care. The old man was bed ridden for few months and expired last Sunday night. He died before he could be shifted to the hospital. After his death, the old lady has also fallen ill and is in serious condition. Anything can happen with her any time. Members of Jaiswal family are attending to the old lady on rotation. This room where the light is on is the room where the old lady sleeps on a low height cot.

The security guard looked at his watch. It is 2AM now. The light at Flat-203 got switched off. Light at other three flats are still on. Another two hours and then this outside darkness will fade away and the entire world will get lighted with the rays of the sun.

Suddenly some street dogs started barking...it started with one dog but later many joined . May be some thief is looking for some opportunity in the darkness. The security guard got up from the chair and started making a round of the campus. Listening to the whistle of the guard, the dogs stopped barking.

MARRIAGE INVITATION

Binaybabu works as a lower divisional clerk in a state government office . He has three children – one son and two daughters , son being the eldest. Son studies in one of the NITs . He is a good student and really worked hard to crack IIT but could not really get it even after two attempts. So he has to be satisfied with the NIT. Two daughters study in the government girls' high school in class X and VIII respectively. Now-a-day's even the expenses at NITs is too much. The cost per semester is nearly one lakh and then pocket expenses of 2-3 thousand a month has to be given to the son. When daughters were small, Binaybabu used to teach them at home and there was no need of a tutor. But at the higher classes , tutors have to be engaged. Every month, the expenses for home tuition is itself 6-7 thousand. Everything in the market has become costly. Therefore even though Binaybabu gets salary as per sixth pay commission, it is not sufficient to meet all these expenses. Somehow he tries to cut the expenses here and there and manages his life. His wife is very simple and understands the financial difficulty and never makes any kind of demand for unnecessary expenses. They hope that once their son passes out from NIT and gets a job , he will support them financially not only for the education of the two daughters but also their marriage.

Invitation from friends and relatives add an extra burden to Binaybabu's life. An invitation means an expenditure in terms of purchase of a gift. If it is a matter of close relative, then the gift has to be special matching the status of host. Every time Binaybabu gets an invitation , outwardly he smiles but inwardly he gets stressed.

Sometimes depending on the nature of the event , Binaybabu reduces the budget. If it is a birthday party , he generally buys a big packet of chocolates for the birthday boy/girl . That is inexpensive and the children love chocolates. And then there are mundane functions like death anniversary, engagement ceremony, house warming etc , where one has to carry nothing or at best a packet of sweets.

Last month Binaybabu got an invitation to attend the thread ceremony from a relative. In thread ceremony, as a part of the ritual the child is dressed like a monk and is advised to beg for alms from all the elders present. And all the elders are expected to give either gold ornaments or respectable amount of cash. After giving the invitation card this relative told Binaybabu , " We have made a rule for all invitees. No one will give anything more than Rs10/- as alms" . It was a pleasant surprise for Binaybabu. The relative requested Binaybabu to surely come to the function with the family and bless the child monk. The ceremony was held at the mandap inside a temple . On the scheduled day , Binaybabu attended the function with his family. They watched the proceedings of the ceremony . Later they ate prasad at the dining hall of the temple. Everyone sat on the floor for the prasad and the host took care to ensure that all guests had a hearty meal. Binaybabu and his family met a number of his relatives and friends at the temple and exchanged greetings and checked their welfare. It was a pleasant experience for the whole family.

Now a days marriage functions are more functions than marriage. Even people who are not very rich are arranging the events like kings would do. Holding the event at home is rare . It is either held at a marriage mandap or at a hotel . Sangeet and Mehendi is not limited to north India , it is part of marriage across India.

Last week Binaybabu got an invitation from a neighbor to attend a marriage reception. The host is a business man and is a rich man. This is the marriage reception of his only son. The boy is a software engineer working with an Indian software company but now posted abroad. He has taken leave for a month for this marriage. The bride is from the neighboring district and she is also an engineer working with a software company at Bangalore. The venue of the reception is the top luxury hotel in the city. Only rich and famous can really afford such hotels.

Binaybabu learnt from his friends that this hotel charges between Rs1000/- to Rs1200/- per plate for such parties. Though the marriage card mentions "Binay Mahapatra & family" as the invitee , Binaybabu is in a fix whether to attend the function alone or with the family. If all the family members attend the function , the cost of the food will be nearly Rs5000/-. The maximum he can afford for the gift is Rs501/- and it looks ridiculously low compared to the cost of the food at the hotel. He discussed the dilemma with his wife and it was decided that Binaybabu alone will attend the reception.

Binaybabu took out his old Bajaj Chetak scooter and drove to the venue. In his shirt pocket, he had tucked a red gift envelope ; inside the envelope there is a five hundred rupee note and a one rupee coin . At the parking place of the hotel , there is a stampede of costly cars. There is no space to park the scooter. So he rolled his scooter few meters off the hotel unto a street and parked it at a corner. He then walked towards the lobby of the hotel ; the lobby manager showed him the direction of the Kohinoor Hall where the marriage reception is being held.

This is a huge hall of the size of three lawn tennis court. At one end there is a podium , backdrop of which has been beautifully decorated with flowers . Floor of the podium is covered with red velvet carpet and at the centre there are two beautifully crafted golden colored chairs , the kind of chairs on which kings sit. The bride and the groom were sitting on these two chairs. The groom was wearing western suit black in color with a red tie at the collar; the bride was wearing a red gown and intricately designed green blouse. Little far from the couple was sitting a young pretty girl with a diary in her hand. She was keeping record of the gifts being given by different guests. Guests are going up the podium one after another , alone or with their family , wishing the couple and then handing over the gift – some in kind but mostly cash in envelopes. Two dozen chairs have been placed in front of the podium. Ladies-old and aged were sitting on these chairs and were taking a meticulous look at the newlywed couple.

Binaybabu looked at the other portion of the hall ; there is a huge crowd busy eating in standing position , with the plate in their hand . Everywhere there are food stalls and food stalls. What one can see is a variety of drinks, soups , spread of veg and non-veg items , sweet dishes and to end it all ice-cream. If one would add up , perhaps the number of items will cross 20-25. And at every stall, there is a long queue and the people are jostling with each other to get the food items of their choice. It is a mad rush , like we see at a film hall booking counter.

Binaybabu wondered , if such extravaganza is really necessary .

FOOD FOR THOUGHT

Amar,Akash,Aditya,Bibhu,Binay and Srikanta are batch mates. They studied together in an engineering college in 1985-89 and now in their late forties. All work at Bhubaneswar except Mr. Bibhu . He works in a central government PSU and is posted at Ahmadabad . Akash and Aditya are into state government jobs and are now senior officers . Binaybabu works with a state government PSU and Amarbabu is a professor in a university. Srikantababu is a an entrepreneur and has promoted an engineering college. Binaybabu and Amarbabau are childhood friends and are from the same village. The interaction among the friends was sporadic till Facebook and Whatsapp came into the market. Now they keep a tab on the events in each other's life like never before.

Once Bibhubabu updated a message in Facebook that he is coming to Bhubaneswar for some official work and will be there for three days. All the friends got excited at the news as they have not met him for more than a decade now. Each one of them started chatting with him over Facebook and gathered more details of his itinerary and the place of his stay.

Among all these friends Akashbabu is known for his leadership qualities. He is always at the forefront in organizing get-togethers and meeting of friends . Even during the college days, he was a popular person and was the secretary of the students' union. He is very calm and takes into account the interest of all. Now the news of Bibhubabu visiting the city made him interested in organizing a get-together. Meeting at anyone's residence was a option, but Akashbabu thought why to put the lady at home in trouble in such men's affairs. He also thought to keep the meeting simple and convenient for all.

A lunch or a dinner party would not suit all considering their engagements. So what he decided is , all the friends will meet at a restaurant in the evening time. During this time, there will be less of crowd at the restaurant and they would get a better environment to chat and can have a good time. The distance factor was taken into account and a centrally located south Indian restaurant was selected as the venue. The name of the restaurant Mr. Idli . The restaurant is known for its menu. One gets all kinds of south Indian delicacy there. The restaurant is famous for their idli manchurian and idli pakoda. Hopefully, everyone will love these items. All were informed the venue over Facebook and Whatsapp . Each one reminded to be present at the restaurant at 7PM and it was clarified that it is a get-together over snacks and no one should have a misgiving that it is a dinner.

Everyone reached the restaurant on time and got seated around a table. They shook hand with each other. Some embraced Bibhubabu , to bridge the arrear of lost interactions over all these years .

Mr.Idli is an air-conditioned restaurant with good ambience. There were just few customers there and they were quietly busy eating their dish.

The waiter left the menu on the table. Adityababu looked at the menu and ordered the specialties. He is very familiar with the restaurant as he is a frequent visitor to this place. He comes to this restaurant almost every Sunday morning to have a breakfast with his family. Adityababu consulted other friends before placing the orders, but more for courtesy than for their choice. He knows his friends' tastes better than the friends themselves. In the engineering days, during the visit to dhabas , friends used to leave it to him for selection of menu.

Binay , " Aditya , we all saw your posting in the Facebook regarding your admission at Apollo. What happened. You did not inform us during your hospitalization. Only after you left the hospital , you made the posting. As friends , we could have been of some use during hospitalization"

Aditya , "Don't know what is the problem really. Even the doctors could not find any issue after looking at series of medical reports. That day I was at my office and was alright till I took my lunch. After lunch , I felt dizzy and later felt that , the left side of my body is just not working, a kind of partial paralysis. I realized there is some problem and informed colleagues sitting nearby. They rushed me to the hospital. I remained in the hospital under observation for seven days and then discharged"

130

Binay , " At our age , we have to be careful. One does not know what will happen when. The other day I was returning home in my scooter with my son at the pillion. Actually, my wife drops my son at the tuition every day and while I return from office I pick him back. I was feeling little tired that day but not anything unusual. But I had never imagined that something dangerous was waiting me to happen. When I was just twenty meters far from my house , I felt like my vision is dropping like a incandescent bulb under low voltage and before I knew I went blank . My sixth sense prompted me to stop and keep the scooter on stand. My son also had got down from the pillion by that time...But I could not stand any more...I collapsed on the pavement and my head mildly hit an electric pole. This unexpected event perplexed my son and he started screaming and calling passersby. Before some people gathered and tried to help me out , I gained my consciousness , resumed driving and reached home safely. I thought it is a heart attack and so without any delay next day visited my family doctor. All tests were done , nothing significant was noticed. The doctor concluded that as a case of excessive dehydration.."

Srikantbabu who has a outward looking tummy opined " You all are not doing morning walk and hence these problems are coming."

Amarubabu who was sitting quietly and listening to the friends could not hold his story any more. He started," Listen , two years back once I traveled to Kolkata by train in sleeper class and the journey was in the afternoon. Inside the train I was feeling very suffocated, because of the hot weather outside and also too much of crowd inside. My head started grilling; I was sweating and later felt like collapsing. I thought, perhaps if I wash my face and make my hairs wet, things will improve. I rushed towards the basin. But before I could do what I had planned to, I started vomiting. That gave me relief till I reached Kolkata. But later again in the hotel, I faced similar problem. All these happened because of the hot weather. Therefore since then I never travel by sleeper class. Even for travelling short distances , I use upper class where one gets air conditioned bogey . You all should also do that"

Srikantbabu always have some expert advice to give. He could not spare this opportunity . He said, "All this happened to you because you are not doing some yoga and pranayam. Why are you not watching Ramdevbaba on Astha channel and do all those breathing exercises. Also always carry glucose water with you whenever you are on journey"

Bibhubabu supported the views of Srikantababu and added " It is all about disciplined life style and pursuing spirituality. You all are running after materialistic pursuits. Tell me why have you all owning two houses in this city. Is not one house enough for you. And then even for small distances you are using this four wheelers. Why can't you all walk a little which is good for your health.". The waiter came with all the ordered items and placed them on the table.

Amarbabu prompted , " Srikanta and Bibhu have given us too much of food for thought.....Now let's have these real food "...Everyone laughed in corus.

INNOCENT ASPIRATION

Govind is a IT administrator in an engineering college. He is married and has a son. Son is just six years old and studies in class-I. Govind is handsome , well groomed and very refined in his behavior. He is an introvert and a very private person ; but once he becomes friendly with someone he opens up. At his home , he has his wife , mother ,two young brothers and a little sister . Father has since expired. Mother is aging and frequently falls ill. Both the brothers work with a private bank as sales executives. They are yet to get married. Govind manages the household expenses . Though he contributes the major share , two young brothers also chip in some money. Overall, they lead a functional life. They have most of the necessities of life . Luxury of any kind is a strict No at their house as they can't afford them too long. Govind's son Krishna studies in a government school which is inexpensive. At times his wife pleads with Govind to admit Krishna in a English medium private school, but Govind is very clear in his mind. One has to cut one's coat according to the cloth available. At his current income, he can at best afford a vernacular medium government school. Only when he will earn higher amount and is in a better financial condition, he will think of private schools.

Govind is also a butcher. One would be shocked at the contradiction between his name and the unusual work he does. He got into this work not by choice but by compulsion.

His father was working in a company which used to manufacture borewell equipments and spares. When Govind was just twelve years old , this company closed down due to poor financial condition and his father became jobless. Since he had no other skill, he could not get any other job. This pushed his family into poverty and it became difficult for them to even have two square meals a day. His father used to suffer from epilepsy. Later because of stress, he developed heart problem.

Govind is Hindu but his ancestors were butchers. His forefathers used to serve the king and their primary work was to slaughter animals as per the wish of the king. Slaughtering is done both for sacrifice before the Gods and also when the king hosts a grand feast . But for the last two generations Govind's family has drifted from this profession. They are no more butchers as the royalty whom they used to serve is no more there. At present, Govind's near and dear ones work in government offices and private companies.

Hunger provokes radical thinking and this happened with the mother of Govind. She thought , " Why can't Govind try his hand in butchering ; after all that is what his forefathers used to do". Govind was in class-VIII then. She called Govind and gave this suggestion. Govind was shocked at the proposal of his mother and reacted " How can we make a living out of killing animals and then I have never done it"..Govind took refuse at his grandmother's lap to absorb this shock . Grandmother was a very old lady but was a warehouse of wisdom. She explained, " Govind , nothing wrong in becoming a butcher. That used to be our profession. Had it been bad or unethical, your forefathers wouldn't have done that job. It is a more respectable work than begging or stealing. If you don't do this job, whole family will die of hunger. Are you ready for such consequences? As far as skill to do the job is concerned, our neighbor Rahimmia will help you...Don't worry about that."

Govind reluctantly agreed to the suggestion and started going to the meat shop of Rahimmia to learn the skill. Slowly he learned the tricks and became a freelancer. He would visit different meat shops in the town and would offer service to the owners. He earned @100 for killing an animal and another @100 for peeling the skin of a slaughtered animal and converting it to eatable meat . Through this work , he earned 3-4 hundred rupees everyday and this brought some relief to his family. He continued his studies along with work and completed his +2 commerce. Later he joined a computer academy in the evening and learned computer hardware and system administration. He started applying for jobs at different places and by God's grace got this job of system administrator in the engineering college.

Slowly Govind's family got back to normal life. Govind also provided treatment to his ailing father and also his grandmother. Later, both expired though.

Govind no more does the work of a butcher on regular basis. But during Ramzan , he helps customers in animal sacrifice. Also it is a tradition in many south Indian Hindu marriages (excepting Brahmins) to sacrifice animal at the altar where marriage is solemnized, both at the bride and groom's house. Govind gets requests from friends and relatives to take care of such necessities. Govind gets service charge for all such work and few customers also give him some meat of the animal as a gift.

His wife and kid has seen him doing this job many times and don't mind it. In fact, his son who is just six years old now wants to follow his footsteps....

WHISPER AT THE MORTUARY

This is a big specialty hospital in the city. Centrally located and constructed over five acres of land. It is a beautiful five storied building. The front part is completely paneled with decorative glass and beautifully illuminated with fancy lights. One would mistake it to be a star hotel till he notices the glow signboard at the top of the building. Inside the hospital, there is a huge marble floored lobby. On one side of the lobby , exquisite leather sofa sets have been placed to accommodate 20-30 visitors. On the other side, there is 4-5 rows of steel chairs fixed to the floors are also available to patients and the attendants. Opposite to the entrance, there is reception. There are three beautiful girls managing the affair at the reception. All of them are wearing chiffon sari of same print and color. Patients and attendants are being directed to the registration and other counters after brief interaction at the reception. At one corner of the lobby, there is a medicine store. Almost at the centre of the lobby, there is a life size statue of Lord Ganesh. An earthen lamp has been lighted at his feet. Doctors , Nurses and other staffs when they are entering the hospital as per their shift duty are first bowing before the Almighty and then they are proceeding towards the biometric to give their finger print attendance.

The hospital opens for the outpatients at 9AM and closes at 9PM. Throughout the day , there is continuous traffic of patients. Large number of patients just take doctor's advice and leave. But many also get admitted in the hospital for operation, treatment or observation. There are different kinds of accommodation in the hospital. For the not so well off, there are wards – separate for male and female. Ward is a big hall where there are twenty odd beds. Near each bed, there is one plastic chair for the attendant to sit. There are cabins for people who can afford quality and privacy. Cabins are small air-conditioned rooms with attached bathrooms. Besides the bed for the patient, each room has a low height foamed bench for the attendant. One person can comfortably sleep on this bench and two persons can squeeze in also. Then there are suits for the rich and famous. These are symbols of luxury and comfort. A cursory glance will confuse one if it is a hospital or a hotel. In a suit, there are two big rooms , separated by a rolling door at the middle : one for the patient and the other for attendants. In each of these rooms there is a TV. In the room , for the attendants, there is a double bed, a refrigerator , a oven and a writing table . At the centre table near the sofa set, there is a basket full of variety of fruits.

Throughout the day, one notices doctors , nurses and housekeeping staffs attending to their respective jobs. Late evening, doctors make the last round and interact with the patients and the attendants. They brief the nurses on night duty all the care that needs to be provided over night. The main entrance of the hospital gets closed at 9PM. So the attendants get hurried up during this time. They come out of the campus to have the dinner at the nearby eateries or take some eatables inside that they can have at night , inside the cabin. At 10PM , the campus bears a deserted look. All the patients and attendants are indoors. Only the watchman is on duty at the gate. The emergency section remains open overnight.

In front of the main hospital building, there is a parking place. It is being managed by an agency. One can use the parking on pay-and-use basis. The staffs of the parking agency have closed the parking area gate. They have rolled mats on a cemented floor, hung a mosquito net and have lied down there to take some rest.

At one corner of the campus , one can see the sign board of the mortuary. It is an air-conditioned mortuary which can accommodate twenty dead bodies. Today between 6PM-8PM , three dead bodies have moved into the mortuary. They are lying on racks adjacent to each other.

It is 1AM at night and the whole world is asleep. Even the security guard has dozed off on his chair. These three dead bodies(A,B,C) started a conversation with each other.

A : Hello Dead men , how are you..This night is so boring. Let's talk a little to get rid of our worries. Hello B , tell us how come you are here. What happened to you.

B: I am a old woman aged eighty . I have four sons and one daughter. All sons are well placed in government jobs excepting the youngest one. He was the naughtiest one and never paid attention to studies. He is a contractor. My husband went to heaven two decades back , few years after his retirement. He was working in a bank. But before he died, we had married off all our sons and daughter. Daughter is married to a doctor and is happy with her family. Each of my son has their own house at different places of this city. After the demise of my husband I felt very lonely and decided to stay with my sons , on rotation , three months each. Each one took good care of me but I used to feel most comfortable at the house of my youngest son. His income is irregular but he takes care of my small personal needs. I came to this hospital from his house last week. I fell down in the slippery bathroom and suffered brain hemorrhage. All the four sons came and did their best to save my life, but they could not. One has to die one day , it is the ultimate truth. But I felt good that I died being surrounded by my four sons. As per my wish , they will take me to Swargadwar at Puri for my last rites.

Hello A , you don't look old, why you died?

A: Sad story. I am just forty and had to die , in fact I opted to die. I am married and have two kids. One son and one daughter. I was working with a private company as a sales manager. I used to earn reasonable amount to lead a functional life. We were staying in a rented house. Sales jobs are very demanding. I used to work very hard just to retain my job. It is not easy to get a job now a days. Everyday young qualified people are entering the job market and the owners of the company prefer them because of their energy and outlook. My wife is a difficult lady. She always wanted to lead a life of luxury which I can't afford. She will pick up argument with me on petty issues and made my life hell. But I used to remain calm considering the future of my kids. But , last Sunday evening I could not control myself. Out of anger , I drank the poison that was there in my house to kill rats. I drank full bottle of it and fell unconscious. Since this

140

hospital is nearby, my neighbors rushed me to this hospital. Doctors tried their best but could not hold my life for more than few hours. I am dead and happy..But I am sad for my kids.

Mr. C , tell us about you.

C: I am an retired government servant aged seventy . I have one son and one daughter. Both of them are married and settled in USA. I get my pension. Me and my wife had been staying in our house for last 15-16 years now. We have a full time servant at home. He takes care of everything at the house, from cooking to cleaning to giving us medicine on time. I died of heart attack. This was my third stroke. I had survived the first two. My regret , I could not really spend much time with my son and grand children in USA .We have gone to USA 4-5 times but I did not like that foreign land. Everything seems so unfamiliar to me there. For the last rites, my son and daughter are coming from USA. I may have to stay here for two days. As per my wish, I will be taken to my village for cremation. I love my village where I was born. I will be cremated at the same graveyard where my parents were cremated by me.

The bell at the nearby temple rang though it is still dark outside. The dead men wished Good Morning to each other.

NO TIME TO REST

Rajiv is a Youngman working in a bank as a probationary officer. He is born and brought up in rural area. His father was the post master of a nearby village post office. Rajiv did his schooling from the village school – both primary and high school. He had to come to the nearby town to study in the government college. He stayed in the hostel and completed his +2 in Arts and then BA in economics. In terms of merit , he is of average standard but he used to put in hard work. This hard work has compensated his lack of merit and he has been able to sail so far. BA is the qualifying degree required for most of the jobs in government , banks and railways. While he was in the final year of his graduation course, he joined a coaching centre which provided coaching for banking jobs. Though Rajiv took coaching for banking exams , the preparation also helped him to appear other exams. With his hard work and God's grace he cracked the PO exam of a bank and joined it. He got posted in a city far from his village. Eating food in the hotel everyday would affect the health of Rajiv and therefore his parents got him married as soon as he completed a year's probation at the bank. The name of Rajiv's newlywed wife is Swapna. Rajiv took his wife to the city , rented a house there and stayed together.

For a newlywed couple staying together is a marital bliss. Swapna is a very good cook and Rajiv enjoyed the items that she prepares. On weekends in the evening hours , they either go to a park or to a temple to spend some good time there. Some days , they also go to a multiplex or a film hall to watch a film. Once in a while , they also make a visit to colleague's place who are contemporaries and are also newly married like them. Life was fun.

But then the inevitable happened ; Swapna got pregnant. Most of the time she would remain indoors. Occasionally , the couple went for a brisk walk in the neighborhood. The doctor advised Swapna to avoid bike ride and also other heavy work. That would strain her body and may harm the development of the baby in her belly. While Swapna is eager to do the household chores, Rajiv would not allow her to do. He started doing most of the work at home including cooking. The D-date came ; Swapna was rushed to the nearby hospital and she delivered a baby boy. It was a normal delivery and the couple is back at home on the third day. They named the baby Rohon.

With the baby at home, the routine got changed. Rohon sleeps less and doesn't have a fixed pattern. He would wake up at the slightest sound or noise. Doctor had advised Swapna to feed the baby in specific interval without waiting for his cry as a sign of hunger. Now Swapna had to take care of house and also the baby. Whole day , she got busy with baby care and got tired in the evening. Many days , Rajiv started fetching dinner from restaurant as Swapna has no patience to cook. Night also did not bring much of relief to the couple. The baby would remain awake over night . He needed either parent to interact with him . If by chance, both the parents fall asleep , he will start crying. So

Rajiv and Swapna would sleep in rotations , an hour each so that they get some rest at night. They thought , with passage of time the baby will get rid of this habit and they can sleep peacefully at night. They were correct . The baby developed proper cycle and started sleeping late night and got up late in the morning . The couple felt good and happy.

After six months or so, the baby made the first turn of his back signaling the end of his inertia on the bed. Sitting on the bed cross-legged and then crawling happened soon after. This mobility brought in new danger. On few occasions , Rohon fell down from the bed while Swapna was busy at the kitchen. She could know the mishap only after Rohon screamed in pain. Therefore at night , Rajiv and Swapna would sleep at either side of Rohon. This reduced the risk of him falling. But even after this precaution , Rohon once fell down from the bed and injured his nose. From that day, the couple would wake up at night intermittently to check the position of Rohon and would realign him if he had dislocated. Rajiv and Swapna thought , Rohon will have the idea of edge once he is two year old and this trouble will be over. He will be personally careful in that age and will not fall from the bed. And they can sleep in peace. True to their judgment , Rohon became independent on the bed little after his 2nd birthday.

Rohon's 3rd birthday was celebrated and this also brought the thought of sending him to the school, to start with a nursery. The couple combed the nursery schools nearby and admitted Rohon to a good school , half a kilometer far from their house . At 7AM In the morning Rajiv drops Rohon at the school and at 11AM Swapna picks him back home by a hired auto. Hiring an auto everyday became very expensive and Rajiv started looking for some cheaper option. Rajiv search ended with a private van operator. He is an aged Punjabi man and ferries kids to school. He is also known to be very caring and responsible. Rohon started going to school by van. Rajiv and Swapna thought , a big issue got solved.

After nursery , Rohon was admitted to a bigger school where in he can study up to 12th class. His parents were very happy as they no more have to worry about a school for next 9-10 years.

Rohon was liked by all in the school for his academics and also extracurricular activities. He participated in all games and competitions and won many prizes. This good show continued till Rohon reached class-VIII. That year because of shuffling of students , he was allotted C section. In that section Rohon came into contact with a number of boys who were not very well behaved and many of them are known for indiscipline in the school. Rohon also picked up their habits and slowly his attention got diverted from academics. He started performing poorly in exams . On some indiscipline issues , his parents were summoned to the school and they had to listen to the unkind words of the principal. When things went out of control , Rajiv and Swapna decided to put Rohon into a boarding school , where he will remain under strict discipline. They searched internet , took the advice from their friends and then put Rohon in a boarding school in the neighboring state. This school is located in the hills and is isolated from all kinds of distractions. The couple felt sad that they can't have Rohon with them but also felt relieved that Rohon's career will be back on track.

Rohon's performance improved. He passed his +2 science with very good grade. He also cleared IIT and got admitted at IIT,Kharagpur. After graduation he got a job with a multinational company and got posted at Bombay. Rohon and one of his friend stayed in a rented house. But food was a problem. Most of the time they had to eat food outside and this affected the health of Rohon. Understanding the issue , his parents searched a good match for Rohon and got him married. Rohon and his wife Mira rented a house at Mumbai and stayed happily. After a year , Mira gave birth to a daughter and they gave her the name Natasa. She was a cute child and grew up to become a pretty girl. Everything was fine . In the meantime Rajiv retired from job , returned to his native village and spent leisurely life with Swapna. They were happy that Rohon is settled and they don't have to worry for him anymore.

One day , while the couple were taking their afternoon nap at their village home , the postman rang the bell. Rajiv woke up and received the letter . The letter was short and simple. " Mom , Mira has taken up a teaching job ; after school hour , Natasha has to stay alone at home , which we don't want. Please both of you come and stay with us....Yours Rohon"

Rajiv wondered.." This responsibility of life will never get over till one goes to the grave yard"

GRATITUDE

1984 ..Residence of Mrs. Indira Gandhi at New Delhi . It is a huge bungalow centrally located in a huge landscape. In the proximity of the residence there is a walking track dotted with large number of big trees . This track is separated from the main residence by a small gate. At the entry point, armed security guards are on duty , so also at other corners of the boundary. Early in the morning, at the lawn, a French film maker is getting ready to record how Mrs. Gandhi starts her day. She has been working on this project for last few months. After morning tea , Mrs. Gandhi came out from her residence, opened the gate that leads to the walking track. Barely she has taken to the track, two Sikh guards fired at her from point blank and she fell unconscious on the ground. This led to commotion among other guards on duty and the house helps at the residence. An ambulance was quickly called and she was rushed to AIIMS . This unexpected action from her loyal security guards is a fall out of the treatment she had given to their fellow Sikhs at the golden temple in the name Operation Blue Star. This news spread like wild fire and caused shock waves across the nation. It was considered a matter of revenge and rejoice for the Sikhs . But it also led to a backlash from the Congress loyalists. In a spat of hysteria and retaliation, they indiscriminately attacked Sikhs and their property. While it started in Delhi, slowly it spread to other parts of the country.

While Delhi had been witnessing dreaded scene, it is a normal day at a military administrative office at Patna . This is a magnificent old building from British era now being used as an office building. More than nine hundred people work in this building. The working time of the office is 9AM to 5PM . All India Radio reported , " PM shot from close range and feared dead" ; in spite of this news most of the staffs have reached the office . The head of this office is Mr. Damodar and his deputy is Mr. Misra , who is also the finance head . While Mr. Misra had reached the office and waiting for Mr. Damodar , the phone rang. Mr. Damodar informed the already known news to Mr. Misra and excused himself from coming to office. Incidentally that day was the pay day for the staffs and cash worth twenty lakh has reached Mr. Misra for payment to the staffs. Though Mr. Misra is responsible for the payment of salary, the actual work is done by Mr. Krisnakumar, cashier.

Little before noon , AIR confirmed the death of PM and hearing that almost all staffs left the office , barring some support staffs of Mr. Misra. The cashier did not turn up till noon and the second key of iron safe was with him. So the option of keeping the cash in the iron safe was ruled out. Mr. Misra was in deep trouble as to where he will keep this cash over night. At the same time, reports have started coming to him that hooligans have started looting the shops of Sikhs and damaging their properties in the town; even their life was at danger and they had no option but to go for hiding.

By 4PM , there were just four staffs at the office – Mr. Misra and three class-IV staffs. Mr. Misra was married and was staying at a rented premises 3km far from the office. He was married with a small kid. But as the fate would have it , his wife had gone to her sister's place that time and he was alone in the house. So considering the situation , Mr. Misra decided to stay back at the office over night to take care of the cash. So he informed his decision to the three odds staffs who were still there; all of them are local people and gave Mr. Misra an assurance that they would handle miscreants if by chance they get into the office at night.

Mr. Misra kept the cash in his room and took rest on his chair ; when it became evening he asked one of the peons to fetch tea from the nearby shop if it is open. His room has an attached bathroom and this bathroom also has a small window from the backyard side . This window had no railing. The peon brought tea . Mr. Misra felt good after having the tea. After tea , he walked towards the bathroom to have a leak. As he pushed the door of the washroom and entered , he was shocked to find a Sikh Youngman standing at a corner . He had beard and was wearing a turban. Noticing Mr. Misra , he folded his hands and pleaded , "To escape the wrath of hooligans , I have got into this washroom through this small window and I am hiding here. I have an electronics shop opposite this building. Please don't drive me away from this place". Mr. Misra was baffled and also scared at the sight of the person, primarily because at his office room he is holding cash of twenty lakh. He thought, allowing a stranger in the bathroom is too risky , but his heart was persuading him to be compassionate to the person at the time of such distress. After thinking for few seconds, Mr. Misra told the Youngman " ok , you may remain here over night , but I am going to bolt it from my side"…The fellow was delighted at the graciousness of Mr.

Misra. The door was bolted and Mr. Misra didn't tell anything to anyone about this strange encounter.

He came back to his room and spent the whole night on his chair. He could not really sleep though he dozed off once in a while. The three class-IV staffs spent time at the other room of the building by playing cards and gossiping. In the morning Mr. Misra opened the door of the bathroom to check the condition of the person hiding. But by that time he had left through that same window.

The money which Mr. Misra carefully protected over night was distributed to all the staffs next day.

Years passed and Mr. Misra got transferred from one place to the other and headed different offices in Defence. In 2008 he was posted at the head quarters at Delhi and by that time he has become a very senior officer. He had a big office chamber and there are two peons on duty at the door , all the time. They would not allow anyone to meet Mr. Misra without his permission, as he is generally busy with important work or meetings.

One fine day when Mr. Misra was at his chamber reading some important file, the peon came and informed him that an aged person wants to meet him for some personal reasons. Mr. Misra nodded to the peon. After some time a person entered the chamber. He looked like a perfect gentleman in his 50's , well dressed , clean shaved and was wearing golden framed specs. He quipped " Can you recognize me Sir"..to which Mr. Misra said "No" after maintaining few seconds of quandary. Then the man told ,"

Do you remember sir , in 1984 one man was hiding in the bathroom of your office chamber on the day on which Indira Gandhi was assassinated....I am that man"..

Mr. Misra quickly recollected the incident and offered him a chair to sit. He asked him, "how is your business and what made you come to my office"..

The gentleman replied," After that incident, we shifted to Dubai and we have a thriving electronics business there. My daughter is getting married here in Delhi ; from your Patna office I got to know that you are working in this office. I have come here to invite you for my daughter's marriage."..."If I am alive today, perhaps it is because of you sir".

GOURMOHON

Gourmohon is now sixty years old , but age has not dampened his spirit. He is still as jovial as a school boy and always happy. He is not married and is a free bird all his life. He is the only child of his parents but they are no more. Gourmohon is always eager to help others in distress , whether they are relatives or just neighbors. He is just a phone call away. He stays in his village alone. The agricultural land that he has inherited has been given to others for share farming . Whatever crop he gets from the farmers is sufficient to meet his annual need. His habits are simple. He hardly has anything as possession. Two pairs of dress , a towel , a gas stove and 3-4 utensils is what he has to lead his life. He cooks his food once in a while. Most of the time, someone or the other offers him food. He sells part of the crop every year and the money that he gets from that transaction becomes the pocket money for him.

He is uncle to everyone – relatives or acquaintances. No one has ever thought of using any other name to call him. He is the affable ever happy Uncle to everyone. With age he has slowed down but with a little opportunity he will regale one and all with his life stories, replete with humor , agony and joy.

When he was in primary school , he was very naughty . Every day he would leave for school on time , but en route would go somewhere else . On days he would go to the village mangrove to play with friends and on other days went to the canal to swim with them. Knowing this mischief , his father would occasionally visit the school to check whether he is present there or not ; also to take feedback from the teacher about his performance. Once during one such visit, his father saw Gourmohon standing on the bench while the teacher is sitting on the chair in the class room. In the evening , when his father asked Gourmohon about the punishment , he was quick to reply " The teacher wanted me to explain a difficult concept to all the students . Since I have a short height , he asked me to stand-up on the desk and explain".

Since his wickedness did not reduce even at higher class , his father put him in a hostel . The warden of the hostel was a strict disciplinarian and put a brake on naughtiness of Gourmohon. All the hostel boarders had to wake up early in the morning , when it is still dark outside , and study. Gourmohon and Mohon were sharing one room. Everyday before they go to sleep , they brought a jug full of water from the nearby borewell and kept that at their door . They used to make this provision for washing the face in the morning . But every day , when they get up , they found the jug empty. To teach the mischief monger a lesson , one day they filled up the jug half with water and rest with their own urine , and kept that at the usual place. Next day , early in the morning they heard the shouting of the warden and came out to see what is the matter. To their utter happiness, they got to know that the warden is the person who has been emptying the jug everyday and had used the mixture that day to wash his face and mouth. But later , the trick of

Gourmohon was detected by the warden and he was rusticated from the hostel.

Gourmohon used to secure just pass mark in his class exams and somehow managed to reach 10th class. He had an one sided love affair with a girl named Malati . She was a not-so-bright student but was a sincere student. They both appeared the 10th class Board examination . Gourmohon hoped to pass the exam in 3rd division so that he could pursue the affair with Malati in the college. But when the result came out , Gourmohon failed and Malati passed in second division. Gourmohon had no regret of failing in the exam but he was very disappointed with passing of Malati. Later he appeared the Board exam 9-10 times , but every time the result was same. Since clearing the board exam became impossible for Gourmohon and he had crossed twenty-five in terms of age , he decided to take up jobs.

Nobody was willing to give a job to Gourmohon since he was an under matriculate. One day while he was loitering in the bus stand , he came across a transport operator who has 3-4 busses. His name was Goloknath. After brief interaction , Goloknath offered a conductor's job to Gourmohon in one of his long route bus. He worked there for few months but found the job very hectic. So he left the job.

Gourmohon knew little bit of palmistry and also some specific puja to expel evil spirit from one's life or home. So one would find him at Kali temples most of the time. He would be chanting hymns and taking the names of Gods to fulfill the wishes of his clients. He also checks the palms of all these people to tell their future. For all these service he used to get service charge from the clients. There is no fixed charge as such. Gourmohon accepts whatever the client pays. The income was not regular and this prompted him to look for other opportunity for earning money.

While he was into this profession, his parents died one after another. It was very painful for Gourmohon to lose both of his parents so soon. There is no one left at home to take care of his life. No one will also marry him because he has no source of regular income. He locked his house at the village and went to the nearby town in search of jobs. He came across a builder who was executing a big government housing project . The contractor engaged him as a supervisor. Gourmohon worked there for two years and got a respectable salary. But it was a very tough job. Throughout the day one has to keep a tab on all the workers at the project site and also the materials at the godown. So he started looking for other better options in the town.

While he was still doing the supervisor's job , he came in contact with a small time local politician. This local politician is very close to a Minister. One day , the minister wanted to show his palm to a good palmist and Gourmohon got an opportunity to meet him through the local politician. The minister took liking of Gourmohon knowledge in palmistry and spirituality ; he appointed him as his personal secretary. This position offered him opportunity to meet different people who visit the minister for favors. Soon Gourmohon became very famous among all . Besides a good remuneration from the ministers, he earned lot of social respect from the public. Lot of people also gifted him money, when they got some work done through the Minister.

Gourmohon's savings soared and it crossed one lakh within few months.

Gourmohon had no bad habits and he used to save most of his income . One day , while he had gone to the market to purchase some grocery , he came across a stall selling lottery. There were big prizes , the highest being one crore. Each ticket priced at five hundred . Gourmohon got excited about the prizes and purchased ten tickets by paying five thousand . The lucky draw happened after few days and the   result   was   published   in   an   English   newspaper. Gourmohon scanned the numbers , but none of his numbers was there. He lost five thousand that day . But Gourmohon had great faith in his luck and so every week he spent similar amount on lottery and waited for the result. Every time , the same fate; he did not win a single prize. Recurring losses did not stop Gourmohon from purchasing lottery tickets. It had become an addiction with him. Slowly , he exhausted all his money that he has saved in the bank. Misfortune doesn't come alone. In the general election that was held during that time , the minister lost the seat to his rival and he could not keep Gourmohon as his private secretary anymore.

When this misfortune happened , Gourmohon was already in the wrong side of forty . It became difficult for him to get any other job in the town. So he came back to his village and lived on the small income that he got from the agricultural land that he had inherited from his father. Whenever anyone seeks advise from him , Gourmohon always says , "Never run after Lottery...work hard , there is a greater chance of winning"

FLORIST SHOP

This is a florist shop at an important junction of the city. Parsuram is the owner of the shop. He started this business a decade back when he was just 20-21 years old. His father was a postman in a post office. He opened the shop in the same year his father retired from the service. Parsuram has not been a good student and is just a matriculate. He never liked studies and so after this matriculation, he stopped further studies. He started doing odd jobs to earn pocket money. His father never expected any money from him till he retired. Being a government servant , his father got pension after retirement ; but that was too meager to run a household in this costly times.

As a child Parsuram was very fond of gardening . In front of their house there was a small land . He had fenced this small patch of land and had transformed that into a beautiful garden. One would find variety of plants in the garden – mostly flower bearing ; but there are some decorative plants as well including cactus. He would plant all kinds of seasonal plants and one would see flowers in the garden throughout the year -marigold in the winter and jasmine in the summer are a must in the garden. Flowers bloom and wither in the garden. Once in a while his mother did pluck some flowers from the garden for offering to the god. Though gardening was the passion of Parsuram in the childhood , later it became his vocation. Flowers became part of his daily life and it provided sustenance to him.

When he started the florist shop, he sold the flowers that are grown at their garden , but later he has to source them from different places . Marigold and Jasmine , he got from Kolkata ; Rose and Tulip from Bangalore. Most of the time , he purchased marigold in kg price and sold them at unit price. Initially, he had to go to all these places to work out business relationship with the suppliers but later everything was done over phone. The suppliers sent him flowers by railway booking and he paid them through money transfer. He had to regularly go to the railway station to receive the consignments from the parcel section of the railways. Flowers came in gunny bags duly packed in banana tree leaves.

After he receives the flowers at his shop, he sprinkles them with water to make them look fresh. He then makes strings and bouquets of different lengths and shapes, using these flowers. Later he displays them at the racks and the hangers at the shop. The illumination of the shop by use of florescent bulbs was excellent and it attracted the attention of potential buyers. At the top of the shop, the name plate said "Parsuram Florist".

Parsuram opens the shop early in the morning. Different people require flowers for different purpose and some requirements start in the morning itself. While most purchase stuff as per his design and craft, there are some customers whose demand has to be met as per their specification and terms.

Today has been a very hectic day for Parsuram. He has been busy throughout the day. As soon as he opened the shop, a woman reached his shop. She wanted a marigold garland which she wanted to offer to the god in the nearby Shivji temple. Parsuram is very superstitious about the first transaction. He would always do his best to make the customer happy. He had this belief that if the first transaction is good, rest of the day's business would be good. So he scanned the best garland from the bunch and gave that to the lady. The price of the garland was twenty a piece but the women offered to give only fifteen . Parsuram did not get into a bargain as it was the first transaction. So this became a sale without any profit. After this lady, few more customers came and purchased garlands for the same purpose. Parsuram thought, everyone wanted to please the god early in the morning.

After the morning rush, there was a dull period for an hour or so. No customer was in sight. But then at about 8AM, Gopal reached his shop. He is a house keeping staff in a big corporate. Every day , he buys a dozen yellow rose sticks and similar number of red rose sticks from him .He uses the yellow rose sticks to decorate the flower vessel kept at one corner of the CEO's table and the red roses are tucked into the flower vessel at the reception. Gopal takes the flowers on all working days but pays the money once in a month. There is some bill approval process in his company and so at times the payment gets delayed, but there had not been any default till date.

Yesterday, Parsuram had got two orders for decoration – one from a political party and another from a marriage party.

159

The leader of the political party is coming to the town to address the party workers at their party office at 3PM. So the podium and the entrance area have to be decorated by 2PM. It takes half an hour to undertake such work. So after lunch he would go there and do the needful. The local leader who has given the order is very slippery in making payment. Last time, Parsuram had to chase him for payment for a month or so and only after that he paid. This time, he has taken full advance payment.

The marriage of the bride is scheduled in the night, but guests from the bride side would start coming in the evening itself. So he has to finish decoration of the marriage hall and the marriage mandap by evening. It is an elaborate work and would take at least two hours or so. So after finishing the work at the political party office, he rushed to the marriage mandap. Completed the work on time, took the payment and returned to his shop in the evening.

As soon as he reached the shop, a big car halted in front of his shop. A person came out of the car and wanted the car to be decorated beautifully with rose buds only. The groom would travel in this car a distance of 80-90km for the marriage in the night. Parsuram was very tired but still agreed to do the job. He showed the decoration album to the person and as per his choice decorated the car using yellow and red rose buds . After the decoration, the car looked magnificent and royal. The man felt good ; after paying money to Parsuram , he drove away.

It is late evening now and the traffic on the road has increased. Today is an auspicious day for marriage. So there are many marriages that are being solemnized tonight. All the marriage mandaps and hotels are booked for today. On such days , the demand for bouquets spikes and to cater to the need Parsuram has maintained a variety of bouquets made of roses and tulip. Many customers came and purchased these bouquets from his shop and then preceded to the respective marriage mandaps.

Hardly anyone comes to his shop after 9.30PM and so there is no point keeping the shop open beyond this time. Other shops in the area get closed by 10PM . So Parsuram also closes his shop at 10PM. It takes Parsuram twenty minute time to reach his home by his bike. He takes dinner latest by 10.45PM and sleeps immediately thereafter.

Today , it is already 9.45PM. After few more minutes he would close shop and rush home. At he was counting the minutes and looking to the watch again and again, a van halted in front of his shop. It was small van , the rear carriage of which resembled a glass paneled transparent box. Inside this box, there was a stretcher. The van was conspicuous by its signage , both at the front and the back. It said " The Final Journey"

Parsuram took out few marigold strings from the rack and walked towards the van....

DESTINY

Suprabhat was a very bright young boy. He was a topper in both the secondary exam and the higher secondary exam in his state, a rare achievement by any standard. He was also very polite in his manners and was very affable among his friends. He was tall and handsome with an innocent face; any girl would fall in love with his looks. He was a charmer of sorts.

Sujogya was the elder brother of Suprabhat ; he was just two years elder to him and was pursuing a medical career. But Suprabhat had a fascination for machines and so he joined an engineering course. It was a big engineering college and offers many streams of engineering – mechanical , electrical ,electronics , computer science and civil. Suprabhat opted for computer science , as the subject was close to his heart. An engineering course is of four years duration and is divided into eight semesters. In computer science department there were forty students , all very bright . But no one could really match Suprabhat. Even in engineering , he maintained his lead in the examinations starting with the first semester. Every time , the college displays the result of the semester examinations , it becomes a foregone conclusion that his name would be there at the top. His performance was always stellar and the next best student is every time a distant runner. But in spite of his outstanding unbeatable academic record , Suprabhat had always been a grounded boy. He was a friend and a teacher to all. He never minded spending long hours with his friends and teaching them complex lessons , which many could not understand in the class. For this empathetic nature , all friends like him very much.

In all the extracurricular activities at the college , Suprabhat is always at the forefront- whether it is a cricket match or a picnic. If he is not participating in the event , he would be there to cheer and support the friends. Suprabhat was so bright that till the 7th semester he maintained the lead not only in his department but in his whole batch. It was an accepted fact that he would conclude the degree as topper and would receive the Chancellor's gold metal as the best graduate.

But a man's destination is not his destiny.

That year , the final semester exam was scheduled to be held in April. As the batch will pass out and there would not be any more opportunity for a get-together , the students of the computer science department planned for a picnic. Ashok , who is a very close friend of Suprabhat and the hostel roommate , was the Class Representative of the department . So he took the proposal to the Head of the Department for consideration . The idea was appreciated and a go ahead was received from the Principal. Everybody was very happy as they would be able to have some fun time together. It was decided to invite all the teachers for the picnic. A committee was formed to plan and execute the picnic . Ashok was made the Head of the committee. With popular consent, a tourist spot was selected. It was a mountain famous for seven springs emanating from its top.

Not a very distant place from the college; required an overnight journey to reach the spot. What was planned is that , they would reach the spot early morning , would spend time there till 2PM and then return so that they can be back at the college by 10PM or so.

The bus reached the campus previous day night at 11PM and all the students boarded the bus after having their dinner. There were forty of them including ten girls. Suprabhat also got into the bus, with a costly camera hanging at his chest . They reached the site early in the morning , located a good spot and put up their tent there. A jumbo carpet was laid and two dozen chairs arranged for the convenience of all.

Boys and girls sat at different places in groups. Some played cards and some others got busy in other fun filled activities. Some adventurous souls attempted to explore the mountain heights and took to the serpentine forest paths. And there are few others who rushed unto the fountain beds to enjoy a splash. The accompanying cook prepared the breakfast and then lunch on time. All sat together and enjoyed the food. It was a unique experience to spend time with nature.

As planned , all got back to the bus at 2PM for the return journey. All were tired and so slept inside the bus as soon as it started rolling. The bus reached the hostel at 10PM. All got down from the bus and preceded to their respective rooms after wishing good night to each other. Suprabhat and Ashok reached their room and started arranging their bed to sleep. At this moment , Suprabhat realized that he has left his camera in the overhead rack of the bus. By this time the bus had left the hostel and had reached the bus stop which is 10km far from the hostel. In those days there was no mobile phone to call and to intimate the driver or the helper on the matter. So Suprabhat and Ashok decided to drive down to the bus stop by their scooter and retrieve the camera. It was already 10.30PM then. They borrowed a scooter from a friend , drove down the National Highway. Ashok was driving and Suprabhat was on the pillion. They soon reached the bus stop. To their delight they could spot the bus at the bus stop immediately and the camera was very much there where Suprabhat had kept it. Overjoyed they took out the camera from the rack and proceeded back to the hostel. Ashok was driving and Suprabhat was on the pillion.

The indicator of the scooter showed that there is almost no fuel and so they halted at a petrol pump on the NH to fill the tank. This petrol pump is just 5km from the hostel. A big mishap was waiting to happen at this juncture. After the filling , while Ashok was about to start the scooter , Suprabhat wanted to drive instead of sitting at the pillion. Ashok had no idea that Suprabhat suffered from night blindness. He agreed to his proposal . Suprabhat kick started the scooter and drove the scooter on the NH , while Ashok was on the pillion. After a kilometer or so , on the NH sideway, there was parked a loaded truck with the backlights off. Suprabhat was driving at 40km/hr or so and could not notice this truck on the sideway and dashed against it. The truck remained unmoved. But both Suprabhat and Ashok popped out of the scooter and fell down at the middle of the NH , both losing their sense. But luckily , before another truck would crush them under its wheel , Ashok got back his sense and pulled Suprabhat to one side of the NH. It must be 12PM in the night then and it was dark all around. Ashok signaled his hands and pleaded to all passing by vehicles for help. By God's grace, a car stopped . The driver helped Ashok to lift Suprabhat from the road and made him lie at the rear seat. The nearest hospital was a km beyond their hostel. At the request of Ashok , the driver took them straight to the hospital and rushed to the emergency. Suprabhat was admitted into the ICU.

Ashok called up the parents of Suprabhat and informed the incident. They reached the hospital next day. The doctors had initially hoped that Suprabhat will regain sense at the earliest. But it did not happen. All kinds of tests made in the next couple of days , but in vain. Instead of recovery , he slipped into coma and the doctors could not do much. Friends attended to him round the clock on rotation. His parents remained with him all the time , with the hope that miracle may happen. But the wait was too long . He remained in coma for more than six months. He was very fond of listening to radio. So a radio was kept near his hand with programs on. The first sign of recovery was noticed when he caught hold of the tuner of the radio and rotated it little bit. It was a painful and arduous wait for all to see a full recovery. It took a long one year for his recovery. He became normal and shifted home for psychological adjustments. A lot of changes were noticed in him. The way he talked and the way he walked changed. He also lost many of his past memories.

Last semester exam had since been over , while he was in the hospital. All his friends had left the hostel and had joined jobs. Suprabhat missed the opportunity to give a finishing touch to his record of being the topper all through. He appeared the final semester exam next year . Later he did his MTech and PhD in one of the IITs. It is a consolation that he is a professor at an IIT , though he deserved much more in his life.

PUPPY

In a small cantonment town named Sagada , there lived a bank officer named Ramakanta. He had a family of six members -his wife , three sons and a daughter. They lived in their own house. It was a one storied pukka house with a small front yard and a big back yard . In the front yard, one would see variety of flowers throughout the year. Ramakanta was very fond of plants . He took care of the garden in the morning before he went to the office and again in the evening after he returned from work.

Daughter was the eldest and was in class-IX and the sons were in Class-VII,V and III respectively. Daughter and eldest son used to go to a teacher's residence , half a mile away , for group tuition. Since the other two sons were small and can't really walk down to another place for tuition , a private tutor named Ashish was engaged to teach them at their house . He is a young boy who had passed his graduation in Mathematics honors and was trying for various competitive examinations. He is a boy from a nearby village. His father was a poor farmer and hence not been able to finance his stay at the town . That is the reason why Ashish had taken up tuition to meet his expenses by himself. Though Mathematics was his forte , he was equally good in science and literature. He used to teach all subjects to the two school going boys . He visited Ramakanta's house everyday in the evening , excepting on Sundays. Ashish was a very strict teacher . He took all care to teach the subjects well and conducted mock tests to check the learning. If the kids performed badly in school exams , he rebuked them and also did not mind beating them with a cane at times.

Ramakanta had a pet dog in his house . Puppy was his name. It had black shinning skin. In terms of height, it was a dwarf. But with regard to its lateral size, it was disproportionately long. Ramakanta had brought this puppy from one of his colleagues whose pet had given birth to half a dozen puppies. Ramakanta and his family members were very fond of Puppy and provided all comfort to it. When Puppy was small, it was housed in a wooden box with one side open . Layers of gunny bags were laid on the floor of that box and the puppy used to sleep on such a quilt . Near the wooden box , two aluminum bowls were kept ; in one bowl , water is made available all the time and in the other food is served . In the initial days , it would only drink milk , nothing else. At it grew up , it started eating all kinds of food , both veg and non-veg. After it grew big , the verandah of the house became its resting place. But Puppy had the liberty to enter any room of the house excepting the kitchen. Puppy ate food , prepared especially for him , as per schedule . But , every time Puppy noticed Ramakanta or some family member eating some food , he would reach there and wagged its tail , hinting that he wanted that food also. To satisfy Puppy , they would throw a small piece unto his mouth . He would quickly gulp that piece and wait for the next bite. Even when a member purposefully ate food in some distant corner of a room , Puppy would know that and would instantly appear there for his share.

On Sundays , Ramakanta helped Puppy take a bath . He would apply soap to its skin and would make it stand below a shower for a proper cleaning of his body. After the bath , Puppy would stand outside the house for sunrays to dry its skin . Later , Ramakanta sprayed a kind of powder all over its body , to prevent insects and germs to take shelter in his body.

Every day afternoon Puppy would take the stairs and sat at the roof top . It is during this time his master returned home from office. As soon as it notices Ramakanta coming towards the house from a distant road , he would gallop down the stair and would welcome its master at the entrance of the house. Puppy was not only dear to the family of Ramakanta but also to the neighbors. At night he would stand guard against all suspicious movements of human beings and will bark non-stop. If a thief trespasses the boundary of any house under its surveillance, he would chase him away.

Perhaps , Puppy was loved most by a Bhujiawala. Known to all by the name Bihari , he is a man in his late fifties . This name had been derived from the fact that he hailed from Bihar. He was a man of short height and used to sport a Maharaja style moustache. He wore a dhoti and a half sleeved punjabi . Bihari migrated to this town when he was a young boy and since then he had been selling bhujia. All loved the taste of bhujia that he made . He carried bhujia on his head in a wooden box and would carry a portable stand in his hand. Every day, in the afternoon , he walked down the streets of the town and sold bhujia to all and sundry . To attract attention of the customers , he had a bell in his hand , which he rang time to time.

While ferrying , Bihari halted in front of Ramakanta's house every day , whether there were any customers or not. Puppy was the special guest to whom Bihari enjoyed feeding every day . As soon as he reaches the street , Puppy would come out of the house , stand near him and would salivate looking at the bhujia. Bihari would take away few spoonful of bhujia in a paper plate and would place it in front of Puppy. It would eat those fast , would lick the feet of Bihari a little and then return to the house of Ramakanta. This was a daily ritual and a kind of unusual relationship had developed between Bihari and Puppy.

Puppy had a knack of spotting snakes. On several occasions it spotted snakes at the house of Ramakanta – sometimes in the front yard and at times inside the house. Puppy would not allow a snake to enter the house if it comes to its notice. It would bark incessantly and would drive the snake away from the house. If the snake is inside the house, he would raise an alarm for Ramakanta to check and kill the serpentine at the earliest. Therefore, when Puppy barks non-stop , everyone in Ramakanta's household gets alerted anticipating such intrusion of snakes.

Sagada being a cantonment town , one would notice military vans and jeeps plying on the road very frequently. One day in the evening time , for some reason , Puppy came out of the house and was loitering on the road. At this time one speeding military jeep flicked him from behind and Puppy was thrown meters away from the road. He was bleeding profusely and was in a very bad shape. Some neighbors saw him in that condition and reported Ramakanta. He was immediately picked up and rushed to a veterinary doctor . The doctor initiated treatment and gave some injection. But Puppy did not recover and succumbed to the injury. His dead body was brought back to home. A deep sense of sorrow engulfed the house . Puppy was like a family member. Children started crying looking at the body of Puppy which was lying still on the floor. Even some neighbors came and sympathized Ramakanta and his family.

At night , the body of Puppy was taken to the backyard of the house where there was a big mango tree. A pit was dug under that tree and it was buried there. All children were present for the burial and they could not believe that their dearest Puppy is gone forever. Ashish , the tutor was also present at the spot. Next day, he wrote a poem in the memory of Puppy . Ramakantababu was so hurt by this loss that he never kept a pet dog again.

Bihari bujiawala was unaware of this tragic incident. The accident did happen an hour after Bihari fed him some bhujia and left the spot to ferry in other areas. Next day Bihari came and waited for Puppy to come and eat bhujia. Since Puppy didn't turn up , Bihari sounded his bell again and again. But Puppy was nowhere in sight. Later, the wife of Ramakanta came out of the house and told Bihari what all happened the previous day. Bihari was deeply saddened and he almost started crying standing on the road.

From that day Bihari stopped ferrying his bhujia in the lane where Puppy lived. Perhaps he was haunted by the sweet memory of Puppy.

CRAZY AMBITIONS

Rahul was a young boy of a middle class family. He was the only son to his parents. His father was a government servant and was honest to the core. He had since retired and used to get is monthly pension. During the service days, he had purchased an MIG house under the government housing scheme. A small house with two bed rooms , which was just enough for their small family. All his life's saving was invested in this house. By God's grace before his father's retirement Rahul completed his studies and got a job in a private bank. He was very sincere and hard working. All staffs liked him because of his simple nature.

Rahul was very handsome and had a body like a Greek god. He did everything to remain fit and fine . Besides a controlled diet , he was a gym freak. He would surely visit the neighborhood gym at least once in a day , either in the morning or in the evening. It was a gym catering to both the genders on the same floor. Rahul was adored by one and all for his sculptured body. Young girls don't miss a chance to discretely peek at his toned body.

Bobita , a young girl barely out of her teens also visited this gym. She is the daughter of an ultra rich businessman. She is the only daughter to her father and lived like a fairy in a mansion. This mansion is a kind of landmark in the city and located at a posh locality. There were servants to attend to

174

her wishes and whims . Her dad had a fleet of cars. The number of cars was so large that Babita used to ride cars matching the color of her dress. Her father fulfilled all her demands even when many of them are unreasonable. She was a pampered child and she knew everything will reach at her feet at the wink of her eyes. She used to study Arts in the city college. But that was just like a pastime for her. She hardly had any interest in studies. College is just a place for her to show off her dress and accessories.

Babita was tall , beautiful and smart. Her behavior was polished. But in the exterior of her refined ways , she had a deep sense of arrogance. She believed , money can buy anything and nothing is beyond her. Whatever she wished to get , she got that by hook or crook. She was not a girl who would accept a No for anything that she wanted.

Incidentally she was also a member of the same gym which Rahul visited . She used to come to the gym mostly in the morning time. While Rahul came in his bike , Babita drove an expensive car. Once on a fine morning , while Rahul was on the treadmill , Babita reached the gym and took up the adjacent treadmill . At this moment, her eyes fell on Rahul and she took an instant liking of him . The thought of winning his heart captured Babita's mind.

That day as soon as she noticed Rahul finished his work-out and was readying to leave , she walked up to him. She wished him good morning and exchanged few pleasantries. Later she invited him for a cup of coffee at the coffee bar attached to the gym. Rahul was reluctant as he might get late to office. But Babita persuaded him and both went to the shop and drank coffee. They spoke briefly at the coffee table and then left for their respective homes. Babita felt very happy that day and decided to deepen the friendship with Rahul. So every day, she would invite him for coffee or for a brisk walk after the work-out is over. Rahul also liked Babita. It was his first real friendship with fairer sex and he enjoyed the friendship. Rahul got to know the social status of Babita but he never considered that an obstruction to their friendship. On some days , Babita would take Rahul on long drive after the gym . At times , she would halt at isolated places and pleaded Rahul to talk to her non-stop. Rahul kept her wish as otherwise she got terribly unhappy.

This friendship continued for few months and Rahul enjoyed it as much as Babita. But there was surprise waiting for Rahul. One day , in one such outing early in the morning Babita expressed her love for Rahul and asked him if he has same feeling towards her. He was surprised and confused at that moment. He tried to explain Babita that they belong to completely different social strata and hence such an affair is unthinkable. But Babita was hell bound to her proposal and wanted to marry him. To defuse the unusual situation, Rahul told " Give me some time. Let me think over on the matter".

Rahul spoke about this personal issue with his parents. They were not very comfortable about the idea of his marrying a girl from a very rich family primarily because there would be adjustment difficulties between the couple and also between the two families. Rahul convinced them by giving them the confidence that Babita is not a typical spoilt girl from a rich family and would adapt to their family easily. After the initial reluctance , his parents agreed . A date was fixed on which the parents of the girl would come to their house to freeze the marriage proposal and to work out the details. Babita's parents arrived on the appointed date with a huge quantity of sweets and gifts. He was a person who would do everything for the pleasure of her daughter. While leaving Rahul's house , he attempted to dump cash worth five lakhs in the hand of Rahul's father. On the other hand , Rahul's father was a very self respecting person and was shocked at this happening. He displayed his utter reservation about this kind of gift , but was almost forced to hold on to the booty as he noticed a kind of silent consent on the face of Rahul.

Marriage happened as per schedule and Babita came to Rahul's house. As was anticipated , Babita felt like a fish out of water in that small house. Even on forth night , she did not cooperate with Rahul to make that a memorable day. She bargained with him that the honeymoon will happen only in the cozy comfort of a five star hotel. Rahul succumbed to her wishes and booked such a hotel next day and enjoyed the night there. But later , it became a regular demand from Babita and Rahul did not have the money to do that. This led to regular fight between them inside the closed rooms at night.

Parents of Rahul could make out the reasons of trouble at home . So to make their daughter-in-law happy they arranged a surprise for her . They gifted them a honeymoon trip to Switzerland for a week , even though this gesture wiped them of whatever small savings they had in the bank. Babita and Rahul were overjoyed when they got to know this. On the scheduled day , they flew to the dreamland and had a fabulous time there.

But when they were on their return journey , bigger surprise was waiting for Rahul . On the way back to their house , Babita expressed her desire to go to her place instead of Rahul's. He tried to explain her the eagerness with which his parents would be waiting for them , but Babita had decided her mind. So Rahul dropped Babita at her parent's house and came back home. His parents felt disappointed for not finding Babita with him but consoled themselves that she would be coming back in few days time. But their hope remained a hope only . Babita had no plans to come back to Rahul's place. She had already got what she wanted . She wanted to win Rahul's affection – mental and physical. It was a kind of personal challenge for her and she had won it.

One full month passed but Babita did not return to her in-law's place. Rahul did meet her almost every alternate day as he had the hope that Babita would come back home. During one such visit Rahul got to know that she is pregnant and felt very happy about the development. He shared the good news with his parents and they were overjoyed. But this happiness was short lived again . Babita aborted the pregnancy without consulting Rahul . When Rahul got to know this from Babita , he felt dejected and also got very angry with her.

In the meantime a new plan had taken shape in the mind of Babita. Having fulfilled her wish to win Rahul , she was not finding any greatness in him. She wanted to get separated from him and look for another life partner matching her status and life style. She took her father into confidence and hatched a conspiracy. As usual to keep the daughter happy , her father asked his lawyer to draft a divorce agreement . The lawyer drafted the agreement and signature of Rahul was necessary to proceed in the matter. Babita's father asked Rahul to sign the papers , but he outright refused to do so. Rahul never knew that Babita's father was a crook. On Rahul's refusal , he reminded him that the money he had given to his father during the engagement was a kind of dowry and receiving such money was a criminal offence. He threatened Rahul that if he would not sign the papers, he would file a criminal case under Anti-dowry Act which will lead to immediate arrest of his parents.

Rahul felt helpless and quietly signed the divorce papers and came back home. He narrated all that happened to his parents. Rahul's life changed completely from that day. He stopped trusting other young girls whom he met at gym or at work. But his parents felt the events that occurred in Rahul's life were a blessing in disguise.

CIRCUS GIRLS

This is the sight of a huge circus tent. The signboard "City Circus" is visible at a height . This huge multi-poled canopy is protected by an encircling fence of dismountable steel grills. Surrounding the huge tent , there are 2-3 dozen low height tents where the performers and support staffs stay. Each tent is occupied by 3-4 persons. girls' tents are located little far from the boys' tent. A row of temporary toilets and a bathing barrack has been there for the convenience of all the inhabitants. The facility provides semi-privacy. There is an aged lady who is responsible to prevent thoroughfare around the girls' tent. But the surveillance is sporadic and hence in the night one would spot a man or a two moving around the tents like thieves. Bathing area is most susceptible to the prying eyes of the boys and men. One has to be extra careful while taking clothes off from the body inside the four walls of the bathing barrack. There is always a risk of someone peeping into the bathroom through the holes and gaps at the joints.

There is a separate area for animals (elephants and dogs) and birds. While the animals are tied to their anchors in the open , the birds are kept in cages.

Salim is the Owner-cum-Manager of this circus and stays in a more spacious tent alone. He is a strict disciplinarian in terms of performance. He started this business two decades back and was doing fine. But in 2002 , due to new laws the use of wild animals and children in circus stopped. This reduced the attraction of spectators towards the circus. Before this time , people were able to see the wild animals like tigers and lions from close-up and also the spectacular gymnastics of small and cute little girls. Circus business is a tight rope walking in terms of profit and therefore Salim never spends any money on non-essentials. Salim is from West Bengal and hence puts up his circus mostly in the eastern part of India. This is a round-the-year business though the best months to attract customers is May and December as during these times schools are on vacation and children are free at home.

It is 4AM in the morning . Darkness engulfed the outside world but the activity at City Circus has started . Boys and Girls have just woke up from their tents and are getting ready for the daily practice. After having few biscuits and a cup of tea , they have all congregated at the area where they perform every day , three shows 1PM-3PM, 4PM-6PM and then 7PM-9PM. Under the strict monitoring of the respective trainers they will practise all acrobatics and stunts till they lose all sweat from their body. The regimented practice ends at 10AM at which they are back at their tents. By 12PM they have their lunch and are ready for the first show.

Rupa , Boby , Madhabi and Ratna are four female performers of the circus. Madhabi is the eldest among them and is around 35years old. Ratna is 30years old. Rupa and Boby have just crossed their teens and have joined the circus seven years back. Madhabi stays with her family in one tent. Rupa ,

Boby and Ratna stay in another tent. Irrespective of the age gaps, all of them share good friendship.

It was the last show at a city where they had camped and after two days the circus will shift to another city . After the show got over , all of them had their dinner at one place and got into chatting on their life . They were trying to recollect the life that they have lived so far and how they had a roller coaster ride of life.

Rupa and Boby are from Jaipalguri , West Bengal. Incidentally they are from the same village. Their parents were poor farmers. One year , there was a famine and the field did not yield any crop. This pushed their parents into poverty and they could not feed them even two square meals a day. There was an aged man in the village named Natwar . He is known as a person who can arrange odd jobs for poor children at Kolkata. Boys get the job of waiters and sweepers at roadside hotels and shops. Girls are mostly engaged as maid servants at the house of Bangalibabus. The parents of Rupa and Boby approached Natwar. During that time , Natwar was looking for good looking young girls for the City Circus which had put up a tent at Kolkata. So he immediately agreed to offer the two girls some job at the circus. Next day , a person from the circus arrived at the village with some agreement paper. Being illiterate, poor fathers of these two girls did not understand what is that has been written on the paper. What they were made to believe is , that the girls will be with the circus for ten years and will be trained for performance . Parents will get a lump sum of ten thousand rupees on signing of the contract and when they start performing , parents will get three thousand rupees per month. After the briefing the contract was signed, the initial amount changed hands and then the two girls are ready to leave with Natwar for Kolkata.

On reaching the circus , they were made to stay in small tents like others. The struggle of circus life started next day morning. Both of them were very scared of heights. But they were coerced to rise to the heights and try the incomprehensible body movements. Their reluctance led to shouting from the trainers and many times it took the shape of verbal abuse. In fear , they did try to act as per the instruction. Many times they fell down and injured themselves. After a week's struggle and oppressive life , they made up their mind to escape from the circus. They attempted that one night when all were asleep but the security guard alarmed the Manager on time. Salim slapped them multiple times and they have to return to their tents with tears in their eyes.

Slowly they got reconciled to their life and tried to learn the performances. The unwritten rule of the circus – maintain your beauty and perform to keep the spectators happy. Even on days when they are going through the hormonal cycle , there is no respite. They have to perform. They have to put up a fake smile on their face even though their body is suffering the acute pain. They have been there in the circus for last seven years. As per the contract, they have to be there for another three years. But by that time , they will have no option but to continue with the same work. Their life will be tied to the circus.

After about two years of their joining the circus , the parents of Rupa and Boby came to the city where they had camped. They wanted to take their child to the village for a brief vacation but the Manager did not agree. The show is on and the girls are tied to the contract. Parents returned to their village disappointed but consoled themselves as their child is at least getting food to eat and a place to sleep.

The life of Madhabi and Ratna have been different. They have stayed with the circus since its inception and there is no looking back. That option is no more there. Both of them have been trafficked from Nepal after they lost their parents and siblings in an intense earth quake. They had nothing to eat and nowhere to go. They spent some time in the government provided tents and survived on relief given by good hearted Samaritans. But that was short lived. They have to fend for themselves. They were small children, not even touched teenage then . Problems brings solutions in the most unfortunate way. They both fell prey to the sweet words of a tout who promised them food and shelter. He brought them to Kolkata in a bus. At the border , he advised them to mention to the officials that they are relatives and are going to Kolkata for sightseeing. They safely passed the border and reached the big city of Kolkata. The tout left them with the Manager of the circus and then went off . He must have taken his due from the Manager. Girls from Nepal are genetically more flexible and are very suitable for the acrobatics. Further they are very exotic to the eyes of the spectators in India.

Madhabi and Ratna have never thought of going back to Nepal as there is no one for them to meet. Madhabi fell in love with Manu who is also a performer at the circus. While she displays her skill on cycle , Manu works as a stunt man. He whirls on a bike inside a big steel cage along with three others. The sight of that stunt used to bring shivers in the spine of Madhabi. But now she has accepted it as a part of their life. Some days Manu gets injured and gets a lot of pain in his limbs. Madhabi takes care of him at the tent. They have a small child of age four. He is learning alphabets from the teacher at the circus. In a circus one doesn't have the scope or the luxury of associating with the outside world as it shifts the camp from one city to the other.

Ratna is not as fortunate as Madhabi. She also got married to another performer named Janu in the circus who used to do aerial stunts. They were married for three years when during a practice session Janu fell down from a height and succumbed to the injury. She is single since then. It is a difficult life to live but life must go on. The birds that she handles at the circus are like her children and she spends most of the time with them. She understands the cacophony of their sounds and the flipping of their wings.

Behind the skimpy shinning dresses and a dictated smile on their face , there lives a story of poverty and irony of life. Rupa , Boby , Madhabi and Ratna keep entertaining spectators as they are tied to their destiny.

BITTER PILL

Today is Eid and there is lot of funfair at Anand Mahal. Gafar Ali and his family stay in this old two storied building. This is the third generation of family members who are continuing to stay in this brick-and-mortar marble floored mansion. It looks like a hexagonal tower with a balcony overlooking the road at each floor. The building stands at an elevation and so the balcony at the ground floor also gives quite a natural view of the road. A mogul style intricate design of the walls makes it look majestic. The terrace is surrounded by a waist height boundary wall . This wall is perforated with small openings in the shape of diamonds and clubs. The building is old - looks more old because of lack of coloring in the recent past. The frontage of the building has many floral and animal designs and looks ancient. At the entrance of the house there is a memorial for some important person of the family. It is a small tomb , over which a green silk cloth with silver border , has been spread. The memorial is a small place of the size of a kitchen , asbestos roofed , with no walls in the four sides; steps are there in one side to reach to the elevated place where the tomb is incorporated.

It is an old style house in the interior also. There is a courtyard at the centre of the house and a concentric verandah. The encircling verandah at the first floor looks like a balcony and one could see what is happening at the

186

courtyard being at that place. In the courtyard , there is a water tap for general use and a big outlet for release of rain and waste water to the drain connected to the main road.

At one side of the courtyard a calf is tied to a hook with a small piece of rope at its neck. It is white in color and has shinning skin . A heap of grass is lying in front of the cow . But the cow is not eating its favorite food. A small streak of liquid has spilled from one corner of its eyes and has soaked its face. Looks like the cow is sad and has sobbed a little, perhaps in anticipation of what is waiting for it to happen.

The maulana has reached the house and is sipping tea at the bench at the verandah. Soon he will descend unto the courtyard to initiate the ritual after which the head of the house has to sacrifice the cow. To help in the kurban , a professional butcher has been hired ; but the ritual warrants the slitting of the neck has to be done by the head of the family. This has been the practice for generations and there can't be an exception

All have gathered at the verandah to watch the ritual which is a matter of merrymaking for them. They included: Three sons of Gafar Ali , his daughter in laws , grandsons and granddaughters. The wife of Gafar Ali is also present. Only one person who is conspicuous by her absence is Madhabi , the youngest daughter-in-law married to Azhar.

Azhar called from the verandah, " Noor , come out from the room; the ritual will start" . Since she got married to Azhar , her name has been changed from Madhabi to Noor. She could clearly hear Azhar but is just not willing to watch something which she can't imagine in her wildest dreams. She is sleeping in her room with her eyes wide open thinking about the turn of events that has reached her at this stage.

Madhabi and Azhar pursued their engineering in the same institute in the city. Both were bright student. Madhabi was very charming and anyone will get captivated at her innocent looks. Azhar was a non-descript kind of boy in terms of looks but his etiquettes are very refined. He is very respectful to his teachers and was very courteous while talking to friends particularly opposite gender. In the 2nd year of their career , they fell in love. It was a most unlikely kind of affair that ever blossomed in the campus. A Hindu girl falling in love with a Muslim boy , but it did happen.

Madhabi belonged to a conservative Brahmin family and she was quite aware that her parents will lose sense if they come to know about the affair. She did confide this issue with Azhar , but neither of them really gave too much of importance to the consequences . The love between them grew and became too strong to be broken as they reached the final year of their college. Both of them did pass with flying colors and also got placement in the same company and same city. They were in seventh heaven and wanted to get married as soon as possible.

Matter reached the ears of the parents of both the families. Parents of Madhabi were aghast at the news and were crest fallen. Madhabi's father called her and conveyed , " We will prefer to die than to see you get married to a Muslim boy". Azhar's father was more accommodating. He was a liberal minded person and agreed to Azhar's wishes though initially he showed reluctance in this inter-religious marriage. Madhabi made up her mind to get married , even though her parents were completely against such a move.

Nikah happened as per Muslim traditions. After spending a week at the in-laws house , she moved to the city and stayed with Azhar.

She has come to the in-laws house again for Eid. She was not very keen to come but Azhar persuaded her and she could not really disappoint him.

Azhar again called Madhabi , "Noor , please come quickly , Abbazan wants you here"

She did not respond to Azhar's call and was thinking of her childhood days at her parent's place before she joined the engineering college and met Azhar. She lived in a big ancestral one storied house; being the only child to her parents , she was princess of the castle . Her parents were fond of cows and had domesticated 4-5 of them. They had a cow- shed at the backyard. Both her parents took particular care of the cows and there was no dearth of milk and milk products at home. Her father would not tolerate any inconvenience to these innocent animals and her mother revered them as God. On every Rakshabandhan , mother used to help her tie rakhi at the horn of the cows. It was such a nice and pleasant co-existence with lovable cows!.

And today , his husband is calling her to witness , the killing of an innocent animal in the name of sacrifice. She was uttering to herself , "God : Forgive these sinners , they don't know what they are doing"

YOUNG AND UNINTERESTED

This is a famous engineering college in the town located on an expanse of fifty acres. The academic building , the administrative block and the hostels for boys and girls are all located within the campus. There is an indoor gymnasium also – first floor meant for the girls and the ground floor for the boys. Little far from the academic building , there are courts for lawn tennis , badminton and basket ball. A little beyond these courts , there is a swimming pool , well protected from public view. Both boys and girls use this swimming pool , but at different time slots. There are four food courts located at different parts of the campus which sells a range of beverages , snacks and fast food. Also available two general stores from which one can buy all kinds of toiletries , cosmetics , stationeries and daily needs. As such almost everything is within reach , excepting the auditorium which is located at the far end of the campus . Whenever there is an event at the auditorium , college buses are used to ferry students to and fro the venue. If the event is inconsequential to the students as per their own assessment , it becomes very difficult to get them out from the hostel , make them sit in the buses and then transport them to the venue.

3PM in the afternoon of a lazy Sunday . After the sumptuous lunch , the boarders of the hostels – boys and girls – are enjoying their afternoon nap. But one notices groups of teachers are standing in front of the hostel.

There is a program scheduled at 4PM at the auditorium. An industry leader has come to give a talk on Power Sector Reforms. Topic is of no interest to the students; therefore even though they are aware of the program , they are lying dormant on their beds. They also know that teachers will not allow them to sleep peacefully and will herd them up to the auditorium. There is no escape from the fact that they have to attend the program. Yes, there is a carrot also. Students who will attend the seminar will get four attendance credits , a great opportunity for all those who have poor attendance percentage in the class and fear being debarred from sitting in the semester examination.

Students from first year to the final year stay in one hostel , each batch occupying one floor.

SMSs from teachers have started trickling in the mobiles of the boarders.....beep...beep... " Buses are waiting outside the hostel. Come out and sit in the bus immediately". Students who have leadership qualities and can help flush out the boarders from their rooms , have even got calls from the teachers , " Inform all boarders in your floor to get seated in the bus in the next thirty minutes time . Also tell them that attendance at the auditorium is compulsory. No excuses will be tolerated"

Obedience is a great virtue when students are in the first year. They are yet to get adapted to the norms and nuances of the new place. So they are the first to come out from the hostel and board the bus. After a while and post few more reminders, seniors also came out from the hostel , though reluctance is apparent on their face. Buses made multiple rounds to ferry all to the auditorium .

After all boarders left the hostel , excepting the sick ones , teachers made their way towards the auditorium in their respective vehicle.

The auditorium is completely filled with students now . The podium is ready. It has been beautifully decorated with flowers . The speaker will arrive very soon. The anchor has already made the announcement that the speaker will reach in the next ten minutes time and has requested the audience to maintain silence . Students are busy on their mobile – some exchanging messages , some playing games and few others listening to music.

1st year students are sitting quietly in the auditorium like the hostages of a hijacked aircraft. They even don't understand the title of the seminar ; had they stayed back in the hostel with some plea of sickness they would have invited bigger trouble. Some seniors have stayed back in the hostel citing some fake reasons , so ragging is a sure possibility. Better to go to the auditorium and sit in the a/c environment . 2nd year students are like birds who have learned how to hop and also little bit of flying. They want to escape from the auditorium at the slightest opportunity but also wish to show off their restrain to the juniors at the auditorium. Pre-final year and final year students are well conversant with the system and are matured in their thoughts. They have settled down at different parts of the auditorium with their respective groups so that they can indulge in gossiping when the seminar is on. And there are couples who have taken strategic positions which allow them a semblance of privacy in this public affair.

All the teachers have settled down at the rear side of the

auditorium and have created a virtual iron curtain to prevent escape of the students from the auditorium till the seminar gets over. Two teachers known to be very strict , have been made responsible to ensure discipline of the students inside the auditorium. They are standing at two diagonally opposite positions and are instructing students through gesticulations to remain silent. They appear as stern as a Samurai.

After the presentation by the speaker , there is a tradition of Q&A session. Students can pose questions to the speaker on the topic. Ironically , hardly anyone listens to the speaker and so the question of asking questions suo moto doesn't arise. But asking questions is a necessity as it gives a subtle feedback to the speaker that his speech has been listened attentively and absorbed by the audience. Not to take chance , teachers have prepared the questions to be asked and have passed the written slips to the identified students for the needful. They have to memorize the questions and raise them verbatim as soon as the floor is made open for Q&A. No need to understand the question or the answer that the speaker gives against that question. Only thing expected is , he should remain standing when the speaker gives the reply and after he finishes , should sit down quietly with a flash of smile on his face to give an impression that he has been enlightened with the answer.

The speaker arrived at the dais. He was welcomed with a bouquet by volunteers . The anchor introduced the speaker to the audience and then requested him to deliver the lecture. The speaker got up from his seat with a small piece of paper in his hand; perhaps he has noted down the points that he will cover in his speech ,quite unaware that he will be engaged in a pointless engagement for the next few hours.

The speaker stood at the podium and started his lecture. While he got busy in his lecture for the next two hours , students got equally busy with exchange of messages on their mobiles.

Hey, what is the evening snacks at hostel today?
Samosa and Tea.
But by the time we will be back at hostel , all those Samosa will be dead cold.
What is there for dinner tonight?
Biryani
After this lecture , only Biryani can make us happy.

Hey, that Top you are wearing in that selfie looks awesome. Where from you got that?
FlipKart
I will book one for sure tonight , of a different shade though.

When will this lecture get over?.
Only God knows.
Teachers are there at the exit gates , no way can we run away.
I took washroom permission and went out , but could not escape…ha-ha…Seniors are on duty like border security force.

How are you finding this lecture?
Intellectual torture…ha-ha…
Hazards of students' life.

It is 6PM...and the speaker concluded his lecture and then drank the glass of water kept near him. The Q&A session was enacted by the assigned students with clinical precision. The anchor announced the end of the program and advised all students to proceed towards the buses waiting outside the auditorium....

OLD-FASHIONED

Bosebabu looked at the new garments purchased by his children for Durga Puja and summoned his son and daughter.

Rahul , "you have paid three thousand rupees for this jeans pant ; but did you check it before you bought it?. See, many places the color has faded. Also look here, at both the knee portion it is torn out. Is this the way you should waste money. Go to the shop where from you purchased the pant and get it exchanged."

Papa , "I have purchased correctly. Faded and torn out jeans are the latest style. You are so old fashioned papa!".

Samina , this pink top looks nice ; but where is its pant?

Papa , this is not a top ; it is a mini frock . This is a standalone dress, nothing more needs to be worn.

But beta , this small piece is just enough to cover the butt. It will look so indecent.

Papa, you are so old fashioned!

This is not the first time that Bosebabu is hearing "Old Fashioned" from his children. Many of his ways are considered pristine by them, though for Bosebabu it is very much sound and appropriate.

Bosebabu works in a bank. He is born and brought up in a suburban town but has settled down in this city for the last fifteen years. He has a 3BHK apartment which he has purchased on loan. Half of the installments are still to be paid. He wears only stitched garments. He believes readymade garments are damn expensive.

His children have been persuading him to buy branded readymade garments from company retail outlets , but Bosebabu will not relent. His logic is simple – if similar garment can be stitched at half a price , why buy readymade.

He still uses the same parker pen that his wife gifted him a decade back. Only the refill gets changed. Children are tired of seeing their dad using the same pen from the ancient times. They like use-and–throw pens . This whole concept of refilling is so boring and un-cool . Since their nursery days , Bosebabu has tried to inculcate the habit of thrift in his kids , but in vain. Unluckily, his wife is an anti-thesis. She indoctrinated the kids to the use-and-throw pens and slowly it became a habit with them.

The other day Bose family went to a restaurant. It was a party from Bosebabu on the occasion of the birthday of Mrs. Bose. Restaurant was beautiful and the food very tasty. After all finished eating , the waiter placed warm lemon water in small bowls on the table. All used that to clean their fingers except Bosebabu. He walked into the wash room of the restaurant to wash his hands. These lemon water doesn't satisfy him. When he came back to his seat , his children looked at him and smiled to convey that dad will never adjust to modern ways.

197

Both the children wear spectacles. In the growing days , their power used to fluctuate and doctor advised eye check up every six months and change the lens if there is a need. Yes , the doctor was correct. The power did change and the glass needed to be changed. But every time , there is a change in glass , children also go for a change in frame. Bosebabu did not like this frequent change of frame , primary because they are costly and the old frames have no resale value. But , who can explain the children. They will do what rest of the world do.

Bosebabu is equally finicky about wastage of paper in notebooks. Children will use only 30-40% of the notebooks and will dump them off with old newspaper to be sold to the kabadiwala. He will invariably tear off the unused papers and keep them aside before he disposes off the note books. Whenever he did this , children will smile at him with a meaning , "Papa , You are so old fashioned"

This statement of "Old Fashioned" many times takes Bosebabu in his memory lane when he also thought his father to be old fashioned. His father died two decades back. He was a factory worker and struggled hard to maintain the family of six members.

Those were old times and people used to take bath in ponds or near wells. Bose family had a big pond where all used to take bath except the female folks. Females bring water from the pond in buckets and then take bath inside the bath room. At a later point in time , municipality laid out the network for water supply and Bosebabu got a water connection at their house. One tap was fixed at the courtyard of the house to meet variety of needs and another tap point was made available at the bath room for the purpose of bathing. All the children started taking bath in the bath room connected with Municipality water supply , but his father's habit never changed. He continued to take bath in the pond. Telling "Papa , You are so old fashioned" was like uttering name of Ram in the land of Lanka those days. But Bosebabu recalls how he and his siblings smile at their dad's habit of taking bath in the pond.

The other thing that captures Bosebabu's memory is his father's penchant to make reconciliation of expenses after he comes back home purchasing vegetables from the market. Those days refrigerators were not there and so people used to buy vegetables on daily basis. There were morning markets as well as evening markets. Bosebabu's father normally goes to the market in the morning. He will leave for the market at 6AM or so in his bicycle and would return at 7.30AM. On reaching home , he would spread all the vegetables at the kitchen and would make a calculation of its total cost to check if the residual money left in his pocket is matching or not. Many days this exercise takes quite a long time. Bosebabu remember giving tangential look to this venture of his father and dismissing it as Old fashioned..

Today is the death anniversary of Bosebabu's father and the priest is there to perform ritual. Bosebabu is sitting with his wife at the altar for acting as per the instruction of the priest. After the conclusion of the ritual , the priest asked Bosebabu to close his eyes , remember his departed father and give obeisance to him. As he closed his eyes , the picture of his father flashed in his mind and he felt like his father telling him , "In the long run we all become old fashioned"

JUST FOR FEW BUCKS

Dead man as a co-passenger! My goodness! How can one do that just to earn little extra money. Pitambarbabu was still not been able to digest the incident that happened with him a little while ago .

Driving a scooter , his son Raghav has reached the city centre where Pitambarbabu is to get down from a taxi , late evening . Pitambarbabu reached city centre an hour late . He sat at the pillion and asked son to drive back home. It is late night now , 11.30PM almost and the roads are deserted. His house is 10km far from this place and it may take 20-25 minutes to reach home.

The mobile phone of Pitambarbabu started ringing. It is his wife at the other end. "Has Raghav reached the place to pick you back home?"

Yes, he has reached at the place on time and we are on our way to home. You don't worry. Roads are slippery due to rain and it may take a while before we reach home.

It was drizzling outside and by the time Pitambarbabu reached home , he was completely drenched. But he did not get into the house and also asked Raghav to stay back.

"Give us two bucket full of water. We need to take bath here at the verandah before we enter the house. "

But what is the matter . Why you want to take bath at such

200

late night and that to outside the house.

First give us water to take bath..I will tell you all that happened with me during the return journey.

Both Pitambarbabu and Raghav took bath at the verandah of the house.

Handing over a Turkish towel to her husband , she told " Change the dress and dry yourself , else you will get fever tomorrow".

Pitambarbabu changed to a dhoti and a sleeveless vest after wiping himself off the water . Raghav also changed to night dress and disappeared into his room and perhaps immediately fell asleep. Pitambarbabu sat at the dining table and started eating the dinner ; his wife was sitting at the opposite side of the table.

His wife quipped , " Why you got so late; you could have stayed back at that place tonight in some lodge and come back in the morning. Why are you taking so much of strain, I just don't understand your ways. Do you think you are getting younger over these years. Unnecessarily you are making us worried".

Yes, you are correct. I should have stayed back. Travelling at night is so dreadful and difficult. You know , my co-passenger was a dead person today!"

What? Dead person? What do you mean by that....

Yes , Yes , it was a dead person who travelled with me for long 200km...and I thought he is like any other co-passenger.

What are you telling ! Tell me what the matter was exactly. What happened , is it that the fellow died while travelling...heart attack?

No, No, nothing like that. Listen to me what all happened to me the whole day.

I finished my work at Collector's office at about 5PM and by the time I reached the bus-stand , the last bus for our town had left. I checked about other options with the ticket counter clerk at the bus stop; he suggested me to go to the nearest NH and get a lift from the trucks that ply there and reach a place called Saruda. From Saruda one gets shared taxies aplenty to our town. So I acted as per his advice.

I mentally calculated that if I get the truck and the connecting shared taxi on time , I should be able to reach home by 10PM.

Since the entire travel will take 4-5 hours , I quickly had some snacks at the restaurant near the bus-stand. Also a cup of tea. I got into an overcrowded trekker and reached the NH. Standing on the NH , I started signaling all the trucks for a possible lift. After about 20-30 minutes , a truck halted and gave me a lift. I felt happy as the first part of the journey was accomplished. The truck broke the journey en route near a temple. The driver and the helper went to the temple to have darshan of the Goddess there. I also got down to do the same as that was a better thing to do than to sit idle inside the truck. Later , the driver of the truck dropped me at Saruda bypass where I intended to catch a shared taxi.

But what happened then...his wife asked..Did you get the taxi easily or you had to wait for some time.

No, it was a bad day for me. None of the taxies were offering shared service. Hiring on reservation was on offer and the price was just not affordable. It doesn't make sense to travel 200km in a reserved taxi and pay a fortune. It was a cloudy night and was also raining. There was no sign of the rain stopping . After a long wait , one taxi slowed down near me ; when I told the driver my destination , he signaled me to seat at the rear . At the front seat , there was a gentleman sitting. He looked at me briefly and then turned his eyes and looked straight.

I opened the door and sat in the rear seat. There were two other persons sitting there. At the window side was sitting a aged man, must be of age 40-45. In the middle , a comparatively younger man was sitting. He was leaning on the back rest and appeared to be in deep slumber. Though it was dark , the driver did not switch on the light. After settling down inside the car , I felt very relieved that I will be able to reach home even though it will be quite late in the night. But bad luck ; after about 30-40 kms of travel , one tyre of the car got punctured and the driver took nearly half an hour time to replace it with a spare one. While the driver was busy changing the tyre , I noticed that the man sitting near me has remained in the same position all the time , without any movement of his limbs. I wondered , how can one sleep so deep inside a car , particularly when there is no air-condition . Then I thought may be the person is too tired and hence sleeping like a dead person.

After changing the tyre , the driver resumed driving. I also closed my eyes to get some rest and leaned on the backrest. The driver called me after he reached the city centre. He switched on the light. I took out the purse , pulled out two hundred-rupee notes and handed them over to him.

I opened the door and came out of the car.

Before I could really push the door back to close it , I saw the man sitting vertically all these time suddenly fell flat on the back seat with his head precariously dangling outside the car. I raised an alarm to the person sitting at the other side . He woke up from sleep and then with tiredness in his tone pleaded , " This a dead body , please help me to keep it in its original position".

I was stunned ....I gave a stern look at the driver and hurriedly distanced myself from the car.

BANK LOCKER

Locker No-13 , State Bank of India. Inside this locker lying valuables of Sarkar family. There are two necklaces , a pair of bangles , half a dozen ear rings and similar number finger rings , two nose tops , two pieces of gold coin , a pair of silver cup and accompanying spoons. This locker has been their home for last two decades. They are born to glitter but have been doomed to spend their time in the darkness of this locker. The locker is well protected with heavy iron grill and an alarm system in the bank . Once in a while , Madam Sarkar picks few of them for use in some function or occasion. But soon after the event gets over, they are back to the locker. Keeping such valuables at house is a strict "No" at Sarkar's family . Burglary apart, they also pose a threat to life and hence Sarkar family always keep their ornaments in the bank locker.

A conversation is taking place among all these ornaments lying inside the bank locker, particularly as to how and when they came to this locker.

Silver Bowl : "Sarkar family has this tradition of Annaprasanna . This is a function wherein a toddler eats rice for the first time and this first bite has to be taken from a silver bowl . Father of Madam Sarkar has purchased beautiful me from a big show room in Kolkata for his daughter , when her first son Abhisek was six months old . I was accordingly used on the day of the function. Since I will not be used anytime in near future , one day they brought me to this bank and left me in the locker"

Later Madam fed Abhi food in a steel bowl. He would cry and nag her to give him food in silver bowl , that is the beautiful me. But that never happened . I languished inside the locker. Abhi is a grown up boy now and is studying in NIT,Silchar ; he would scarcely believe that it is me from which he ate the first spoonful of rice.

Gold Coins narrated ," We came to Sarkar's house along with his new car , ten years back. During that time , the car dealer had an interesting offer. Anyone buying a car during Diwali will get 20 grams of gold coin free. That time, Sarkarbabu had their little daughter who was just six months old. The scooter is what they had then and there was not enough space to carry four members of the family. Abhi was 4-5 years old and Priya was just a toddler. Abhi used to stand at the footrest of the scooter holding the handle and Madam Sarkar used to hold Priya at her lap. Lot of difficulty they faced while they did this. This gold coin offer prompted them to buy a car. They had kept me at their house for few months but after that they thought it safe to put me in the locker. The more costly you are , the more chance that you will be kept in the locker....ha-ha..."

Designer Necklace broke silence and said, "When Madam Sarkar came to this house as a bride , I was adorning her neck . After few days , mother-in-law asked her to remove me and keep inside an almirah. Once in a while when there is a function , she used to take me out and wear it. That practice continued for few years. But after 5-6 years , one day Sarkar babu persuaded her to keep me here in this locker as there was some danger of thieves then".

Other Necklace joined the talk...."me?....ha-ha...I was a gift from Sarkarbabu to Madam when she came to his house. She used to wear it all the time as a mark of love. But one day a mishap happened because of which Madam kept me inside the locker. Madam and Sarkarbabu had gone to the market to fetch some vegetables . The market was crowded and it was evening time. While both were little absent minded and were busy in selecting vegetables from vendors , someone tried to snatch away the necklace from Madam's neck. But before the thief could snatch away the necklace , Madam could got hold to it and saved it. But this futile attempt by the thief bruised her neck very badly. Next day , Madam came and left me in this locker."

Ear-rings said in chorus , " We all have come as gift from relatives to Madam when she came here as a bride. Some of us are gifts from her in-laws side but mostly we are from parent's side. She used to wear us in rotation in her initial years of marriage. But later she settled with just one pair of ear-ring and a finger ring , which had been gifted to her by Sarkarbabu. On that finger ring , there is a engraving of S , which is the first letter of   her name Savita. After she developed a kind of intimacy with those rings , one fine day she dispatched Sarkarbabu to leave rest of us in this locker."

Bangles which were listening silently to all the observations of other ornaments broke their silence and told . " Hey , listen to us . We have a breaking news to share". " We are privy to the discussion that Sarkar household did when Madam wore me last month for a function ". "They were telling , since the ear rings are of very old design , they would exchange all of you for some new design   at the new jeweler show room that has opened in the town. I felt sad , but what they   planned sounds very logical. Who would like a wear old designs, tell me?"

Silver cups and Spoon muttered , " But will they exchange us also."

"No, No, they were telling , they will retain you and will pass on to the next generation. That means, you will be used to serve the first rice to the kids of Abhisek and Priya. Good luck and best wishes to both of you"

Necklaces also got worried and asked ," Did they discuss anything about me"

"Yes, Yes...what they plan , the better of the two necklace will be given to Priya when she gets married and the other necklace will be given to the would-be wife of Abhisek when he gets married. So you both will continue to remain in the locker till the children grow up and get married....ha-ha... But nevertheless, you both are lucky as you will adore the newlywed beautiful brides."

Finger rings got very anxious and wanted to know their fate.

Bangles said ," Many of their close relatives are in the pipeline to get married and it is customary to give some gift to the newlyweds. So what they have thought of is that they will gift all of you , on by one, to aforesaid relatives as and when they get married. They will of course polish you to glitter before they give out to others as gift."

As they were engrossed with deliberation about their life inside the locker, they felt like the locker is being opened by someone . It must be Sarkarbabu or his wife.

All the ornaments kept quiet in anticipation as to who is being taken out from the locker that day and for what purpose.

STRANGE INTERESTS

As he got down from the car at the main entrance of the five star hotel , the waiter ran towards him and got hold of the luggage . The guest is a old gentleman, must be in his seventies ; he is fair with wrinkles on his face and has a dropping chin ; his gait and posture makes him look much younger to his age. He walks straight with majestic looks . He is wearing a tussar pyjama with a matching kurta . At his feet , a pair of Kolhapuri sandals. The steel frame spectacles makes him look sharp and elite. There is a suspension chord at his neck knitted to the two arms of the spectacle. Surprisingly his head is full of hair even at this age. Those have been dyed pink and pepper almost in equal proportion ; eye brows look dark and broad .

The darwan at the gate , wearing white dress from neck to toe with a red turban at his head , saluted the guest as he proceed towards the reception.

'I have a booking in my name for three days. Mr. Sampath is my name' said the old man to the manager at the reception.

'Sir, may I have your ID card please' the Manager prompted and the old man handed over the ID card.

Wearing surprise on his face the Manager quipped ,' Sir , you look so different in this ID card.' . Hearing this , the old man removed the wig from his head.

'oh..sorry sir . This wig created the confusion in my mind. Hope you didn't mind my apprehension'

'No, not at all. You are not the first one to get confused. I use wigs , not just one but many. So I look almost like a new person everyday...ha-ha'

'Raghu , take sir to Room No-302' the Manager instructed the waiter waiting with the luggage of the guest. Both entered the lift and the liftman opened the lift door at the third floor. It is a beautiful hotel . The corridor is fully covered with Persian carpet and the walls have been decorated with huge paintings. There are some antiques placed at different corners. The waiter escorted the guest to the allotted room. He opened the door and made way for the old man to enter the room. Later , he also entered and left the luggage at one corner of the room.

'Sir , the calling bells are here : Room Service , House Keeping and Laundry' . Please use them as and when you need some service. Would you like anything now sir?

No, the old man said and he took out a hundred rupee note and handed over to the waiter. The waiter showed his ten teeth to express his happiness and left the room.

2nd day of his stay at the hotel.

In the evening , Mr. Sampath went for a stroll in the lawn of the hotel and then absent mindedly went towards the pool. It is a beautiful oval pool, of the size of a badminton court. The water looks sparkling blue. Around the pool , plastic chairs of assorted sizes with centre tables have been laid out. Some tables have been occupied but most are vacant. Mr. Sampath occupied a chair at a vacant table. As soon as he got seated , the waiter reached him and asked , ' would you like to have some drinks sir?'

No, just bring lemon juice. No sugar. Add a table spoon of black salt.

He glanced at the people gathering at different tables briefly and then looked up towards the sky. Winter has set in ; though it is early in the evening , world looks completely dark.

Mr. Sampath heard someone prompting from behind 'Can I join you?'. He turned back and saw a young man standing near him.

Oh, yes. You are welcome.

The young man got seated opposite to Mr. Sampath and said 'Thanx'

The old man asked , ' so what made you come to my table young man'

Sir, I have come to this tourist place with my parents. You may be knowing there is a famous temple here and also the beautiful sea beach. In the morning we all went to the temple. Now , my parents and sister left for the sea beach to enjoy the nice breeze. My cute little sister is very fond of playing with the waves. But I don't like sea beach much and so stayed back at hotel. I just happened to see you alone and thought of joining you.

Sir, are you also a tourist here; have you visited the temple and the sea beach.

Yes, I am a tourist ; but I have not come here for the temple or the beach. I have seen the world , all kinds of temples and all types of beaches.

Then what else you plan to see here.

Oh, you may get surprised if I tell you that.

Tell me what else is there to see here. I will tell my parents to take me there.

Ha-ha...don't tell that to your parents. They will curse this crazy old man me..ha-ha.

Ok...tell me what is that you saw here that was so interesting.

Young Boy , in one part of the sea shore there is a graveyard here , very dear to all Hindus. The grave yard is just a small piece of land of the size of four lawn tennis courts but everyday more than two hundred dead bodies are cremated here. There is cremation round the clock. It is said that the funeral pyre at this place never gets extinguished. It is a kind of assembly line operation that we usually see in factories. Dead bodies are kept in a queue and then one after the other is taken to a wooden platform for consigning them to the funeral pyre . It takes just an hour for a body to turn into ashes. Is that not amazing?

But how is it possible for a body to be completely burnt in just one hour sir?

The sea breeze that we enjoy at the beach also touches these pyres and speeds up the burning of the body.

But what is that you like about this graveyard?

This place is a great leveler. There is no distinction between rich and poor. All end up being ashes. We are born unequal , we live unequal ; But at the end we die equal.

SILVER JUBILEE CELEBRATION

In the midst of hectic day at office , the mobile of Mr. Manmohon started ringing.

"Mr. Manmohon , I am calling from IDBI Bank. Your EMI cheque towards repayment of house building loan has returned dishonored. This has happened for the third time in a row".
Oh, I am sorry. The salary is yet to be credited. I will deposit the amount as soon as I get the salary.

Yes , please do that as soon as possible as there is a penal interest for such delay in payment. While making payment add Rs250/- as penalty for cheque dishonor.
Is there a way in which this EMI date can be postponed beyond 10th ? I am not getting the salary on time from my employer every month.

No Sir , there is no such provision in our bank. We advise you to make necessary financial provision before the due date.

That day , as Mr. Manmohon was driving back home on his decade old scooter , he was thinking of this nagging financial difficulty and the way to solve that. But there is no solution at sight. Expenses are mounting from all sides and the source of income is just one. He has a family of five to take care – wife , a college going son and two school going daughters.

Little after he reached home but before he changed his dress , his wife prompted , "Did you get your salary today?" No, he said faintly.

"How do I run the house, if you don't give me the money on time. I have told you thousand times , you must give me money on the 1st day of the month. I just don't like reminding you"

Manage somehow. I understand from accounts department that the salary payment may get delayed abnormally this month. Very less chance that I will get that before 15th of the month.

What ? 15th? You have gone mad or what. I don't care where from you get that money , but I want my part tomorrow.

You know the problem; still you don't want to bear with this difficulty.

No, I don't care. You beg, borrow or steal; I can't wait for the money beyond tomorrow.

Tired he was , now stressed because of wife's outburst . Mr. Manmohon sat down on the wooden sofa and then switched on the TV. A comedy program was at the channel. He looked indifferently to the TV screen and was thinking of ways to get rid of the personal tragedy.

Beep,Beep,Beep…a message on the mobile phone.

Your insurance premium is due on 12th…ICICI Prudential.

The message got him thinking; this life insurance coverage of 25Lakh he has taken to shield his family in case something happens to him. He took this coverage when his third child , the cute little daughter was born. It has been ten years that he has been paying the annual premium. Never has he failed in paying the premium. But , it seems this time he will not be able to pay the premium on time. God forbid something happens in between; these insurance companies will not pay the claim because of slightest fault once the fellow is dead and not there to follow-up with them.

Not before Mr. Manmohon has abandoned the thought of how he will pay the insurance premium, the phone started ringing.

"Good Evening Sir; This is a call from Tanishq. There is an offer on the eve of Dhantaras. If you buy gold or diamond ornament worth fifty thousand , you will get a gold coin , absolutely free."

Without bothering about the value of that gold coin he responded " ok , ok...thank you for the information"

"Who is that" wife enquired from the other room.
"A colleague from office"

Mr. Manmohon pulled the newspaper from the rack and lied on the bed to scan the news of the day. Suddenly his eyes fell on the two pages supplement carrying employment advertisements. So many organizations looking for so many kinds of candidate. But nothing fits him. Age is the real problem. Everybody wants young and energetic candidates.

The phone started ringing again...
"Hey Manu, how is life"....engineering batch mate and friend Ashok on the line.

Yes, Ashok..how are you. After a long time….
Yes, Yes…after a long time..But there is a great news for you.
You will be overjoyed.
News?....Tell me.

This is the silver jubilee year of our passing out. We are celebrating it at Simla this time and making it a family affair. Will that not be fun?
Yes..Yes…

We have worked out the contribution to be five thousand per head which will take care of accommodation, food and events. Travel part to be managed individually. There is direct flight to Simla…so no issue on that count.
But Ashok…..I will not get leave during that time.

Manu….tell me who is your boss..I will have a word with him. I will ensure that he allows you leave.
No…No…Ashok..I am also not keeping well these days. Doctor has advised not to take too much of strain , particularly long distance travel..

Manu…you will travel by air dear…not by bullock cart; there will be no harm to your health.
Ashok…it just came to my mind..if I go for that trip , my son has to miss many of his coaching classes. He is preparing for IIT…

Manu…if there is a will , there is a way. All friends are joining..will it be nice if you don't come?.
Ok..ok…let me think over…I will let you know.

DANGEROUS NEIGHBOUR

She sat in the Starbucks cafe, sipping her coffee and staring out of the window. The blood stained knife lay next to her handbag, covered with her blue silk scarf. She had done something that she never thought of doing. No one would ever believe that she had done that. But she was not apologetic about what she had done. The modesty of women is her best ornament and whatever she had done is to protect that sanctity . But when she thought about the turn of events that forced her to take this extreme step , her mistakes glared at her. Three months is what it took to turn her life upside down.

Mitali and her husband Rakesh were a newlywed couple and stayed in a colony as a tenant. It is a nice colony with beautiful houses on both sides of a lane. Owners stayed at most of the houses but there were few tenants also. Some owners offered paying guest service and few young boys stayed in such facilities.

Rakesh was working for an MNC as a senior executive. There was too much of work pressure in his job and he was also very ambitious in his career. On working days he returned home late , tired and exhausted. He would take dinner and would sleep like a dead person. On Sundays and holidays , he used to get busy with all kinds of official paper work at home and would be talking to staffs and colleagues all through . Some days he will join friends for party and would come back late to house completely drunk. He had little time to spare for his wife.

Mitali was a sweet girl and took care of her husband like a devoted wife. But she was disappointed about her life as she was not getting any attention from her husband and had to lead a lonely life at home most of the time. Even when she pleaded her husband to take her to the nearby market for shopping or to a multiplex to watch a movie , he would not do that. Also Rakesh never liked Mitali go anywhere alone. Mitali spent her time mostly attending to household chores. During the spare time she would watch programs on TV , else would read newspaper. In the afternoons, she used to sit at the balcony and looked at the people passing the street.

Opposite her house, there was a two storied building. One of the occupants of the house was a paying guest. He is a young handsome man, similar to the age of his husband. The name of this young man was Mahesh. He worked in a private bank as an executive. Every day in the evening time, Mitali would notice Mahesh passing time on the terrace and at times found him looking at her. After few days , eye contact developed and later it matured into a kind of acquaintance and friendship. Mahesh started visiting Mitali in the evening time almost every day. Mitali would serve him tea and they indulged in small talk. This relieved her mental stress to great extent. Once, on one such a visit to her house, Mahesh held her hand and attempted to get intimate , but she resisted and reprimanded him. Mahesh corrected himself after that incident. In any case he had not much of sexual desires . His intentions were different. He was basically a kleptomaniac, that is a habit of stealing small items. Every time he visited Mitali , while she would be busy at kitchen , he would pick up a decorative item or two and would put those into his pocket. Later he started stealing money from her purse also , which Mitali at times mistakenly left at some place in the drawing room.

In the building where Mahesh stayed as a paying guest was staying a childless couple in the ground floor as tenant . Though they are married for five years , the couple did not have a child. But the lady was pregnant for the first time then . Her husband Kaluram was a petty contractor and most of the time stayed at home. One day the visit of Mahesh to the house of Mitali came to his notice and he became suspicious and intolerant at the same time. From that day he kept a close watch on both of them and even started taking their snaps in his mobile from the close-up of open windows or other places which offers a sight into the drawing room. Kaluram had a crooked mind and an idea of blackmailing Mitali had germinated his head . Kaluram's wife was aware about this cranky activities of her husband but she was not sure what exactly his husband was doing. Once or twice , she confronted him on the subject , but he would evade the suspicion by showing sudden affection towards her and suggesting her to take rest for the proper growth of the child.

Once , in the afternoon when it was quite isolated , Kaluram knocked at the door of Mitali. She was alone at home. Since she knew that this man stayed opposite her house , she allowed him to come inside the house. Kaluram got seated in the drawing room and then disclosed to Mitali that he is privy to her relationship with Mahesh . He tried to bargain a physical favor from her in exchange of keeping the matter secret. He even attempted getting physically close to Mitali as he was burning with desire. But Mitali knew she had done no wrong and so she resisted his advances and drove him away from her house. But back in her mind , she was scared as Kaluram had threatened her that he will show the snaps to her husband.

Next day when Mahesh came to Mitali's house in the afternoon , she told him her apprehensions and advised him not to come to her house again . Mahesh was indifferent to her fears and was only worried that he would no more be able to steal from the house. In a spate of irritation, he left the house. Before leaving , he blamed Mitali that she used him for time pass at her home and wasted his valuable time. Nothing could be more ironical than this statement from Mahesh.

Mitali thought of informing the wrong doings of Kaluram to his wife as she stayed next door . But an afterthought restrained her. Kaluram's wife was pregnant and this bad news may be too much for her to bear . Mitali was a very sensitive lady and hence remained silent.

In the meantime Rakesh noticed that a number of items were missing from the drawing room and asked Mitali about that matter. She conveyed Rakesh that she is also noticing this issue for last few weeks and with suspicion had dismissed the maid servant from the job.

Everything was fine for a week as Mahesh stopped visiting Mitali. But one day he again came to her house and knocked the door. When Mitali reached at the main gate , he pleaded to meet her just for one last time. He was carrying a bottle of cold drinks with him . With reluctance Mitali allowed Mahesh to enter into the house. He came and got seated on the sofa at the drawing room. After exchanging initial pleasantries , he opened the cap of the bottle and poured the cold drinks into two glasses. At this point , he secretly dropped one sedative pill into one of the glass and handed that to Mitali. Without any suspicion, Mitali started sipping the cold drinks from the glass and before she could understand the trick of Mahesh , she fell down on the sofa partially unconscious. Mahesh adopted this plan to create the last opportunity to loot all the valuables from the house. Everything happened as per his plan and he decamped with all jewelry and cash from the house.

The fact that Mahesh has come to Mitali that day did not go unnoticed by Kaluram. He hatched a plan to blackmail Mitali again . Therefore , as soon as Mahesh left the house with the loot , Kaluram entered Mitali's house and found her in half conscious state. But at this point in time she was regaining her sense and understood that Kaluram has entered her house. She pointed her finger towards him and asked him to leave the room at once. But Kaluram was in no mood to leave. He wanted to take full advantage of the situation. Even Mitali's threat that she will shout did not stop him and he was inching towards Mitali to fulfill his desires.

As Kaluram neared her , Mitali stood up. But she was feeling very weak because of the affect of the sedative. In a raised voice she asked Kaluram not to proceed any further and threatened him with dire consequences. She even caught hold of the mobile phone and mocked as if she was calling the police. But all these were in vain. Kaluram pounced on Mitali and gripped her tightly from the front. Mitali got enraged. She shook him away and ran towards the kitchen. From the kitchen she quickly got hold of a knife and turned towards Kaluram.

The sight of the knife created some fear in Kaluram. He stood still at one place. Mitali chased him with the knife and before he could run away , she stabbed him at the shoulder and at the hip. Blood oozed out from these places . Kaluram with acute pain on his face , left the house without making any hue and cry. He limped towards the dispensary nearby.

Mitali closed the main door of the house , came back to the drawing room and sat on the sofa. She thought what next. She was scared of telling all these to her husband and contemplated to go to the police station. But then she was unable to garner courage to go to the police station alone. At this juncture, the thought of her friend Madhabi, who is a lawyer, came to her mind. She called her over mobile and narrated all that happened. Madhabi consoled her and agreed to accompany her to the police station. As per her advice, Mitali reached the Starbucks opposite the police station and was waiting for her.

Mitali was thinking aloud, all these happened because she allowed a stranger to get friendly with her without the knowledge of her husband.

A SIMPLE QUESTION

Close to the city of Paithan, in a small village called Sauviragram, which lay along the banks of the great river Godavari, lived a woman named Ilaa. Being cotton farmers, her family was well to do, but not among the richest in their area. It was the harvest season, and cotton had to be picked from the plants. The wholesalers and traders from Paithan would be arriving in just a few weeks, carrying gold and goods for barter. They would exchange what they carried for the cotton that the farmers grew. The bales of cotton had to be ready in time! Work was at its peak!

But Ilaa was not to be found in the fields. She wasn't working. Instead, she was sitting by the banks of the great river-Godavari.

'I am sick of this!' she grunted loudly.

It was too much of a discrimination that she had been witnessing at her in-laws house which she calls her home now. Sitting at the bank of the river, she was thinking about her past, her present and the possible future.

Though she was born a girl, her father always treated her like a son and in that spirit named her Ilaa . She was allowed to live a carefree and unrestricted life. The name Ilaa was given to her based on a legend , which goes as follows;

226

In the ancient times , there was a king named Ilaa, who ruled the kingdom of Bahlika . Once during a hunting trip, he strayed into Lord Shiva's forest and was cursed to become a woman by Shiva. But by praying to Shiva's wife Parvati , he managed to stay as man and woman alternatively every month. He would not remember events of one stage in the other. When Ilaa was a woman, he married Budha , one of the 'Navagrahas' . She had a son from this marriage named Pururavas . Budha helped Ilaa to attain his former self by pleasing Shiva through 'Ashwamedha Yagna' . Later king Ilaa left Bahlika and established the city Pratishthana which is now known as Paithan.

Ilaa's father Ramnath was a farmer and had a large piece of land. He cultivated cotton in that land and the income that he got from the harvest was good enough to maintain a descent life of his family. It was a small family of four members – Ramnath , his wife Radhadevi , son Gopinath and daughter Ilaa. Gopinath was four years elder to Ilaa. Both the children went to the pathsala in the village and learnt how to read and write. Being the children of a farmer, there was no need for too much of education. After all, the son would help the father in the field and daughter would get married once she attains puberty. Cooking and serving food was a basic skill needed for one to become a house wife. So Radhadevi had taught Ilaa the nuances of cooking. She quickly learnt how to cook everyday food items and also special items for special occasions. Ilaa was very cultured in her upbringing but was very progressive in her thoughts. She had great interests in the teachings of Pundit Eknath. She had read all holy books written by him and has been greatly influenced by his reformist ideas.

Unlike many other farmers, Ramnath didn't sell all the raw cotton to the traders . He had installed a handloom at his house and used part of the cotton harvest to weave beautiful saris. He sold those saris in his village and also at the nearby city market. Paithani saris had a good name in the city market and customers were ever willing to pay a premium to get one from Ramnath. The saris were beautifully designed and were very durable.

Maratha kings were ruling Paithan those days. Through their valor, they had been able to dethrone and drive away the erstwhile mogul rulers. In Comparison to the Mogul rulers, Marathas were more compassionate towards their subjects. They treated the people of all religions equally. The jijiya tax that the grandfather of Ilaa used to pay , had been abolished by that time and people of all religion were being taxed uniformly . Ilaa's father had to pay only one fifth of the harvest to the Desmukh of the village who is in charge of collection of tax and deposit with the rulers. In lieu of the tax , the rulers provided protection to all villagers. But there was no respite from the plunder of Thuggees . The rulers were clueless about their identity and their modus operandi. These thuggees had spread their tentacles everywhere and one never knew when and how he would fall prey to their tricks. A week back. a group of twenty farmers from Sauviragram went to the city of Paithan with different crops to sell to the mahajans there . They were supposed to return to their home in two days , but they did not. A search by near and dear one made , but there was no trace of them. It was then presumed that they had been preyed by the dangerous thuggees . Thuggees were either Musalman or Hindu ; but both worshiped goddess Kali before they went out for their prowl. They operated in groups of 20-100 ; they would trick unsuspecting travelers to isolated places and then killed them by strangulating with a handkerchief. They would loot all the valuables from the dead bodies and then bury them in pits dug by them in advance.

Ilaa was very extrovert and participated in different events at the school. Whether it is a debate , sports or a drama , she is always there. She recalls how in one of the epic drama , she acted as the princess and selected her prince through Swayamvar. There were ten odd princes sitting in a half circle and each one demonstrated his skill in warfare and knowledge in scriptures, based on which she selected her husband. It was a hilarious scene when so many boys were trying to woo one girl, but Ilaa felt very good that day as she was the centre of attraction.

Ilaa's father was very fond of cows . He had domesticated 4-5 of them and had a big shed for them. While he took care of them , his wife milked the cows every day in the morning. Two of these cows were very unruly and Ilaa used to help her mother control them . Some days Ilaa would hold the horns of the cows tightly so that they stand still and her mother milk them with ease. And some other days, she would tightly hold the rear legs of the cows to prevent them from kicking her mother while she milks . Cows were revered and also loved in those days. On the days of Rakshabandhan , Ilaa would tie rakhi on the right hand of her brother and also unto the horns of these cows.

Illa was married off when she was just fourteen years old. Her in-laws were rich farmers of the nearby village. It was a joint family of ten members – old parents , three sons , their

229

wives and children. His husband was the youngest and was just twenty years old when she married him. They had a big house with an open court yard at the centre. Each couple has a separate room. Children used to sleep at a separate huge hall where the elderly parents also spend their time. All the male members work in the field and the women folks take care of the household. The farm is located two miles far from the house and so the female folks have to carry the lunch to the field at midday so that their husbands can have a stomach full of food at the farm itself, under the shade of banyan trees. The eldest son had two wives. The first one could not bear a child and hence the need for the second wife. The wife of the other brother died three years after the marriage , but he had a daughter born from her. Six months after the death of the first wife , he got married again to the younger sister of his wife.

Ilaa had a fairy tale life at her in-laws place. Her husband Mohon was very loving and caring towards her . He did everything to keep Ilaa happy. He bought her new saris every month even though she had a pile of saris to wear. Everyday Mohon used to leave for the farm early in the morning after taking the breakfast. Ilaa carried lunch to the farm and Mohon would eat that there , sitting under a banyan tree. After the lunch , she would spread a bamboo mat for Mohon to take a nap. She returns home only when Mohon gets up and resumes work at the farm. He returns home in the evening and spends time with Ilaa talking with her all that happened throughout the day. Mohon had a God gifted hand in farming . Crops grew splendid under his care and attention.

But this joy of life remained very short lived. Before Ilaa could bear a child from Mohon , he met with an accident. One day when he was working in the field , a snake bit him at the leg. It must be a very poisonous snake . There was no one around to help Mohon reach the village hakim. When Ilaa reached the farm at the lunch time , she found Mohon lying unconscious at one part of the field. She shouted for help . Some farmers working nearby reached her and took Mohon to the hakim but it was too late then. Mohon's life could not be saved and Ilaa became a widow in just one year of her marriage.

Life took a hair pin turn for Ilaa. Without Mohon around , she felt completely helpless. The behavior of the in-laws also changed for the worse. She was expected to live a mundane life bereft of any pleasure and happiness. She wore a white sari and shaved all the hair from her head , which Mohon used to love so much. It was almost the end of the road for her. She had to be the first to get up from the bed and do most of the household chores . She was the last to eat and last to go to bed. With time she realized the reality of life and understood that she can't spend her life by cherishing the memory of Mohon. When Mohon was alive , she used to jokingly suggest him , " If I ever die , don't remain single ; get married again". Mohon wanted to reciprocate by saying similar things to her. But she would stop him from uttering anything relating to his death. But after a year of death of Mohon , the thought of another man in her life started crossing her mind many times. She realized how difficult it is to live a solitary life without a husband, particularly when one didn't have children.

Since the death of Mohon , she stopped going to the farm . Most of the time she remained indoors. Only in the afternoon , she would come out of the house and would sit in the verandah for a while. The verandah faced a road that connects the village with the city. One would notice village folks walking down this road ; occasionally a bullock cart or two would also pass that road. Ilaa would be giving a blank look unto the road , as if waiting for her husband to return from the farm. A dead man never comes back . Ilaa retreats to her lonely living room as the evening sets in and darkness grips all around.

Ilaa was generally indifferent to all the passersby on the road. But for the last few days she has been noticing a young man taking the road every day , almost at the same time in the afternoon. As he strolls on the road , he would give a tangential look at her and continue walking . Ilaa initially discounted this sight of the same man everyday as a coincidence , but later she felt something purposefully being done by the man. Who is this man , why is he looking at her every day , what is that he wants from her are some of the questions that haunted her mind all the time. At night , while she would be lying on the bed , the thought of the man would cloud her mind and she could not get sleep easily. At times she would feel guilty for thinking about a stranger but later she tries to rationalize ; may be God wants her to have a life partner again and he is the man meant for her .

Months passed, but nothing significant happened.

But one day the inevitable happened. Illa had gone to the nearby well to fetch water. While she was pulling the rope to get a bucket full of water , she noticed the young man standing under a palm tree few meters away. She looked at him and smiled. The smile prompted the man to walk towards her ; He reached near the well , stood there quietly for few seconds and then expressed his love for Ilaa. He was indifferent to the fact that Ilaa is a widow and instantly proposed to marry her. Ilaa was not very sure how to react to such a sudden and unusual expectation from the young man; But by that time , a kind of affection for the young man has already taken shape in her heart . She intuitively asked the man to make that proposal to her in-laws and left the prospect of a marriage to the decision of her in-laws.

Next day, little before the noon the young man reached the in-laws house of Illa. There was no one at home except his father-in-law and mother-in-law. All men were in the field and women folks had just left for the farm carrying lunch for their respective husbands. Children had gone to the pathsala and would return in the afternoon only. Hearing the knock at the door , the old man came out and opened the door. Guests were messengers of God and so the old man asked the young man to sit on the mat lying on the verandah. After he settled down there, the old man wanted to know the purpose of visit from him. The young man had made up his mind to marry Ilaa and so without any sign of hesitation he expressed his desire to the old man. Hearing the absurd proposal, the old man got very angry and shouted at the young man. He ordered him to leave the house at once and never to show his face again. The young man begged for Ilaa's love , but the old man had gone deaf. He shouted uncontrollably till the young man left the house and disappeared from his sight.

The old man returned to his room and sat down thoughtfully on his bed , his face still glowing red with anger. Ilaa reached his room with a glass of cold water and gave that to her father-in-law. He gulped the water and returned the glass to Ilaa. She remained standing in one corner of the room. The old man quipped, " Anything that you want to tell?"

Yes, replied Ilaa, "If your sons can get married twice, why can't I?"

The old man got agitated seeing the audacity of Ilaa to question his decision . Maintaining silence for sometime he said , "I have never seen the remarriage of a widow in my life time. How can I accept your wishes when the whole society is against such an preposterous idea." . Ilaa reacted , " What is popular is not always right and one should have the courage to do what is right even when it is not popular" She continued , " I would raise the issue at the Panchayat court for the consideration of Nayadhish".

Ilaa raised the issue at the court of the Panchayat . Nayadhish listened to all her arguments in favor of the remarriage of a widow. But at the end decided that the tradition has to be respected and a widow should not get married again.

This decision greatly disappointed her and she felt very sad. The place which gives her solace at the time of such distress is the bank of river Godavari. She did not return to her home that day and instead went to the banks of the river. She sat there and thought perhaps a revolution is required for women to be treated at par with the men.

WE MEET TO PART

I observed him carefully as he walked to the door. I knew that time was running out but suppressed the urge to check my watch. I took a deep breath and started counting in reverse under my breath. "Ten, nine, eight, seven..."

This is going to be a very awkward encounter between Lalat and Manasi and I hope this to pass like a non-event. Both are close to me. Lalat is very dear to me as a batch mate when we did MBA together and later as a colleague when we worked for the same organization. We even shared a rented premises when we picked up our first job in the same city. I knew Manasi as a very affable colleague.

As I looked at Manasi and Lalat , I tried to reconstruct the paths they have traversed so far.

Lalat was a handsome boy from a semi-urban town. He was Khetriya and his father was a government servant. They were four brothers and three sisters. All of them were good at studies. Lalat was eldest among the brothers and worked in a government organization as an executive. He was very polished in his manners and refined in his tastes. He had a penchant for fashion; his wardrobe contained garments of all shades and he was always well dressed for different occasions. When it comes to work at office ,he was very sincere and can impress anyone with his friendly gestures. He used to drive a scooter and he maintained that vehicle like a baby.

Manasi worked in the same organization where Lalat worked. She was graceful , smart and very matured in her ways. She belonged to a Brahmin family and his father was a chartered accountant. She had two elder sisters, one elder brother and a younger brother. All of them were educated in English medium schools and were therefore very extrovert and outgoing in their ways. But her father was very conservative in his principles and ways. Manasi was a very talented girl . She was known to have cleared almost all the job related exams that she ever sat for. But she was selective in picking up jobs as there was a big issue with her health. She had a chronic asthma problem and used to suffer a lot. Besides regular medicines she would always be carrying an inhaler for emergency. She was allergic to dust and smoke ; she would never miss to carry the inhaler with her where ever she went . She used to feel breathless even with few meters of walk . Many times she gets hospitalized as the illness thickens. But she had learnt to live with the disease as it is not curable. She took all kinds of precaution to ensure that the disease do not aggravate anytime.

In terms of work she was always at the forefront. She had excellent command over English language , both written and oral. She used to execute the assigned work seamlessly and all her superiors were very happy with her performance. Her disease rarely stood against her excellent performance.

It was a small office and there was frequent interaction between Lalat and Manasi in the course of work. As luck would have it , with time , this professional interaction took the shape of personal liking. They fell in love and started dating each other. Initially they kept the relationship closely guarded but later they had to make it open to their colleagues. Colleagues also felt very happy about the development as they would be able to see two of their staff becoming married couple.

After a year of courtship the issue of marriage cropped up in their discussion and both decided to take up the matter with their respective family . Lalat's parents were ok with the idea but were little skeptical because of the health issue of Manasi. Girls with asthma problem face difficulty in pregnancy and delivery and that was a reason of concern for them. They tried to make Lalat understand the future implications but having realized the interest level of Lalat , they agreed to the idea. Manasi was not that lucky. Her father was enraged at the proposal. Brahmins are considered a higher caste and hence he was not willing to get his daughter married to a Khetriya boy . Besides this there was one more issue. The two elder daughters were not married yet and hence Manasi has to remain in queue. So the whole plan of marriage got into a stalemate. Manasi was very decisive kind of girl and would not accept anything that is against her wish. So she kept on pleading and convincing her father regarding her choice. Things moved in a positive direction after the two elder sisters also joined Manasi in this pleading.

Almost after a year of constant persuasion , Mansi's father agreed for the marriage of the youngest daughter bypassing the elder ones. Since it was a inter caste marriage , it was decided to hold the marriage at Arya Samaj. Parents of Lalat met the father of Manasi at their house and the marriage date was finalized. Friends are relatives were invited to the marriage. With the chanting of slokas , marriage was solemnized in the presence of all. Both Lalat and Manasi felt fulfilled after the tying of nuptial cord.

Lalat and Manasi were staying in a PG arrangement before they got married. After marriage they took a rented house and stayed there. It was a joy to live together and to indulge in marital bliss. Lalat was very caring towards Manasi and did everything to keep her happy , all the time. He would take her for a outing every evening after they come back from work. Manasi had excellent culinary skill. She cooked variety of items and Lalat was very happy to have them with Manasi at his side. He helped Manasi in all kinds of household work as he was fully aware of the health problem of Manasi. Many days he would not allow Manasi to go to the kitchen or do any house work. He would do everything while Manasi would take rest and enjoy music or would watch TV. On Sundays and holidays they did not cook food at home. Invariably they would go to some restaurant and would have food there. And then they would watch movies or would go to a park to have a good time there. Whenever they got a holiday of 2-3 days , they visited tourist spots nearby. Life was a joy for the first few months.

But soon crack appeared in their life in the form of frequent disagreement on different issues. Manasi used to wear salwar suit to office , but Lalat wanted her to change over to sari after the marriage. While she did not have much of a problem in wearing sari once in a while , doing that every day became a sour point. Lalat also wanted her to wear sindoor at the forehead prominently when she went to

239

office ; also he did not appreciate her interacting with other male colleagues. Manasi tried to accommodate the wishes of Lalat as much as possible but at a point it became too much for her and she felt irritated. Manasi could figure out that Lalat is too possessive a person and she felt suffocated to follow his diktat all the time.

Perhaps reality had also set in the mind of Lalat after the initial euphoria of a marital life. The bout of breathing issues that Manasi faced due to her chronic asthma added to the irritation of Lalat. During one of the visits to the consulting doctors , Lalat got to know that it would be a difficult proposition for Manasi to get pregnant . He wanted to have a child as soon as possible , but Manasi knew the constraints and refused to put her own life to risk. She thought may be with time she would get better and then would try for baby. Discussion on this topic led to arguments and counter arguments. The environment at home became very alien and uncomfortable. This matter came to the notice of their close friends and relatives. They tried to bring in understanding between them but the undercurrent remained and there was hardly a day on which there would not be an argument at house. On some days because of too much of irritation , at odd hours in the night , Manasi would walk out to the street in a hush. Lalat would follow her and bring her back to house.

Things turned nasty with time. During the altercation , the possibility of a divorce also cropped up and both mentally considered that as an option. The incompatibility was too much for any kind of adjustment. The parents of both Lalat and Manasi got to know the development in their life. Since the marriage has been against their wishes , they remained mute to this escalating marital discord.

Manasi was unable to bear this emotional turmoil and one day after a big fight with Lalat , she left the house in a hush and boarded the bus to her parent's place. She took a long medical leave from office and remained at her parent's place . Lalat was not a person to melt in such a situation. He got even more angry and met an advocate to know the process to go for a divorce. The lawyer was a good soul and advised him to think over the matter calmly and then take a decision. Lalat came back from the lawyer that day but again met him after a week and confirmed his mind . The lawyer drafted the divorce notice and it was posted to the address of Manasi's parent. The reason cited was irresolvable mental incompatibility. The notice reached Manasi on time. She went through it and felt bad. But she was a very matured girl and thought the move to be a right one for the interest of her life. She could not visualize to reconcile with Lalat and try again to adjust her life with him. She signed the notice and returned it to the lawyer indicating her consent to the separation. Lalat though very angry had the belief that Manasi would mellow down on receipt of the notice , but when he found it otherwise he felt even more agitated and made up his mind to take it to the logical conclusion.

In due course , both of them were called to the court for deliberation on the matter. They were staying separately for quite some time and were mentally miles away from each other . They had reached a point of no return . The Judge checked their conviction to get separated and ordered as they wanted. That day when the court sealed the divorce document , it became legitimate and permanent. They became strangers.

A year after the separation , the parents of Lalat persuaded him to get married again. He was reluctant initially but could not really counter their justifications for long. Life had to go on. First marriage did not work as he wished for , but there is nothing wrong in trying once more . He mentally got ready to get married again. Parents looked for a suitable girl for him. After a long and careful search , they got the match. A village girl to poor parents. She is the seventh and the last daughter to her parents. Date was finalized and the marriage happened in a simple function at a temple. After marriage Lalat shifted to one of the metro cities and got settled there. He started his own business there and prospered. In due course two cute daughters came to his life.

On the other side , Manasi never thought of getting married again. One marriage was enough for her to understand the hazards of marriage. She had married to Lalat after a courtship of 2-3 years and even then there was so much of incompatibility that she has to consider separation as an option. She did not have the courage to repeat that mistake. She remained single. She changed the job and started working in another office as the memory of Lalat in that old office haunted her like a ghost. She kept herself busy with her professional life and stayed with her parents.

Lalat and Manasi had vowed to be couples for next seven births but got separated in less than seven months. Their life moved like two parallel lines since then.

After a gap of nearly two decades , today they will meet face to face . I have invited both of them to my house warming function. Manasi has reached my house and having a small talk with my wife at the drawing room. I noticed Lalat opening the gate at the front court and walking towards the main entrance of my house . His wife and two teenaged daughters are with him. As I waited with tight breath, Lalat reached the main door and gave me a bear hug with a big laughter in his face. As he did that , his eyes fell on Manasi in that room. His smile faded, as a shinning sun would under the influence of a floating cloud , and he attempted to divert his attention to other people in that room. Manasi glanced at Lalat and thought time is such a great healer...

ALL WELL THAT ENDS WELL

Time has made Rhea tough. She used to be a sweet and simple girl but the destiny has made her rock hard in her thinking. She is not as innocent and as forgiving as before. To bear a child out of wed lock and then being constrained to walk away from the live-in partner was a double blow. She had never anticipated that life has this curvy path defined for her. It was nothing short of a nightmare when she thought how her life changed and how she was left alone not only to rear a toddler but also to bear the humiliation of all and sundry.

Rhea was the only child to her parents. She grew up with all love and affection. To her father , she was a little angel at home. He would not keep any of her wishes unfulfilled. Whatever she wanted, he met those without a wink. She was never allowed to believe that she is a girl and hence no restrictions and limitations in her life. She was treated like a boy and given all freedom . She did whatever she wanted to do. She played cricket and kabbadi with the boys in the colony when she was in her pre-teens. Later she reduced interaction with boys but she led a carefree and unrestricted life style. She rode bikes and would give a chase to her boy-friends. Even she dressed herself like a boy.

Rhea was top class at her academics. She was not so good at Mathematics and science , but her command over language was very strong. She won prizes in essay competitions and also won awards whenever there were debate or elocution competitions. Besides her grip over language, she was very good at creative thinking and was very quick to get simple solutions to complex problems. She was very persuasive and can influence people very quickly. Out-of-the box thinking was her greatest strength. She used to get lot of appreciation from her teachers and friends for all these good qualities. Though she was a cut above the rest in these fronts, she was very modest and ego never touched her. She remained as modest and sweet as before.

Parents never imposed on her what to pursue as a career. Her interest lied in literature and creative activity. So she opted for journalism and mass communication as her subject for higher studies. As expected she did extremely well in this course and earned a good name in the institute where she studied. Her articles and poems appeared in the college magazine and were highly acclaimed. She planned to join a media company after completion of her course. But she was destined to join an advertising company. On the first day of the placement, one advertising company named Sharp Ads came for recruitment. Without much of thought, she appeared the selection process of this company and did extremely well. The recruiter made the offer and she quickly accepted it as she needed a job first. She thought that after working in that company for few years , she will shift to a media company which she aspired to work for all these years.

Working in an advertising company was a different ball game. She joined the copy writing department and got needed orientation . The main work of the department was to prepare catchy tag lines for different advertising campaigns. Though there were many aged people with years of experience, Rhea could pop up interesting catch lines and soon became very sought after writer of the company. She became very prominent and famous after some of her tag lines became hugely popular. Slowly, the entire media world got to know her talent and she started winning prizes in award functions.

It is at this office that Rhea came in contact with Aman , a genius in creativity. He was the Creative Director and most of the advertisement ideas are conceived by him. He was couple of years elder to Rhea . Because of his immense talent he has rose through the career ladder to occupy such a high position in the agency. Aman was very smart in his interactions with others and any girl can easily be swept by his charm. Rhea used to have very regular meeting with him for development of the ads for different clients. Aman also started liking Rhea because of her talent and the discipline with which she executed her job. In the advertising world , the work culture is very open and modern . "Work Hard and Party Harder" is the philosophy that governed them. Therefore Rhea and Aman got more opportunity to interact at parties and other social gatherings. Later both of them confided their love to the other and the relationship blossomed like a flower. Once Aman suggested Rhea the idea of staying together . This would help them to understand each other more deeply and help them taking the marital decisions forward. Rhea was then staying with her parents and used to travel to office by public transport . She evaluated the offer of Aman and agreed to stay in a live-in kind of arrangement. Aman used to travel by car and Rhea thought she could travel with him to office without the hassles of the public transport. They set up an elementary household facility inside the 2BHK house where Aman was staying and started living together. Most of the days they would have their food at the office mess or at some restaurant. So the cooking at home was limited to tea/coffee and occasional snacks. When two young persons stay together , it is almost impossible not to have physical intimacy. So it happened in the case of Rhea and Aman. Soon , Rhea got pregnant and she broke the news to Aman. When Aman got to know about it , he wanted to fast track the marriage and wanted Rhea to inform her parents. Telling such a thing over phone will not be a good idea and so Rhea took leave from office and went to her parents place , which was 40km far in the suburb . She did not tell Aman when she will be coming back , as she was not very sure how her parents will react to the news since she was already pregnant. Rhea was feeling guilty but was courageous enough to tell the whole story to her parents and convince them.

Rhea was a very sweet daughter to her parents. When they heard the whole story from Rhea , they understood her plight. Rhea was even ready to abort if her parents were not ready for the marriage. Her parents thought over the matter and consented Rhea to go ahead with the marriage. It was decided to hold a simple temple marriage to solemnize the couple. Happy with the words of her parents she left her home to meet Aman and convey the good news.

The day she reached Aman's house changed her life for

good. She reached the house late in the evening. Normally , by this time Aman is back at home and so she rang the door bell...waited for few seconds and then again she rang. There was no response. She thought may be Aman is inside the washroom and so not able to hear the bell. She waited at the door patiently but at this moment her eyes fell on the door opening that gave a peek into the master bed room. She saw two men sitting coyly on the edge of the bed in the dimly lit room and are kissing each other. She could figure out that one of them was Aman and the other one is a stranger. She could immediately guess what all is going on inside the room.

She did not wait there even for a second and left through the lift in a hush. While moving down in the lift she could hear someone opening the door but she was in desperate hurry to leave as fast as possible. She even did not think where she would go then . She scurried to the nearest bus stop and only there started thinking where to go. She googled the contact numbers of working women's hostels and called them to find out if there can be any accommodation. She was lucky. There was a vacancy and she was asked to come over as soon as possible. She took a taxi and reached the hostel. Stayed there. After dinner she lied down on the bed and thought over her future plans. She was already pregnant – whether to abort it or to give birth the baby was a big question which clouded her mind. She was unable to make up her mind and so for guidance called her father. Narrated everything in one breath. That day her dad did not give her any opinion or suggestion; he just said whatever is her decision, he will stand by it. Next day , she came face-to-face with Aman at the office and gave him an indifferent look.

He tried to catch up with her to find out the reason of her changed behavior. She bluntly cited what all she had seen and declared the end of their relationship. Aman did not tell anything and moved away from her life.

In due course, she gave birth to a baby boy. She took a sabbatical for one year and stayed at her parent's place. Rhea was happy spending time with her cute little baby. Her parents were also very supportive and caring. But her having a baby out of wedlock was news at the colony. Inhabitants were conservative minded as usual. Most of them started talking ill about Rhea and even did not mind passing caustic comments tangentially. She ignored all these but they were hurtful in any case. She remained silent against all these nonsense. She knew , her counter or reaction to these comments will lead to more trouble for her. She took it very maturely and remained busy with her baby boy.

But one neighbor was most caustic and his comments always pierced her heart. It was very unbearable for her but she maintained dignified silence. He was an aged person, a retired government servant and had a young son. He was a good looking boy , a freshly passed out MBA and was working at a multinational in another city. This aged man who was a pensioner and his wife used to lead a very comfortable life with the pension they got and perhaps what their son sends every month.

Once this young boy fainted at his office . Office staffs took him to a hospital for check up. The doctors diagnosed an acute heart ailment. He needed a heart transplant at the earliest. The condition was very critical and sooner it is done the better. The doctors cautioned that the ailment could aggravate anytime and might become fatal also. This bad news reached his parents. They rushed to the hospital to have the first hand information from the doctor. After hearing the doctor, they got crest fallen. Came back home and started wondering how a donor heart can be arranged. It was as difficult as snatching the moon from the sky.

As they were exploring the possibility of getting an organ, its price and the paraphernalia, physiological endowment of Rhea came to the mind of the aged man. He told to her wife that Rhea had two hearts and can afford to donate one to their son. The idea of taking shelter of the whole colony struck his mind at this time. He canvassed the whole colony and next day a group of people gathered in front of Rhea's home with placards pleading for the heart . The aged man did not had the courage to meet Rhea and make direct request for her heart . But her wife pushed him to make a try. After lot of reluctance , he went to Rhea's house and narrated the need to her mother. While this meeting happened in the drawing room, Rhea was busy giving a bath to her little baby in the dining hall. Her mother came inside and told the story to Rhea. When Rhea heard about the person sitting at the drawing room she got agitated and sternly told her mother , "The man who had made his mission to shame me is at our door step for a favor...a Himalayan favor. How dare he come here and has he lost all shame to plead for such a favor". She continued, "Mom, you just inform that aged man that he has come to the wrong place and there is zero chance of getting his wish fulfilled."

'Are you sure, Rhea?' asked her mother, with emotional tone.

'Of course I'm. Survival of the fittest, mother. I'm not going against Darwin. Also I don't want unnecessary scars on my body.'

"It's a known fact that we are all born to die. And frankly, I don't understand why it has to be made into such a big deal. Tell that to the bunch of people outside our house shouting slogans, waving placards, literally wanting me to cut one of my beating hearts out.

"Save A Life. Donate!" they were sloganeering and pleading.

Rhea had two hearts , a God gifted physiological endowment. For someone who is one in billions, 1.12 billion to be exact, she expected to be treated better. Scientists are still befuddled regarding her condition that gave her two hearts in her mother's womb. But years of research and sticking needles into her have led them nowhere, and they have labeled her as a freak mutation. It's so rare - literally one in all humankind - that they didn't even name the anomaly

An IQ of 180, increased concentration, exceptional athleticism and a phenomenal metabolism rate - are just the few boring benefits of an increased blood circulation. Why would she ever give that up?

Next day in the evening time the door bell at Rhea's house rang again . When she opened the door , she found a young man standing at the door. She looked at him inquisitively expecting him to tell his identity and what he wants . After few seconds of eye contact, he said , " I am Rajiv , your neighbor. Can I talk to you for a while?". Though he was a neighbor, Rhea never had the occasion to speak to this young man though she had seen him once in a while at their front court. She asked Rajiv to come into the drawing room. Both of them got seated , opposite to each other . After a brief pause Rajiv started , "I don't know how to start the subject , but perhaps you know what is the purpose of my visit.". Rhea thought, being tough with the critics is easy but when one is talking to someone who is counting his days , it is not that easy to be blunt and direct. She nodded her head in conformity. He resumed, " I know how foul my father has been towards you and I appreciate your reaction to his atrocious expectations. I know I will die in few days if a transplant is not made. The doctor has been very open to us regarding the urgency and the consequences of delay. Getting a heart is not something one gets just like that. I thought, before I embrace death , perhaps I should make one last attempt and meet you. But that is not the only reason why I am here. I have a bigger aspiration. I know you are a single mother. I would like to make you my life partner if I survive with your heart."..Rhea listened to him intently without almost any blink and then went inside the house. Rajiv remained seated at the drawing room. She spoke to her parents on the proposal and almost expressed her acceptance to Rajiv's proposal. Rhea's mother came to the drawing room and got seated. She conveyed Rajiv the decision of Rhea. He was overwhelmed at the news and touched the feet of the lady out of deep respect.

Heart transplantation surgery of Rajiv was successful and he was discharged from the hospital in a month's time. Rajiv's father visited Rhea's home, met her and apologized for his behavior. He also met the parents of Rhea to fix the date for the marriage.

The marriage of Rhea and Rajiv was held in a grand manner. They became husband and wife with the blessings of their parents and other elders. They lived happily ever after.

LIFE IS LIKE THAT

"Goats of FakirMia again sneaked through the fence and eaten away the plants"..Malati prompted to her husband Asitbabu as soon as he reached home from office riding his bicycle. His face paled at the news. Leaning the cycle against the front pillar of the house, he looked at Malati and asked," Could you not scare them away?"..No , "It all happened when I was taking afternoon nap"....She paused and resumed , "This FakirMia is leaving his goats in the field adjacent to our backyard. Next time, these goats get into our garden, I will beat them up; they will never again enter our garden".

No..No...Malati , goats are animals. They have no brain to know what is right and what is wrong. So beating those up will be of no avail. That will be cruelty to innocent animals. They are eating up the plants as they are hungry".. Better... today, I will meet FakirMia and appraise the matter to him.

Asitbabu , changed to his house dress . With eagerness in his mind about the extent of damage to the plants, he walked towards the garden. Malati followed him. Amol , their only son , used to help him in gardening . But after he left for USA , Asitbabu is taking care of the garden alone. Amol works for a software company and will be in USA for next five years on a project.

This is a small garden, of the size of a badminton court. It is fenced with bamboo strips and reasonably well protected.

There is a water tap at one corner of the garden and a long polyethylene pipe for watering the plants.

"If you wish to have a nice garden, you have to take care of the plants like your children" Asitbabu uses this statement at the drop of a hat. In the morning, he would surely spend an hour mending the soils and watering the plants. He also sprinkles water over the plants and they shined as the early sunrays fell on them . He would sweep and clean the dry leaves littered in the garden to make it look tidy and beautiful.

Again in the afternoon after he comes back from office, he would walk straight to the garden to repeat the ritual. It was a kind of addiction to him. If a plant has been affected by some insect, he would get serious as if a person has fallen ill. He will quickly rush to the nearest shop to buy the insecticide and would spray them over the plant at the affected parts. Each day, he would inspect the plants like a doctor till they get rid of the infections.

Malati , used to tease her husband..."These plants are your first love, my number comes after all of them'....and he reacts ," They are mute and can't express and it is our duty to take care of them diligently."

That day, Asitbabu and Malati were very happy as Amol was coming home . He had taken fifteen days break from job. He reached home late evening.

Amol who was lying coyly on the sofa to recover from the jet lag , looked at his parents. Sitting on a wooden chair his dad was reading a newspaper and mom sitting on the floor and cutting vegetable.

Amol's dad prompted , "Me and your mom are aging and are thinking of getting you married. We want you to settle down in your life "

"Dad...it is just third year of my service and I am on this very important project...Company has sent me to USA with expectation that I will wrap up the project on time...."

"Amol...we understand...but it is our responsibility to get you married..how much more time this project will take."..Malati scooped this question with a sign of urgency on her face.

"Mom , another two years...at least...But then mom why are you in such a haste...I don't want to marry now...give me some time..let me settle down with a good company"

"Amol...don't delay this matter unnecessarily...This company where you are working is paying you well , what is the problem in getting married..."..Malati countered.

No..mom....I am not ready for this married life...wish to work for a bigger company and then get married. Once married, I will lose all this freedom that I have now. I am able to work non-stop , remain awake whole night and travel as much as I wish...all these will go for a toss once married...

Malati gave a emotional look towards Amol and said , "Your dad is ailing now..the complications of this diabetics is showing some signs. Last visit to Apollo , the doctors hinted that the kidney has been marginally affected. He is taking a fresh list of medicines and also some change in diets..."..

Asitbabu folded the newspaper and kept that on the centre table near the sofa. Removed the spectacle and kept that on the rack. He remained seated on the chair with his right palm forked at his chin...in a thoughtful mood...."

Malati looked towards him and muttered , " Why are you remaining silent..tell your son that he has to get married as soon as possible. We can't wait indefinitely"..

Malati , "Give him some time to think. It is his life. We have lived ours. He must decide what is good for him. He is educated and matured. Whatever he thinks correct, we should accept. It is not good to force something when one is not ready".

I know, you will never support me Malati countered . You are not even looking for a prospective bride for him. If you drop the message at the ears of your colleagues, they will get you many candidates...Tell me who will listen to you after you retire...You will sit at home like a owl doing nothing. Everything has a time..And Amol's marriage is also due.

You will not allow me a minute of peace...Asitbabu muttered in irritation.

Next Day Morning:

Amol got up little late . His dad is a early riser. After the morning walk, he was already at the garden . Amol was feeling guilty because of his self centered statement previous night. He walked into the garden to say sorry to his dad.

When he reached the garden , his dad was leaning over a plant and inspecting something. He felt the presence of Amol , turned his gaze towards him , smiled and then again fixed his gaze on the plant. Amol stood near his dad and said , " Dad , I guess I hurt you yesterday , by telling that I am not ready for marriage..I am sorry"..Asitbabu straightened himself and looked at Amol and smiled...He tapped his hands on his back and said , "No...Amol..I understand your priorities. But your mom is worried about me. She thinks I will die before you get married....ha-ha.....and she will be left all alone to take the responsibility...she is over stretching her imaginations...."

"Dad...That kidney thing that mom referring to yesterday.....I think , you need to be extra careful in taking your medicine and food".

"Yes..Yes...your mom takes care of my needs. But these complications are very normal with chronic diabetic patients. I have to live with it..You don't worry"

The voice of Malati was heard from indoors..."Tea is ready....Come quickly...else it will get cold"..

Both Amol and Asitbabu got back to the house and seated in the drawing room...Malati appeared with tea for Asitbabu...and looking at Amol enquired , "would you like to have tea or coffee?"

"Don't worry mom..I will make coffee little later and have it..You sit here."

Malati raised the issue of marriage again, "Amol , you must get married. Do you have anyone in your mind "

"No Mom....whomever you fix , I am fine with it"

This answer rang sweet bell in the ears of Malati...she got up and disappeared from the scene for few minutes...and returned with a bunch of snaps. These are the snaps of prospects that she has collected from the nearby marriage bureau..

She placed the snaps on the centre table and asked Amol , "Have a look at these..and tell me your choice....pick up 2-3 of them...we will then talk to their parents and finalize...marriage will be during your next visit from USA"

Amol , was amused at the promptness of mom in bringing the prospects in front of him. He smiled to himself thinking ,"in this time of internet and hundreds of matrimony sites , mom is still in ancient times" and then he said ," mom....my next visit is after six months...that will be too early for the marriage...can't you wait for a year or two.."

Asitbabu was quietly sipping tea broke silence , " Malati...Give him some time....I am not dying...even if I die, what is the problem. Get him married in a temple, hand over the keys of this quarters at the office , shift to USA and stay with him"

Malati reacted , "You are never serious on these issues....."

Amol muttered, "ok...mom..no more discussion on the subject. I will get married in my next visit"....Then he picked up the snaps and started looking at them one after another. "

Little later he passed on three snaps to Malati and

remarked.."Any one of them will do...you finalize"

Amol's stay at home was pleasant and Malati remained in happy mood. ..

After fifteen days , Amol had to say good bye to his parents and travel back to USA....he looked at his dad and said ,"dad..take care of your health. I will be back after six months"

After about a month:

When Amol was getting ready to leave for office , he got a call from his mom .."Dad fainted while he was taking dinner. He is now admitted at Apollo hospital. Doctors diagnosed kidney malfunctioning and shifted to ICU. He will remain in observation for 5-6days..will update you later"

Amol wanted to know from mom , if he should come home at once....but the news was so sudden , before he could think , mom had disconnected the phone..he was not sure if it is alright to call her back again...

Two hours later:

Amol was at office. He was unable to focus on his work. How can he. His dad is in ICU and he is unaware of his condition. His phone rang and it is mom again..This time..he could hear the sobbing sound...he in a raised voice asked , "Mom...mom....how is dad..."...There was no response from the other end....He became even louder.."Mom..why are you not telling anything...is everything alright with dad?"..

After a long pause in a faint voice she said, "He is gone...your dad is gone"...and resumed crying..

Amol felt like crest fallen..He wondered..how can God be so unkind...Could he not keep him alive for few more months to see him married.

Same day evening :

Amol flew to his home. It was a long journey. The thought of loss of his dearest dad made the journey appear even longer...almost like never ending. He wanted to see the mortal remains of his dad..

As he entered his house , he came across a motley crowd of relatives . His mother sitting at one corner of a room , silent. She burst into tear at the sight of Amol. He gripped her tightly and consoled, "It is God's wish...life and death are under no one's control"

With deep grief he entered into the room where his dad's body has been kept. He was sleeping on a body length ice slab , looking up.......silent. Cotton balls have been plugged at his nostrils. A earthen lamp was glowing at his head. Petals of marigold flower have been sprinkled over the white sheet which covered his body. His eyes closed..never to open again.

With the arrival of Amol , everyone got activated for the last rite. They were all waiting for Amol to reach home as he has to lead the funeral procession and will lit the funeral pyre.

Amol came out to the verandah...

Six pieces of bamboo poles were lying on the front court – two long and four short. Two persons tied these bamboo pieces with ropes to give it the form of a bed and then laid a mat on it.

The funeral was completed soon.

After 12days:

The long drawn ritual got over. The house which remained crowded during this period slowly became vacant place. Only Amol and his mom were left at the big house. The room which was known as "dad's room" has been bolted from outside.

Amol made her mom agree to travel to USA with him . It would be good for her . That is also what his dad wished. As per the tradition, no auspicious event can be undertaken in a year's time because of dad's demise . So the search of a prospective bride was abandoned. And now that dad is gone, there is no reason to be in a hurry.

They have to catch the late morning flight to Delhi and from there the connecting flight to USA. Malati slept early so that they can get ready on time. The alarm rang and she woke up with a jerk. It was still dark outside. She looked at the garden through the window and wondered how life changed so abruptly…..how something unexpected can happen and can change all plans of life.

It was the first thought that came to her as she woke up. He was gone. And, soon, this bedroom, the house in whose eastern corner it sat, and the tiny garden outside with its gnarled old red hibiscus and the half-grown mango tree they had planted together, all those would be gone as well. It was the strangest feeling ever.

This thought got interrupted when Amol , standing at the door , prompted "Mom , get ready . The cab will reach at 7AM to drive us to the airport"

WISE RETREAT

Syed and Gayatri didn't mean to fall in love. But love happens when you least expect it. It touches you quietly. When someone needs attention, care, conversation, laughter and maybe even intimacy. Love doesn't look at logic, or at backgrounds and least of all, religion. It is restricted by nothing.

Gayatri was from a very conservative South Indian family who went to a temple every Saturday. Syed bought goats for his family every Eid. That said it all. Their paths would never have crossed if it hadn't been for that fateful day.

That day when she walked into Malini Cafe and waited for Syed at the corner table , Gayatri wondered '" if destiny chooses our loved ones for us? ; did we have any role to play at all?". She looked at her watch. Syed was late. They met every Thursday at 5PM to catch up. Their conversation lasted for hours. Sometimes at the cafe, sometimes in his car, sometimes in places that she could never tell her friends about. They would never understand. And yet Syed made her feel happy, very happy through his witty and lovable talk.

Suddenly her phone beeped. He had sent a message. "On my way. Have something important to tell you." Gayatri stared at it and realized she had knots in her stomach. Thoughts flooded her mind. What did he want to tell her?

Sitting alone in that lonely cafe , Gayatri impatiently looked at her watch again . It was winter time. The sun would set after a while and it would get dark soon . She had lied to her mother and on the pretext of going to a friend's house she had come to this café to meet Syed secretly. Purposefully she had occupied a table at one deep corner of the café. She was worried that someone known might spot her with Syed . There were hardly any customer at the restaurant and most of the tables were vacant – those present were all strangers . She breathed a sigh of relief. But every time the darwan opened the door to a new customer , her heart beat faster . It could be someone who knows her and may just walk up to her for a chat . Anxiously waiting for Syed , she was wondering if there is no other private place where they could meet and evade the prying eyes of relatives and acquaintances. They have explored many places in the past , but at every place the fear of meeting known persons haunted them . On many occasions , they had spotted them when they were least expected. On every such instance they had escaped by immediately rushing to a more secured place . She thought ," Love is such a beautiful emotion , yet the whole world conspires to disrupt that.....irony of life ".

Gayatri's father worked at the local LIC office and used to return home in the evening . She thought , there is not much of a chance of dad passing through this area and walking into this café to pick up some snacks . So not much of a fear from dad. She then thought of her younger brother .He was in class-X and had this habit of whirling around the city with his friends in his bicycle. She felt scared thinking of the possibility of his group just stopping in front of the café for a round of chatting .

Gayatri wiped her sweating face with wet tissue paper and tried to get rid of all these apprehensions. She consoled herself that everything would be fine.

"Virbhadra Singhji , Jindabad".... "Your leader , Our leader , Virbhadra Singhji Jindabad"...these slogans fell on the ears of Gayatri even though she was inside the café.

It was election time in the state for legislative assembly . The city was abuzz with campaign. Auto rickshaws and jeeps with loud speakers were moving through the narrow lanes of the city to canvass for the candidates. There were more than ten of them in the fray but actually there were just two real contenders – one , the son of the royal family Virbhadra . Returned from USA last year with an MBA degree from a reputed university , he was young , aggressive and ready to take over the legacy of his father . A large segment of the city population still had that mai-baap kind of reverence towards the members of the family. For many years father of this young boy , popularly known as "Rajasaheb" represented this constituency as an MP. A first time contestant Virbhadra was not leaving anything to chance. He had enough money to spend in this election . A platoon of party workers were campaigning for him. One of the big halls of the old palace had been converted as election war room. There was arrangement of food for the party workers through a dedicated caterer as well . Some party workers were even staying at the attached guest house of the palace to ensure 24X7 support to the campaign.

Virbhadra provided the strategic direction for the campaign and oversaw the allocation of money for different purposes. He had pinned his eye on the Hindu voters . He was sure, most Hindus - poor and rich - would vote for him ; what worried him was the votes from Hindu middle class . They are very rational voters and could really swing the result in any direction. He was well aware that Muslims who constitute nearly 30% of the voters will not vote for him . The calculation was very simple - 40% Hindu rich and poor will vote for him , 30% will vote against him. So the real game is on that balance 30% fence sitters – Hindu middle class people. They can't be bought and they can't be coerced. He was breaking his head how to influence that segment. Election was two weeks away and something concrete needed to be done , else he would have to bite the dust. Virbhadra was sitting with his seven key advisers in the war room and was brainstorming. The palace servant appeared in the room and served tea to all.

The candidate who had stolen the sleep of Virbhadra was Jalaluddin Ali , known as Jallu in his community. He had been the councilor of Ward No-34 for two terms. A social worker and friend to all. Young and affable, he was always ready to help anyone in problem. Muslim by birth but a deeply secular person at heart. Whether it is a Muslim festival or a Hindu festival , he was always there . He stayed with his parents in the cluttered Muslim dominated area under Ward-34. His father worked as a cleaner at the city Maszid. His mother , a very simple and caring women . She carefully managed the house with the small money that her husband earned from the work. The house where they inhabited was of non-descript type – a two room asbestos roofed house with a small verandah which doubled up as a kitchen and a visitors' sitting area . In the verandah two rickety steel chairs took care of guests.

The club house of the Ward no-34 was the place where Jallu coordinated his election campaign. He was contesting this legislative election as a first timer . He had no money power to roll a massive campaign; what he was sure of was full support from his community. The young boys of the club were his lieutenants and they were campaigning for him. He had adopted a different strategy – a door to door campaign and distribution of leaflets mentioning his poll promises.

Virsaheb Namaste , "I have a bomb like news for you which you can use in the campaign"..a party worker prompted while entering into the war room. Remaining calm , Virbhadra said , "Have a seat , drink tea and then tell me what news you have brought for me" . Immediately, this fellow was served tea . Sipping tea he disclosed, "This Jallu has a younger brother named Syed , works as a helper in a tailor shop . I have firsthand information that he has an affair with a Hindu girl, daughter of an LIC officer. This is Love Jihad and we can use it in our campaign. I am dead sure this will push a lot of middle class people from Jallu to our party". Listening this interesting news , Virbhadra gave a crooked smile and looked at the war team for their opinion. In chorus all said "Yes , we must exploit this weakness of Jallu".

Syed had left the tailor shop on time to meet Gayatri that day . He never kept her waiting. He knew how risky it is for her to come out of her home. Parents aside she was very scared of the group of vagabonds who often stalked her. In fact these vagabonds were the reason why Syed came into her life . That fateful day, like every other Saturday Gayatri came out from the temple after offering puja. She was wearing a white salwar kameez with a purple dupatta. Holding the small puja basket in her hand , she was waiting to cross the road and then take the side lane to reach her home hundred yards away . She was looking very sober and divine that day . But that did not stop the vagabonds standing at the tea stall to pass some teasing comments at her. She remained indifferent, waiting for the speeding vehicles to slow down so that she could cross the road. The traffic was too much that day and she got stranded on one side of the road for quite some time. The longer she waited, more irritating they became. As it got too much , Gayatri gave a disgustful look at the vagabonds and said , "Idiots"..This remark offended them , they got enraged and walked up to her perhaps to bother her even more. Syed who was taking tea at this tea stall was observing this drama from a distance. He felt the need to help the innocent girl ; he dumped the tea cup in the dustbin and rushed to the place where Gayatri was standing. He stood between Gayatri and the vagabonds and looked at their eyes . Seeing the muscular body of Syed , the vagabonds calmed down and later retreated. Had Syed not come out to shield Gayatri that day ,they might have harmed her. Gayatri said, "Thank You " to which Syed replied ,"That was my farz". This chanced meeting ignited many feelings unknown to both of them. It had been more than three months that they were seeing each other.

While on his way to Malini Café , Syed got stranded by the crowd which had gathered to listen to Virbhadra. The meeting was being held at the mini football field but the adjacent road was jam-packed and the traffic had come to a halt. Syed had no option but to wait till the traffic gets cleared. While he was sitting on his bike and waiting for traffic to disperse, his ears fell on the speech of Virbhadra . He was roaring ," My opponent Jallu is the anchor of Love Jihad in this city. He has used his brother Syed to woo an innocent Hindu girl. This is sacrilege of our religion...Will you all tolerate this nonsense?"...and the crowd replied in chorus.."No...Never"

Like wild fire this proclamation of Virbhadra spread in the city and in no time Jalaluddin came to know about it. This came as a shock to him. To check the truth , he ringed Syed and asked, "Are you having some affair with some Hindu girl...Is that true?"..Syed remained silent for few seconds and then meekly said ," Bhaijan.....I wanted to tell you before but then thought to wait till this election gets over". Jallaluddin reacted, "Idiot..you did not get any Muslim girl to fall in love..Are you aware of the repercussions..Abbu and Ammi will not allow a Hindu to come to our house till they are alive.."..He paused for a moment and uttered, " In the evening while returning home , meet me at the club house. I need to speak to you."

By the time Syed reached Malini café , he was sweating badly and the upper part of his body was almost visible through that wet white half sleeve shirt. The sight of Syed made Gayatri happy but her heart started beating even faster. He got seated opposite to Gayatri. Took out his hanky from his pant pocket and wiped his face. Later drank the glass of water that was available on the table. After taking a brief pause , he said , "Sorry , I got late"...She reacted, "It's ok". Syed prompted, " You know my brother is contesting this election and his biggest enemy is Virbhadra. That rascal is using our names to further his electoral prospects...He is canvassing that my relationship with you is a kind of Love Jihad"....he continued...."This will not only impact my brother's election but also will tarnish your parent's reputation"....he took a deep breath and then resumed " I was wondering can we get rid of this affair and remain just friends "

Gayatri had never expected such a blunt suggestion from Syed. She gave an intense look towards him and said ," What do you mean by that?"..Syed tried to explain.."Yes, we like each other. But we are also matured to understand each other's limitations. I know you will yell at me if I now say "inter-religious marriage is a big taboo" , "but that is a fact. Tell me, can you bear to watch the sacrifice of a goat inside our house on the day of Eid..I am sure you can't"...."Our food habits are at loggerheads...we eat that animal which you worship....I know, these things I should have told you long before..but better late than never."

Gayatri fell silent and thought over what Syed told. She felt sad but she understood the reality. She looked at the eyes of Syed and said , "Yes, You are correct. Sometimes it is wise to retreat". She paused for a while and then said , " You had done your farz when we met for the first time; I have a plan to do my part of the farz this time"..Syed looked at the

271

stoned face of Gayatri and quipped , "What farz you intend to fulfill?"..Gayatri responded , " Look, this Virbhadra has already spread a negative message which will adversely affect the election interest of your brother. Let us do something dramatic to counter his strategy.....Lets call the local news channel and give a joint statement that we are just friends and highlight that Virbhadra is indulging in nasty politics"...Syed smiled at Gayatri and said ,"Brilliant idea, let's do that today"..Gayatri replied , "Before we do that lets meet your brother and give a status update of our relationship"..

THE PRINCE OF MY HEART

It was early winter morning and dark outside . Jyoti could not sleep properly last night and had woken up early . Her parents were still asleep. She sat down on the couch in the living room and tried to close her eyes to catch some sleep. Her brief nap was interrupted when the hawker pushed the newspaper of the day under the main door of her house. She walked up to the door, collected the paper and glanced at it.

" Biplab Escaped; Police is on Hunt" was the headline.

Jyoti felt relieved that Biplab has escaped police ; but she was scared that he may get caught again. Biplab had been a friend, philosopher and guide to her for a decade now. But more than all these , he was her soul mate , her lover.

Biplab was from Naxalwadi. He was unorthodox in his thoughts. He did not accept things as they were. He believed , things should get better and everyone , rich and poor , should get equal opportunity in the progress of the nation. He was intolerant towards any kind of injustice particularly when it is inflicted on the poor and down trodden.

After completing his schooling and graduation at his native place , Biplab came to Kolkata and joined Presidency college to pursue Law. He opted for law not because he wanted to

273

become a lawyer but he wanted to understand the long arm of law which can be positively used to solve the problems of the poor and marginalized. Biplab was a voracious reader. He had read the life of all oriental and western philosophers and was greatly influenced by Marx. The catch-line he mostly used , "Market decides survival of the fittest; Leaders ensure survival of the weakest". In college debates , he made his opponents half dead with his fierce arguments ; when he talked rest of the crowd listened . He was very passionate about his opinions on different controversial issues and would go to any length to prove his point.

His intellect and grip over social issues made him a natural leader; everyone saw in him the seed of a great leader who could really bring in change in the society. Friends reposed faith on him and he became Student Union's President . He won the election by a huge margin. His opponents were nowhere near him in terms of popularity and votes. But Biplab was very down to earth and gracious. After winning the election, he built relationship with all, even with those who had a completely opposite point of view . Soon he became the pivot of all students' activity and the leader of all.

Jyoti was also a student in Presidency college , but she was one year junior to Biplab. Like Biplab , she had a social bent of mind and was a great believer in welfare of the poor. Born and brought up in Kolkata , she had a cosmopolitan outlook but her parents had ingrained in her the fundamental values of service , service to the have-nots. She was tall , dusky and had sharp facial features. She had great oratory skill and had won many prizes in the debate competitions at the school and the college . But Presidency college was too big a place to make a mark. She was a kind of junior leader among the girls in the college; She did not take up any formal position in the Students' Union but she was an active participant in all the students' events , particularly social programs.

Once in the college auditorium , Biplab gave a fierce speech regarding social injustice and how the government after government had perpetuated the tradition. He even tangentially mentioned how socio-economic isolation had bred naxals and why even intellectuals are getting constrained to support their cause. Sitting at the front row , Jyoti clapped loud and long after Biplab ended his speech. She walked up the podium and congratulated him for the spirited speech . Biplab liked the sweet gesture of Jyoti and thanked her. He also smiled at her almost meaning 'Love at first sight'.

Next day , in the hallway of the college Biplab and Jyoti came face to face. They both slowed down and moved to one side of the wide corridor to have a small talk. The exchange was introductory : their native , subject being pursued , local address and lastly their career aspirations. While Jyoti wanted to join a teaching profession , Biplab was evasive in his answer. He just mentioned , " I would like to do something for the marginalized."

This chanced interaction slowly matured into many purposeful and intentional meetings- sometimes inside the campus but many times outside. They would decide the time and place for meeting and both would reach there on dot.

No delay , no waiting , no excuses. The place could be as crowded as the footpath of the Howrah Bridge or as romantic as Victoria Memorial. Someday , they would take up trams which would move in snail's pace through the busy roads of the city. At other times, they would get into the Metro train to reach a place which gives them privacy.

Once they visited Belur Math in the banks of The Ganga. They were mesmerized by the serenity of the surrounding. There was peace and tranquility everywhere. Only sound that one can hear was the gurgling sound of the river . Hundreds of monks in their purple robe were in deep meditation at different places of the Math.

That day , after making a round of the Math , they sat at the banks of The Ganga and looked at the flowing waters. It was scenic indeed. Jyoti was an exponent of Rabindra sangeet and Biplab liked some of the revolutionary songs of the poet. He asked Jyoti to sing a particular song of Gurudev and she obliged. In that song , that day Biplap found the great calling of his life. He expressed his love for Jyoti and she smiled in consent.

Time passed pleasantly for both Biplab and Jyoti. After passing out his Law , Biplab joined a reputed lawyer of the city as a junior. A year later , Jyoti passed in flying colors. She did not take up a job and stayed at home. Perhaps , she intended to get married to Biplab as soon as possible and lead a happy family life. But as a junior , the earning of Biplab was meager and the marriage was nowhere in sight.

Biplab was not at peace with the kind of work he was doing.

He wanted to be of greater use to the society . Soon he met political leaders of all hue in the city. He liked some but hated most. What surprised him is that , politics is a kind of commercial activity for most leaders and they are not interested in things where there are no financial benefits. They don't mind fleecing money from the poor for getting some elementary work done. All these blood suckers take advantage of the illiteracy and innocence of the poor and rustic. Biplab somehow could not digest this state of affair and wanted to do something about it. He decided to plunge into Politics and become a leader as soon as possible. But that was not so easy. The old timers would not allow him rise through the ranks so early. But he was clear in his mind that politics is the only way in which he can add some meaning to his life.

But as fate would have it, his life took a hair-pin turn.

One day , while he was doing his work at the lawyer's chamber , a middle aged man entered the chamber. This man was wearing an off white dhoti and a brown punjabi. At his shoulder was hanging a square sized cotton bag. He had unkempt hair at his head and equally cluttered beard at his face.

The man enquired , "Where is Okil Sahib ?" . Biplab offered him a chair and replied, "he is off to Delhi and will not be available for a week". The man appeared disappointed and worried. Biplab asked him , "Anything important that you wanted to discuss". He responded , " Nothing..Okil babu contributes some money for a social cause and I had come to get that"

Oh..ok..but if you tell me the cause which you are pursuing , I can also help out.

No..No…Young man , you will not understand those things. But you can try and check if I fit into that or not.

The man quipped, " This is an underground organization. You understand underground?"

Yes I do understand.

We are spearheading a movement to guarantee rights to all marginalized poor people of this great country. The British have left the country, but there is another kind of colonial power who are ruling over us now . They are wolfs in reality and can do anything to fulfill their interest. Poor people are dying of hunger; but they are just not bothered. It seems, this country is only for the rich and well off, not for the poor.

Oh…if that is your mission , I am game for it. I wish to join your organization as a full time member . If you say yes, my dream will come true ; whole life I have been thinking of working for the poor.

Ok..said the man..and after few seconds of thought added "Have my contact number ; sometime you come and meet me and the core team."

This encounter with a radical changed the life of Biplab for good. He joined and got indoctrinated into naxal movement. With no time his brilliance was seen by the cadre. He was not only a strategist but also a great organizer and motivator. He started adding more and more young people into the movement and built up the organization. He rose through the ranks and soon became one of the key functionaries. He also got involved in some of the violent attacks on the police and government officers.

His name started appearing in the newspapers as a sought after naxalite and government even declared prize for information about his where about.

Though Biblap got busy with his passion of doing something for the poor , he remained in touch with Jyoti , all the time. He would call her once in a week or send her an sms. So the flame of love remained burning but what got sidelined was the plan of their marriage. It became increasing unlikely as Biplab got underground and was always under police radar.

Jyoti was in the know of his activities and place of stay on any day , this was through the sms that he exchanged with her. Few days back , she did read a newspaper report that there would be a massive combing operation to nab Biplab and other key members of the banned outfit.

She felt very worried about Biplab and pleaded with him to surrender and join the mainstream. She had lost count of SMSs that she had sent him to change his mind , but in vain. The last message that she sent was a kind of SOS (Save My Soul).

She willed herself to not check her phone to see if he had replied. It had been about three days now. She hated that she was constantly checking his 'last seen at' status and yes, he had logged in just five minutes ago. Yet she couldn't stop herself. This sinking feeling to find absolutely no communication from him was becoming unbearable, almost torturous.

And then, just as she sat down in her chair, her phone vibrated. With her heart thudding in her ear, she unlocked her phone and stared at the screen. Finally! It was his message.

But when she opened it and read it, she nearly stopped breathing. She didn't know if he was joking or not. What was this?

The message said , "Police captured me just now"

VIRTUAL FLIRTING

'I never wanted to lead the life of a pauper' grumbled Maya and looked at her husband with disdain.

'If luxury is what you wanted all the time , you should not have married me. After ten years of marriage , this statement of yours sounds ridiculous' reacted her husband Iswar . After a brief pause he added 'We have a beautiful flat to stay , a car to drive and there is enough money to meet the necessities of life. I can meet your needs but there is no way I can fulfill your greed'

'You may be a saint, I am not. I want to enjoy my life and you have to earn enough for that. I am least concerned as to how you do that' , Maya countered.

'Do you want me to steal? Money that I earn doesn't come so easily, I have to work hard; appreciate that. It is easy to demand money, but very difficult to earn that. Money doesn't grow on trees'.

'Look at your friends and your batch mates. All of them are in big positions and are minting money. You are nowhere near them. You should feel ashamed for your professional status and also the pittance you make every month.'

281

'I can only try for better jobs; everything is not within my control. There is something called luck also'

'What luck? Don't take shelter of these excuses. If one try hard, nothing is impossible'

'I have told you hundred times and telling you again, I can't earn more. We also have to save money to take care of the education of our only daughter and also her marriage. Please don't expect a life beyond our means'.

'Go to hell. Why don't you die? I can marry once more and can have a better life'. Maya shouted.

With irritation on his face ,Iswar left for office . Even before he entered the lift at the fourth floor , to reach the basement of the apartment where his car is parked, Maya closed the main door with a bang.

Iswar is the Manager in a private bank. With increased competition, job at banks have become very demanding. One has to chase the targets set by the management and make sure that the customers are happy.

Being treated rudely by wife is not something new to Iswar. It has been happening with him for couple of years now. He talks less at home and generally absorbs the caustic comments of Maya . Only when it gets too much , he opens his mouth. There is no peace at home and happiness is a distant dream.

Facebook is where Iswar takes refuge for some happiness. He had a long list of friends : class mates , colleagues and relatives ; but there are a few strangers also . When he gets bored , he exchanges messages with some of them . Recently, he has befriended a lady named Sarika . Her Face book profile says she is married and is from Indore; Nothing more. She keeps posting nice short poems on her profile page which are spiritual and very motivating.

Everyday Iswar sends a message or two to Sarika , but she responds occasionally and that too very briefly. But with time , the chatting got more regular and frequent ; but always limited to few messages, never a long hook-up . Iswar liked Sarika for her matured thoughts ; She liked Iswar for his romantic lines.

One day , while Iswar was exchanging a message with Sarika in the late evening , Maya suddenly entered the room and saw the profile of Sarika which was open on the laptop. She wanted to see all the chats that Iswar had with her , but he did not agree to show.

She shouted , " Why are you not showing me what kind of chat you are having with this lady. Who is this lady. Give me her number . I want to speak to her and check what is she up to"

It is just a FB kind of chatting. Time pass only.

Oh! You don't have any male friends to chat ? . Why is that you are fond of women"

"Please don't bother me. I am thoroughly disgusted with your ways. You lead your life. Leave me to have mine"

Next day after Iswar left for office , Maya summoned Sanjay , best buddy of Iswar in the town. As the best friend he was aware of all that is happening in his friend's life including his innocuous chats with some ladies on social networking sites.

What the hell is going on between my husband and that stranger lady?' Maya's patience was at its lowest ebb and she was ready to burst. She was burning in anger like hot coke.

Sanjay knew that she was serious. "Look, Maya. There is nothing going on between the two of them. Just a little bit of healthy flirting, I'd say. Now a days it is so common."

'Flirting? Healthy flirting? Really Sanjay . . .' she rolled her eyes in disgust. 'That's what you men call it? There is nothing healthy about flirting, Sanjay, not for a married man.

'Healthy flirting is a term introduced by perverted men who want to lend legitimacy to their extramarital dalliances. Flirting invariably has a sexual connotation to it'. She got up from her seat and walked around the room gesticulating and muttering something to herself. Suddenly she stopped, turned back, looked at Sanjay and asked, 'Did my husband sleep with her? You are his friend. Did he ever tell you anything about it?'

Maya , I know Iswar . He is a simpleton and can't do anything bad. I am aware of what all happened between

284

both of you yesterday night. You are justified in doubting Iswar, but trust me there is nothing between them that you should be concerned about.

Don't fool me with these stories. I have heard enough of it.
Ok . if you wish I will log into his FB account and show you the chats. Will that satisfy you.

"Yes, that is what I wanted yesterday. Your friend felt scared and did not show me."
Ok , I will show you the chats.

Sanjay , logged into the FB account of Iswar and the chats read as follows:

Sarika , by this time you must have known everything about me from the profile, but I find your profile too sketchy . Tell me something about you. I know nothing more than your name. Hope the profile picture is a genuine one..hahaha.

Sarika wrote , "I am not going to produce my CV before you , so stop there."

My mind is like a butterfly...in spite of all my restrain, it is flipping its way to sip the nectar of your sweet talk . It is such a wonderful feeling to indulge in forbidden pursuits, like talking to a lady who is a stranger.

Oh..great !! There must be thousands minus one !
Good luck !

I am a human being , not a passenger train. And this breed of beauty with brain is so rare now days . I have spotted you after a long and careful search at FB ..Be with me some time...You will not be disappointed.

Hello Sarika , you remind me of a tube well ; one has to put many stokes before water oozes out ; Only after I write 4-5 messages do I get a reply (one liner) from you. Nevertheless I am thirsty and hence have to put those strokes every day .

Hi Iswar , even I find you like a clever crow ..hahaha

You know Sarika , I like the way you talk ; I get a kind of punch that one gets while drinking a bottle of Pepsi.

Good , at least you did not mention , rum or whisky , I would have blocked you then ...hahaha

I enjoy talking to you , but back of the mind I am also scared of my wife. If she gets to know about my amorous adventure, there will be Mahabharat at home.

I am not going to report to your wife, be assured. There is no thrill in any adventure where there is no fear factor.

The day you report, next day you will read a newspaper headline " Banker hangs himself , reasons unknown"

hehehe... logical conclusion

I am very scared of my lion wife when I chat with others . Are you not afraid of your mouse husband....haha.

Never , freedom of expression is my fundamental right.

"We stay in a duplex on the hill top from where the world appears like a beautiful sketch , why don't you look for me on the floating clouds moist with early monsoon " ...Sarika

I would surely look up to those clouds...will relish those lightning smiles on your face. I plan to take the form of a sweet breeze and pierce through the gloomy clouds and coerce you to drench me with the rains that you hold within you.

Prosaic Banker , stay in your own prose domain , don't kill the business of so called poets of this world.

My imaginations going wild . I am reminded of the shepherd who impressed the princess by the skillful play of his flute , when she was taking a bath at the lagoon besides a hill under the shield of her servants.....I am just a shepherd and you princess at the hill top...Show mercy on me...Beg you your affection...I know your are tied to the destiny...but if not here , May I meet you in heaven.

Hey, married I am. Chain your imaginations. Be aware of my hubby.

Hey apple of my eye , who is that prince charming who stole you away from the horizon of my sight. Blessed must be the man who got the sweet heart you. Me must be a sinner in last birth; why else you would deprive me even from some wishful imaginations. Make me your slave; let my eyes see you in flesh and blood. Fairy, mercy on me , mercy on me.....Iswar

Viral fever or infatuation , both manifest in similar way , symptoms are same, mild to high temperature, feeling of cold often with shivering , running writings, lack of sleep and hunger, weakness in body n mind....however go away with time with or without medication !! Just wait and watch !!....Sarika

Hey dream girl , tell me which is more permanent - love or lust. The later overpowers all my good intentions...I can feel your vibes from miles and without you perhaps can't survive....Love thy ways..Enigma you are.

Trust me, I smell lies staying miles away from you!! Botanical longevity of lust is equal to a mushroom and love is fleeting; comes fast and leaves even faster.

Hey damsel...pity on me...after showing all your love on your dear ones, if you have some left-over love, do sprinkle on me. Let me take a shower in the fragrance of your senses and cherish it when I lie on the bed. You look so innocent, but your words are piercing. Don't make me a Bhisma and force me to sleep on the bed of arrows...Pity on me...Send me to hell, but Love me a little before I go there.

Bed of Arrows!....Perhaps you have back pain and so the wish for acupuncture treatment.

I will crawl if you wish me to just bow ; I have not seen any sign of romance in your eyes...not getting sleep...will you come...we will go for a long walk on a sea beach...only you, me and silence....Iswar

Sounds romantic ....Sarika

While the white sands will be rejoicing the soft touch of your feet and sweet breeze will be fondling your hairs , I will look at your futile attempts to return the hairs to their original position . I will be sitting cross legged on the beach and you sleeping on the sand with your head rested on my lap...and I looking at that sweet smile on your face..it would be divine sweet heart. As you look towards the dipping sun at the horizon, I will be mesmerized at the sight of the beautiful mountain from the close-up....Iswar

You need a sleeping doze. Goodnight....Sarika

How do I sleep dear ...Your memory is neither allowing me to live or to die...The sweet memory of you is touching my soul like a breeze...It is such a nice feeling...Is that a one-sided affair again with me dear.

Any doubt ?

Yesterday there was a flood of messages from you and today there is a drought...Guess you are busy otherwise...Would love to read a message from you before I sleep.

Got busy with work at home...Sorry.

Make me Your partner...I will do all your spade work...and I will not ask for any remuneration..At the end of the tiring

289

day , just look at me once and smile a little , that will fill my stomach.

Oh My God !!! Am I born for these lines !!! Killer lines !!.....Sarika

Made For Each Other...Separated by Destiny...It is nice to feel like a teenager again....I am surely blessed. "Mission Impossible" for me to win your heart....You have stolen my sleep.

May God bless you !!! I am a virtual existence, may vanish within a blink...Sarika

Miracles do happen....Tell me has it ever crossed your mind to fall in love with me...

Yes, miracle happened, I tried and just failed!!!! Can you tell me the reason wise Banker!!!!!
I may fall in love with your answer, I m afraid...Sarika

Oh...It did not cross your mind? That is exactly what I wanted. It should stay at your mind and then slowly and steadily it should slip in to your Heart....oh...that unbelievable charming heart....The distance between your mind and heart is just eighteen inches...wow...I can see the light at the end of the tunnel...
You and Me in This Beautiful World....Green Grass, Blue Sky....Hope to see you in my dreams tonight....

Ha-ha...Intelligent you are...Sarika.

Every time you reply to my message, I live a little longer. Every time you remain silent, I die a little.

You have Reasons not to say who you are. I have Reasons not to ask who you are....but it is a beautiful season for love...It is early morning here and there is a drizzle outside...Roads are lonely...Wish to hold your hand and go for a walk and get wet in your love and the shower from the heaven...

Hey Beautiful lady, evasive you are...you can't fathom the curiosity that I have about you...when I walk few miles, I notice hesitation in you in stepping few yards. Why are you so cautious...walk a little...my little sweet girl...

Am I just an admirer of your beauty and worshiper of your divinity. You appear to me like a beautiful fountain flowing from the mountain tip and you are pure like a pearl. I am at my wits end and struggling to find words to match my feelings.....I don't know how occupied you are at home..If I am piling too many messages , bear with me...I need daba and dua to get rid of this illness...help me Goddess of my heart...

You write so well Banker , that is another reason I am not blocking you , I have fallen after the accomplished writing as I ever remained as a passionate lover of literature ....Sarika

I was thrilled with the hope "I have fallen" will be suffixed with "in love with you"...but despair knocked at my heart when I read "after the accomplished writing"...It is the emotion that brings out the best out of me , language is just incidental...and there are three causes of those emotions- You , You and You.

Hey anchor of my life , blessed I am to get such a nice message from you. I am on voyage in the deep sea of love. You are the captain of my Titanic..Steer me slowly in the turbulence of these love waves , lest I may drown...Have a wonderful Sunday.

Titanic?...good luck Banker......Sarika.

Talking to you is like listening to a melody...one keeps humming the tune long after it is over.....Charmer You are..Good Night.

I am on a pilgrimage of love and hope to get salvation in the shape of a bear hug from you some day....Good Morning..You have brought happiness to my life...

I just read at one place no matter how beautiful your dreams are , you have to wake up some day. I suggest you spell your loving words on your wife and live happily..Sarika

Ha-ha...I wish making my wife happy that simple . She just doesn't appreciates all these . She thinks money can bring all kinds of happiness. Who can explain her that money can buy pleasures , not happiness?

After going through the chat , Maya cooled down and looked towards Sanjay and remarked 'why is that he is indulging in this virtual romance"

Sanjay reverted , ' because he is not finding real romance at home'.

Sanjay left Iswar's house in the afternoon. On his way home he told Iswar all that transpired between him and Maya.

In the evening when Iswar returned home , he looked at Maya lovingly and said "Sorry" and she responded "Me Too"

LOVE IN THE AIR

It was still dawn when I stepped out of the cab and walked towards the entry gate of the Delhi airport. The early morning February air was pleasantly cold and soothing .

I was travelling to Bengaluru to attend a college friend's wedding. It had been four years since we graduated from the same college. This wedding was also going to be a reunion of our batch mates. But what I didn't know was that the reunion would begin much ahead of time; right in the queue in front of the airline counter, in the most unexpected way.

I was almost sure it was she. Same height! Same long hair! Same complexion! Curiosity had my eyes glued to her. And then about sixty odd seconds later, when she turned, she proved me right. My ex-girlfriend stood two places ahead of me in that queue. We had never met after the college farewell. She looked back , perhaps to see the length of the queue. Her eyes fell on me. She surely recognized me , but turned her glance away as if she has not seen me. I wondered if she was still upset with me , if she had still not forgave me for that bad habit . Standing in the queue , I was thinking if I should come out of the queue , walk up to her and say "Hi..Sarika. How are you"..But I was not able to garner courage to do that. If she reciprocates my wish , it is ok. But if she ignores me   , it would be embarrassing .
What if in a rage of irritation she shouts at me   and the

public suspiciously look towards me ? My absent mindedness was interrupted when the boy standing behind me muttered "Uncle , move forward , there is lot of space in front of you". I recovered from my strayed mind and moved few steps ahead and closed the gap . My intelligent mind guided me not to meet her then and there . Instead I planned to meet her when she gets comfortable at the waiting lounge after the security check. I saw, after getting the boarding pass , she walked up for security check to the area meant for the ladies . I was standing in the gents' queue which was quite long and the security on duty was taking time to check each passenger. The checking was elaborate and careful as week before there was a bomb blast at a nearby city.

After the security check , I reached the waiting lounge and scanned the people sitting at different places. She was nowhere in sight and I was thinking where she vanished in few minutes. I felt disappointed not finding her at the lounge and remained standing at the centre of the lounge holding my handbag. My search ended when I saw her coming from the wash room towards me. She was wearing sunglasses and I was unable to make out if she has seen me or not though she was walking straight towards me. I thought, perhaps she does not want to see me eye-to-eye and hence wore the sunglasses...I was unable to gauge the emotion on her face. She looked indifferent. She almost reached me but then took left turn and walked along the rows of perforated steel chairs. She reached near her red hand bag kept near a chair and sat there. She lifted the sunglasses over her head , pulled the front zipper of the bag , took out a magazine and started turning pages. She was not reading anything, just turning pages. Perhaps that was her method to avoid me. I could read the name of the magazine. It was "Femina"..This used to be her favorite magazine in the college days and she still reads the same magazine.

She was wearing a brick red salwar and a bottle green panjabi which had a rounded cut at the neck and had long sleeves. She always wore such long sleeve dresses and preferred covering the body as much as possible. I used to tease her for such a conservative dress sense , though in her mind she is very liberal and modern. I was still not sure if she has really seen me or not. The thought that she has seen me and avoiding me haunted me. But then I garnered courage to meet her and wish. I walked up to her and stood in front of her. Her eyes were still on the magazine. She did realize that someone is standing close by but she remained unaffected. "Hello Sarika.." I said tentatively scared of the response this statement of mine may ignite. She looked up , gave a forced smile and said ,"Good Morning"...and then continued, "Are you also going for the marriage function?". I replied, "Yes". Pointing to the vacant chair next to her she said , "Sit here" and returned her gaze to the magazine . I sat next to her but I remained muted. In my mind , I was trying to figure out a topic to resume the conversation. But the boarding announcement aborted that effort at my end.

On hearing the announcement for boarding, she got up and straightened her dress a little. She caught hold of the red handbag, looked at me and said , "Boarding call" and then proceeded. I followed her but soon she got lost inside the hustling and bustling of the passengers pushing their ways to reach their designated seats. I found my seat at the middle of the aircraft and got seated. I tried to find where she is sitting. She was not there at any of the front seats. I presumed that she was sitting at the tail end of the plane.

The plane took off after a while and settled at high altitude. I looked at the floating clouds and smiled at the beauty of the nature. I closed my eyes and rested my head on the head rest , not to sleep but to recount all the good times that I had spent with Sarika in my college days.

The first thing that struck my mind is the fresher's meet , the day on which it all started when I was a fresher and just a month into the new place . It was tradition in the institute , for the seniors to welcome the juniors through an elaborate function. The auditorium was looking like a bride decked up with flowers and colored balloons . All the fresher were sitting at the front rows and the seniors at the rear rows. Many activities were lined up for the function, "Mr. & Ms Fresher" being the major attraction . It is a kind of fashion show for boys and girls , through which the best boy and the best girl is selected , based on their dress-up , ramp performance and Q&A session. I was wearing a designer sherwani that day , brown in color. She was in a white gown. She looked like a fairy in that outfit. She was tall , fair and had long curly hairs. The gown was long and when she walked the ramp , the lower part of it swept the floor. There were twenty contestants – ten boys and equal number of girls . I still remember the answer I gave to the question from one of the judges, "What is your goal in life?" and I had replied with poise, "Life is too big a thing to be limited to a single goal. I have many goals – to work , to love , to travel , to make friends , to learn singing …and many more…but among all the biggest goal is to fall in love with right girl".

She also gave equally interesting reply . To the question, "How do you define your ideal husband?", she had said , "There is nothing like an ideal husband in this world. Pursuit of ideal can only bring disappointment. Each man will have his own imperfections and I accept that fact of life. I want a man who is a man not a machine. I wish a man who can give me things that money can't buy".

After each component of evaluation got over , the judges asked for ten minutes time to calculate the score and declare the result. All were waiting in tight breath. The waiting got over when the anchor came to the stage to make the announcement. All the participants were standing in a row near the backdrop of the stage..The anchor prompted "Now the time has come to declare Mr. and Ms Fresher...any guesses?...The crowd roared with names of their favorite participants..There was a lull for some time as the anchor withheld the result for 10-15 seconds to keep the people guessing further. But then at last she declared, " Mr. &Ms Fresher for the year 2010 are Manab and Sarika"...There was euphoria in the crowd and the whole place got choked with the sound of the clapping. Sarika and myself walked up to the centre stage and were crowned with grandeur. She was blushing like a school girl that day and I instantly developed a liking for her.

This fresher's meet started a new chapter in my life. Almost under the spell of social recognition, we became lover and beloved. I was very sharp in academics, she was not. She was good at extracurricular activities – in sports and in music . But the affair did bring improvement in her academics. She started spending more and more time with me in the library. Teachers would cite our examples to others as our affair was very controlled. We never indulged in public display of affection , which many other couples did in the campus. Teachers cited our affair to be a kind of ideal love affair.

Four years in the college passed like a fairy tale. I enjoyed each moment of life at the campus. With her in my side , I have nothing more to wish for. She was sweet and charming. She would always encourage me in my work and if I am depressed some day , she would boost my morale by saying good things about me. I was not very expressive. But she had no complaints. She understood the typical emotions of boys like me. She loved me because of my good nature. Only thing she was not happy about me was my habit of getting drunk once in a while. I picked up this habit at the college because of friendship with some boys who were into it. In the final year , I almost drank every Saturday evening with my friends at a nearby bar . She understood that I had become an addict. On Saturdays , she would call me at late night to check if I am ok or not and would advise me not to drink almost like a ritual. In every such call from her , I promised to get rid of the bad habit. But habits die hard; it remained part of my life.

On one such Saturday night she gave me the ultimatum, " Manab, I am tired of your drinking habit. All my friends are taunting me as the beloved of a drunkard and I am getting deeply hurt every time they say those unkind words. I can't bear it any more. If you don't stop drinking, please forget me. Forget that I have ever come to your life."..I felt like she is crying at the other end of the phone ; I understood her plight and promised not to touch liquor ever. When I made this promise to her , perhaps I was not aware that liquor has become part of my life and I loved that red liquid as much as I loved her.

I continued in my ways. She stopped meeting me. She stopped talking to me. Soon, our lives ran like two parallel lines with no chance of ever meeting. If by chance she came face to face with me, she either turned her face away or gave an indifferent look. I did stalked her few times to explain how I am unable to get rid of this addiction, but she just did not listen to me . I felt deeply pained at her behavior but after few such pleading I felt angered. I did not realize that I have a problem with me. I considered her avoidance a bigger sin than my addiction. One day I was in a very foul mood and shouted " I am going out of your life. I will never come back again. I will not drink from tomorrow and will punish me that way"..She was sitting with the group of her friends on the central lawn of the college. She remained silent as before. Her friends gave me disgusted look. That day I went to the bar alone and drank double of what I am used to. I fell down on the floor of the bar and vomited and almost lost sense. The bar owner had to call my friends to take me back to my hostel.

College placement season came. I joined an MNC and it was a news that I was the highest paid recruit at the campus. She opted out of placement. I was not in talking terms with her. I also did not check why she opted out from placement. I gathered from her friends that she wanted to devote herself to social work. After I left the campus and joined the MNC , I got busy with my career and life.

Pilot made the announcement , "Ladies and Gentlemen, we will shortly land at Bangaluru. ". The announcement broke my sleep. I looked through the window. The plane was slowly lowering its altitude and readying for touch down at the runway. The city looked beautiful from a height. As the plane stopped and crew member advised exit , passengers started pushing through the rush. I remained seated at my place for the rush to subside. I noticed Sarika passing through my seat. She gave a tangential look , perhaps she also wanted to know where I sat during the flight. But she did not smile. Only my eyes met with hers.

Both of us joined the wedding party. It was being held at a famous hotel of the city. The venue was exquisite – the pool side lawn. That huge lawn was beautifully decorated with colorful lights. In different parts of the lawn , squared tables had been placed with four chairs at each table. In one part of the lawn , there was a grand podium decorated with flowers. The newlywed couple was sitting on two royal looking chairs at the podium . I went up to them , handed over a bouquet to the bride and congratulated her Hugged my friend and shook hands with him. He thanked me for attending the party.

I turned back , stepped on the wooden stair to disembark the podium. While doing so , I noticed most of the tables at the lawn were filled up with guests excepting one . At that table sitting a lady , alone . I looked intently and realized that she is none but Sarika. I could hear a romantic music that was being played at low volume. Without much thought , I walked towards the table . She was wearing a full sleeve purple colored salwar suit with intricate embroidery work at the neck. At her wrist , bangles of matching color were shinning. She was wearing simple white stone tops at her ears which were sparkling . I reached near her table and stood there. She looked up , smiled and said , "Sit". I sat opposite to her and started thinking how to start the conversation.

She understood my predicament and asked , "So , how are you Manav. How is life". I looked at her eyes and said , "Yes , I am doing fine in my professional life"…and after a pause said "I am a saint now"..She gave a puzzled look and quipped , "Saint?"…I clarified , "Yes, I have got rid of that red water addiction"..Hearing this , she appeared very happy and said , "Good for your health. Congrats". I resumed, "But , the sweet girl for whom I did this forgot me..life is such an irony"..She paused for a moment and muttered , "How did you know that she has forgotten you. She might be loving you as before". Encouraged at this statement I asked, "Are you sure , she still loves me?". She did not say anything but bowed her head and smiled. I understood the sign and shifted to the chair next to her. I held her palm lovingly and asked, "Will you marry me?"…she gave a bigger smile..and I understood it to be a Big Yes.

HONOUR OF MY FATHER

Hello Rishaan , how is life?..What are you doing in this lazy Sunday? ...Asutosh Pathak this side. Yes buddy , tell me what made you remember me.

Yaar , Did Ashok not to tell you anything?...
No...

That liar Ashok will die a liar; told me , he informed everything about our plan..
What plan..?
Buddy , this time we are having our batch-mates' get-together at Goa on 25th December..24th is a Saturday. Are you coming or not?..I am not ready to listen a NO from you.

Asutosh, let me check my engagement at office first. I will confirm you tomorrow. But tell me , is it a family get-together or just the batch-mates?

Yes, Yes...I forgot to tell you , most of the batch-mates are married now, so it will be a family get-together. Bachelors can bring their girl friends...hahaha...He continued, "15k per head. Transfer the money to my a/c ...I will sms the a/c number".

As Rishaan finished with the call and left the phone at the charging point , his wife Kaira busy putting clothes into the drum of the washing machine, gave a angled look towards him and asked, "Who is that?"

Get-together at Goa of   MBA batch-mates... Rishaan muttered in a nonchalant manner.

Smile sparked on her face; she prompted " Goa?....I have never been there. Kajol was telling the white beaches there are awesome"

Rishaan lifted his gaze from the news paper and asked ,"When did she visit Goa?"

Teasingly , Kaira replied , "Bro-in-Law does not know about the last outing of sis-in-law, sounds strange...?"

How do I know. She is your sister. You speak to her daily, so you know.

Kaira almost with an wish to hear yes from her hubby asked. " So are we going or not?"

He smiled and said , "Yes"

Kaira came running from the washing machine , arched herself in front of Rishaan and parked three kisses on his forehead and said , "I love you my dear."

Rishaan had already drank two cups of coffee in the morning and had this urge to have one more. As Kaira was busy with the dirty linen , he was not daring to ask for that. But now seeing her in jubilant mood, he quipped , "Let there be one more cup of coffee at this good news."

Next Day:

Rishaan called Asutosh from office to check who all are coming to the get-together and also to confirm his joining .

Out of sixty batch mates , forty have confirmed. Rest will also confirm. It will be a mega event. ..Asutosh told in a euphoric mood.

Rishaan made a innocuous query , " What about Diya?"

Oh your ex-flame?...ha-ha....Yes...she is coming. She is still single. Are you not in touch with her?..She is in the same city as yours since last 4-5 months. Relocated with promotion. She is now a big shot in that MNC.

Rishaan reacted," Oh...I was not aware. In any case, after my marriage never had the face to talk to her again. She ignored my FB and Whatsapp request also"

That day , after dinner Rishaan lied down on his bed at 10PM as usual. But sleep did not come to his eyes till late in the night. He was turning sides again and again , but in vain. Old memories are clouding his mind and he was feeling uncomfortable even on the soft bed.

The memory is so fresh in his mind. Appears like it all happened yesterday. His affair with Diya was the talk of the Institute where both studied and everyone thought they were made for each other. It all started in the first year of his MBA course. He was the topper of the entrance examination; She was most charming, smart and gregarious.

In the batch of sixty students , there were just eighteen girls. Each boy was vying to get a girl friend as soon as possible. But he never got into such a contest . After he joined the institute , his goal was to maintain his academic excellence and continue to be the topper in the semester exams also. Diya on the other hand was enjoying the attention she was getting from all. But she was not someone who will melt for anyone.

Lack of attention from Rishaan was actually burning her heart. How can a boy , however brilliant he may be , can't be swayed by his feminine charm? That is what was bothering her. Every day she would wear a new dress and come to the class looking like a Barbie. Many days she would sit at the bench just in front of Rishaan to get his close attention , but nothing was enough to influence him.

Slowly it became a challenge for Diya to win the heart of Rishaan. She decided to take a bold step in that direction. One day she reached the class earlier than usual and to her surprise the class was almost vacant excepting half a dozen other boys. She sat next to Rishaan and gave him a look. He was indifferent and was busy reading a book. She tore a piece of paper from her notebook , wrote , "My cell no : 9237178199. Congrats for being the topper of the entrance exam"..He picked that up and read. Diya noticed him smile also. She waited for his response in anticipation . For nearly five minutes he got busy with his reading. With each passing minute she was feeling more frustrated . Each minute seemed like an hour to her . She was also feeling worried ; rest of the crowd will soon reach the class room and her adventure will remain unfinished.

He thought it is impolite not to respond to a sweet girl. He tore a small piece of paper from his note book and wrote , "9933322789..and drew an emoticon meaning Happy". He pushed that piece towards Diya . She swiftly picked that like a kingfisher will do to a fish. Read the content and thought , candle has been ignited.

Same day 11PM in the night:

When he woke up to go for a leak to the washroom and pressed the mobile to see the time , he saw a miscall from a number..He matched that with the slip in his shirt pocket. It was Diya's. He looked at the time of the call...it was 10.10PM. He was in two dilemma – first to call back or not ; second if 11PM is a good time to call a girl. Then he made a logical analysis – if a girl can remember a boy at 10PM , it is alright to disturb the same girl at 11PM..By the time he was mentally ready to make a call it was 11.15PM..He pressed the key and could hear the rings of the call.

There was no response..perhaps she was in deep slumber by that time..He felt awkward for calling at that point in time and was waiting for the rings to end. ..His guilt feeling was abruptly ended when he heard from the other side , "Not slept yet Mr. Academic?"

Rishaan naughtily replied , " Somebody's memory is not allowing me to sleep. What to do?"

"Oh...who is that fairy who is troubling you at night?"...she countered in more naughty tone.
"Her name starts with D...ha-ha" ...he created mystery in the mind of Diya.
There was no response from her for few seconds but then she in a teasing tone prompted ,"D for Doll?"

No, I am not in nursery school dear …the meaning of her name is LIGHT…Now you guess.
"Hey Rishaan don't kill me with such lines…Is that me?"
Yes…Yes…Yes….It is You…You and You…
She almost screamed with joy at the other side of the phone and said , "Now I will not be able to sleep rest of the night…You Devil Rishaan …I love you like mad"

This maiden chat started the romance between Rishaan and Diya. They were often found at the isolated culverts in the campus talking for long hours and soon friends tagged them "Couple of the Campus"..

Two years in the campus passed like few months. Both of them passed in flying colors and they joined MNCs . Though they wanted to work with the same company and the same city , luck was not in their side. Before they left the campus , both promised to be in touch. Rishaan took the responsibility to share their relation with his parents and initiate discussion for their marriage.

What stood between their relationship moving towards marriage was their caste…rather class. While Rishaan belong to a Brahmin caste , she was from a Rajput family. Rishaan did persuade his father to take up the matter with the family of Diya..hoping that they will agree considering their affair at the institute. His father was reluctant as he knew how snobbish those Rajputs can be. But for the happiness of his son , he visited the patents of Diya one fine day.

Before visiting their place , he made a phone call and spoke to Diya's dad and intimated the purpose of his visit. He consented coldly. But when he arrived at the big palace , the darwan at the gate even did not allow him to walk the stairs that led to the main door of the palace. It required some patient waiting before he was allowed..The darwan spoke to someone over the intercom and then opened the gate.

That day , when he returned home , he was not only looking dejected but also angered. The kind of humiliation that he had to suffer at the palace was too much for him. He narrated everything to his wife while Rishaan was standing nearby... Rishaan also made up his mind..He can't get married to Diya if that is the kind of treatment mooted to his dad . He walked into his private room and called Diya on his mobile ; in a single breath he said , "It is all over. I can't marry you. I hate them who ill-treat my parents". Diya understood the anger of Rishaan and tried to pacify but he was in no mood to listen. He cut-off the call abruptly in a rage. She ringed him back a number of times but he did not respond.

Since that day , interaction between Rishaan and Diya stopped..Each stuck to their ego. After three years Rishaan got married to Kaira , a simple girl from their own caste. It was an arranged marriage. Diya did not think of marriage after Rishaan parted his ways. The day she got to know about Rishaan's marriage from a common friend , she cried a lot. She starved herself for two long days as a kind of revenge on Rishaan.

On 24th evening , Rishaan was waiting at the airport lounge with his wife to catch the Goa flight. He saw Diya standing in the queue for the boarding pass and thought she is also travelling by the same flight. As fortune would have it , when Rishaan got into the aircraft , he found Diya sitting at the window seat with two other seats left for him and Kaira to occupy. She was looking outside and perhaps did not take notice of his presence there. Rishaan hinted Kaira to take the middle seat and after she got seated , he sat on the seat at the aisles end. At this time , Diya turned her eye towards them. She gave a quick look at Kaira and then riveted her eyes with Rishaan for few seconds. He could notice the sorrow in her eyes.

Lights were switched off to allow passengers to sleep. It is a long three hours journey.

In the middle of the flight, Kaira woke up to go to the washroom. When she returned, she was too lazy to push her way into the middle seat. And with Rishaan readily offering to shift seats, the seating arrangement changed. With twenty minutes still remaining for the flight to land, a sleep starved Kiara took another power nap, this time holding Rishaan 's right hand more firmly. Rishaan's other hand, though, nervously moved to touch Diya's. Her heart skipped a beat. Diya pulled her hand away. But a defiant Rishaan held her wrist again, this time firmly and more reassuringly. The changing behavioral dynamics between the three perhaps gave out a foreboding of what was to come in Goa.

When the flight landed at the Dabolim Airport, Rishaan felt uncanny...his excitement seemed replaced by an unknown fear that he found very difficult to decipher.

Rishaan was thinking , if Diya will remain quiet excusing his misadventure in the darkness of night or she will create a scene in the presence of all friends and his wife when the party is at its peak.

HOW BLUE IS MY SAPPHIRE

Times of India , 22nd April

Kota : IIT Result will be declared today . Kota , nerve centre of IIT coaching is waiting for the ultimate news – how many cleared , how many in top-100 , how many in top-10 and then the ultimate who is the Topper, the blue eyed student on whom hinges the fate of the coaching institute. Many will crack it but there will be many more who will not make it. The whole air will be filled with joy and despair at the crack of the news. Even today , when the result is still to come out , the city is abuzz with this topic only. As if there is no other issue worth talking about. It is only IIT, IIT and IIT. This is such an exam that catapults one into a different league altogether. Perhaps this is the gateway to all good things in life. You become uncommon , you become the cynosure and everyone looks up to you as if you have earned a demi-God status.

Royal Garden Apartment at Kota:

This hostel houses two hundred odd boys who have come to Kota from different parts of the country to take coaching. Most have one dream – to crack IIT. But there are a few who are here because their parents wanted them to get into IIT. They never wanted to become engineers. Rohon is one such boy from Delhi. He came to Kota two years back. His parents put him in this hostel. He wanted to share a room , but his dad forced him to stay single in one room. He had his own logic – in single room Rohon will have privacy and can focus on his studies, no one around to disturb him. He never cared for what Rohon wanted.

Rohon has been attending the coaching classes religiously. Every day six hours of class; even on Sundays there is no respite. There is a test for sure. He can't miss even a single one. His parents get an sms from the coaching centre if he misses one and almost instantly he gets a call from his dad. He has to tell some stupid lies to escape the anger of dad. He is not comfortable telling lies; so he keeps attending classes. In the class room also he is stressed. In one big gallery hall, close to two hundred students sit. Teachers use collar phone as otherwise their voice will not reach the last bench..They hardly know anyone by name. But they are the best in the subjects. Physically Rohon is there in the class , but mentally he is just not there. He has no interest in the class. He waits patiently for the class to end. His mind travels hundred miles to the cricket field at Delhi where he used to play cricket. He loved that game. When he played cricket , time just flew. He would be playing for hours together, yet there will be no sign of any tiredness in his face. It was all joy – batting, bowling or fielding…the activity does not matter.

At Kota, he is like a fish out of water. He did tell his dad that he liked cricket and would love to pursue that as a career. But his dad revolted and rebuked, "You have to first get into IIT".."Cricket can wait....You can play cricket at IIT" . Rohon took refuse with mom , hoping that she will appreciate his wish and will plead with dad. But in vain. In front of the ruthless aspiration of dad , the advocacy of mom vanished like vapor.

Central Park, Delhi

Mr.Rakesh , father of Rohon is a bureaucrat at Delhi secretariat. He is very health conscious. Morning walk is a must and then in the evening few swings of the ball at the golf course. He is taking a stroll at the Central Park . Damodar who is a regular at the park and a colleague of Rakesh came face-to-face and wished ,"Good Morning Rakesh..how is life"...Rakesh smiled and said , "Life is good. But today I am very anxious. IIT result will be coming out today"...Hearing this Damodar picked up the thread and quipped , "Yes , Yes...your son has been taking coaching at Kota...I know...how is he doing". Rakesh posed a confident face at Damodar and said ," Yes, he will crack the exam for sure. I am concerned about the rank. Unless he gets in the Top-1000 , it will be difficult to get a good IIT and good branch of engineering."..He remained muted for few seconds and then continued, "IIT,Kanpur is best for computer science..Hope his rank is good enough for that"...Damodar , who was listening intently suggested , "But , there are so many IITs...he can join anyone'..Rakesh dismissed the idea by raising his hand and reacted ," Those new IITs are like ITIs....ha-ha....no reputation. In the worst case scenario, I will allow my son to study at IIT,Delhi. He can stay at home and study. At least he will not have to eat those lousy hostel food."...Damodar did not counter Rakesh but said to himself , "Too much of ambition leads to disappointments".

Rakesh reached home after the morning walk. By that time his wife Sabita has already woken up and was preparing tea. She knew the exact time at which he needs his tea. There can't be any deviation in that. He went to the bathroom , washed himself and wiping his face with a small Turkish towel he settled down on the sofa. She brought tea in a tray , kept that on the centre table and then sat opposite to him. She noticed his pale face and enquired, "You look worried today. What is the matter"…"IIT Result will come out…."he said and she understood the rest. As a caring wife she looked at him with concern and said, " Today is Sunday and you don't have to go to office. Take rest. Don't worry about the result. Whatever happens , it will be God's wish and will be good for Rohon"…He gave a stern look at her and said , " I will be deeply disappointed if Rohon is not in Top-1000….I am not asking him to be the topper"….She looked at him , gathered courage and countered ,"Just cracking IIT is so difficult….expecting Top-1000 rank…." She did not complete the sentence.

Royal Garden Apartment at Kota:

Rohon is very tensed today..he knew he is a borderline case, a fence sitter. He may or may not get the cut-off mark. It may swing any way. He is scared of his father's reaction to a poor show at his end. What can he do. In spite of the fact that he does not like the subjects, he has put in hard work and has tried his best. He has not taken the breakfast today. He doesn't feel like eating anything. He is feeling like a convict waiting for the gallows. He came out of the apartment and stood in front of the main gate. A street dog has become a new friend to him. As soon as it saw Rohon , it came running towards him and looked up to him wagging its tail. He arced himself to reach its back and rolled his fingers on its shinning skin. The dog felt the love and started licking the feet of Rohon. He felt good. He was touched by the unconditional love of the animal...a street dog , loosely called...but it surely has a soft heart , softer than many humans.

Vasant Vihar bungalow, Delhi.

10AM..and IIT result out. Rakesh opened his laptop , connected the wireless modem and logged into the site. He entered the roll no of Rohon and then his birth date...and he pressed the OK button...his spine chilled as the computer fell silent for seconds before popping up the rank..Rank...20391 it said. Stunned , he stood-up and looked towards his wife who was standing nearby.

His face turned pale with disappointment and then red with anger. He rushed towards the bed room to get his mobile phone. Sabita followed him in anticipation of the horror that she will witness soon.

He dialed the number of his son and asked sternly , "Rohon, did you check your result?"..he meekly replied, "Yes,dad"...He burst like an atom bomb , "Idiot , is this the result for which I put you at Kota? Shameless . I hoped Top-1000 and you are not there even within 10000. Did you study or were busy in something else...Don't know what to say...How I will show my face to my friends...colleagues....relatives..?"...

There was silence at the other end. Rohon listened to dad's

outburst and calmly asked, "Dad , how is your respect linked to my performance?..If I have failed , I have failed...You have not failed"

Times of India 23rd Apr

Kota does it again. 1242 students cleared IIT with 32 in Top-100 and the icing on the cake is the Topper is from Kota. There is jubilation all around. Students and the Teachers at the coaching centers burst fire crackers and distributed sweets. Some institutes even celebrated the achievement with musical night. Congratulatory messages are flooding the topper. This paper tried to contact the Topper for an interview. But he is indisposed as he has a tight schedule of felicitations by Ministers and various organizations. But amidst this good news, there is a pall of gloom. Yesterday night two students who could not make into the merit list committed suicide. This kind of extreme incidents are happening too frequently at Kota. Educationists and psychologist are blaming this on parent's over-expectation from their children and forcing them to try for something they really don't love. Regular counseling of the students by the parents and also by professional counselors at the coaching centers can alleviate this social problem. The District Collector has directed all the coaching centers to write letters to all the parents advising them to be more humane and realistic with their kids. In fact the collector has enclosed the draft letter in English which has to be translated into vernacular and sent to the parents. The theme of the letter is – There is life beyond IIT. Hopefully, this communication with parents will have positive impact and will reduce suicides at Kota.

Rohon was not one of the boys who committed suicide that day . He had made up his mind to pursue is first love..Cricket.

5 Years later:

Rohon is a well known cricketer today . He is a member of a famous IPL Team and has an enviable bidding price. Among the girls , he is also a heartthrob and wherever he goes youngsters rush to him for getting his autograph. Sometimes he thinks about his Kota days and smiles to himself.

In the last IPL match , he scored the fastest century and declared man of the match. When the commentator asked him the secret of his success , he said ," Most of us live with our past. Most of us allow it to shape our future. But some of us know how to shrug the past. I think that is who I am....."

ABOUT THE AUTHOR

Amarendra Pattnaik is a native of Odisha(India). He graduated in engineering from University College of Engineering,Burla in 1989 and later pursued MBA at Xavier Institute of Management,Bhubaneswar. After working for twenty years in the corporate sector , he shifted to academics and currently he is a Professor at KIIT University.

Watching people and writing about their emotions is his passion. He loves talking to people and listening to their stories. He writes stories with two objectives – to make the readers smile and to make them think.